Advance Praise

"A light, charming story of best friends in a small Florida town who navigate conflicting relationships, careers, and values on their journey to love. Inspired by Shakespeare's *Much Ado About Nothing*, this novel will especially appeal to young adult readers."

— Kathleen Anderson, Ph.D., author of *Jane Austen's Women: An Introduction*, SUNY Press, 2018

"*Welcome to the Paradise Motel* by Olivia Taylor is a delightful retelling of *Much Ado About Nothing*. While it follows the basic plot structure of Shakespeare's comedy, it is perfectly adapted to contemporary Florida. The two main female characters—Bea, a quick-witted journalist, and Honey, a pink-haired schoolteacher— are protagonists readers can and will root for. This book has everything a reader could want—pirate tales, exciting fight scenes, true love. Brilliantly executed."

— Maura Jortner, Ph.D., author of *102 Days of Lying About Lauren*

Welcome to
The Paradise Motel

Welcome to The Paradise Motel

Olivia Taylor

Apprentice
House Press
Loyola University Maryland

First Edition

Library of Congress Control Number: 2025932637

Casebound ISBN 978-1-62720-596-2
Paperback ISBN: 978-1-62720-600-6
Ebook ISBN: 978-1-62720-598-6

Editorial Development by Rory Durso
Design by Maxx Lao
Promotional Development by Kate Tourison
Cover art created by Karen Samuelson

Published by Apprentice House Press

Apprentice
House Press
Loyola University Maryland

Loyola University Maryland
4501 N. Charles Street, Baltimore, MD 21210
410.617.5265
www.ApprenticeHouse.com
info@ApprenticeHouse.com

In memory of Kayla Harris

Contents

"Thy grace being gained cures all disgrace in me."
William Shakespeare, *Love's Labor's Lost* 4.3.66

INTRODUCTION

This book began with a production of *Much Ado About Nothing* at the Fernandina Little Theatre, so named because it was about the size of a double-wide trailer. I was an enthusiastic middle schooler and confirmed Shakespeare nerd playing a catch-all character comprised of Margaret, Ursula, and Antonio, officially called Margaret.

Despite playing three characters, I had a lot of offstage time, so I would sit out in the audience and listen, fascinated, as the older actors who played Beatrice and Benedick rehearsed. It was one of my first times experiencing a live performance of Shakespeare. I was amazed at how these dusty old words came to life when acted aloud. I never got tired of it—the playfulness, the sharpness, the rhythm of the language. Even now, I still hear a lot of the lines from the play in the voices of that cast. *Much Ado* was already one of my favorite Shakespeare plays, and that production cemented my love for it.

The idea to adapt *Much Ado* into a novel came about several years later. It was early in the pandemic, and the beaches in my hometown had just reopened. I had decided to write a creative thesis for my masters' program, and had gone to walk and mull over potential story ideas. I wanted to write a story set in an old beachside motel that had been converted into an apartment complex. I had lived in several places like it in college, and it seemed like the perfect setting to write about what I, along with everyone else at that moment, was desperately missing — a community. The main character would be a journalist whose news articles contrasted hilariously with what was actually happening.

I had been thinking about this idea for several weeks, but the plot refused to budge. Over the years, I had encountered a few Florida-themed productions of Shakespeare. Florida, in many ways, is to the rest of the world as Shakespeare's Italy was to his Elizabethan audience. The Italy of *Much Ado* is a larger-than-life "faraway" land, but it also plays on English views of Italy as a place associated with commercialism and vice. Having lived in Florida most of my life, this sounded very familiar. So, why not write a novel about *Much Ado About Nothing* at the Paradise Motel?

Delighted by this epiphany, I started working the old familiar characters into the new landscape. Like most people, I was drawn to *Much Ado* because of Beatrice and Benedick — they are smart, sophisticated, and brilliantly funny. They are also deeply flawed, and maybe a little crazy, but there is a kind of purity to them — they are unapologetic about what they think and feel, and they are fiercely loyal to those they love. They take a lot of living up to, but I loved every minute of writing them as Bea and Ben.

Beatrice became my journalist, Bea, forced to write well-mannered news articles that contrast with the way she truly feels and speaks. She lives next door to the Hero character, Honey, whose mother, Leonata, owns the motel. Don Pedro and his soldiers became successful businessmen—Peter Prince, Ben Constant, and Charlie Love, videogame entrepreneurs who have somehow managed to plaster a façade of charisma over their deep nerdiness. Using videogames gave me a way to bring in the swashbuckling element that colors the soldiery of Benedick and Claudio.

I set the play in the fictional city of Paradise because I needed the town's inhabitants to be a lot more gossipy and tightly-knit than real cities typically are. The townspeople needed to have a unified presence for Charlie's defamation of Honey to make an impact. Using a fictional city was also practical, because the worldbuilding and geography can be a little more flexible. Paradise is a kind of fantasy remix of several places in Florida, including my hometown, Fernandina Beach, along with Daytona and West Palm Beach.

I think my overall approach to writing can best be described in terms of playing games. I started writing fiction when I was pretty young, and it was mostly a more organized version of playing make-believe. As I got older and more serious about writing, I realized that it requires a lot of discipline, but I have tried to keep the spirit of play in everything that I write. One of the reasons that I was drawn to *Much Ado* is that it is a very playful story, even though it is also pretty dark. There are all these games going on—the wordplay between Beatrice and Benedick; the masquerade; the plot to make them fall in love. I decided to take the idea of gameplay and role playing and run with it.

If anyone believes that all the world's a stage, it is the characters in *Welcome to the Paradise Motel*. They are constantly playing a series of roles, some of which they create and some of which they have thrust upon them. From a technical standpoint, the games were a way for me to capture the spirit of play which runs throughout the original —Don Pedro's elaborate love-plot becomes Peter's tabletop campaign; the *Swashbuckleriad* video game allows the characters to practice being adventurers. These layers of games also invite you as the reader in to play.

I will close with the memory of another Shakespeare performance. It was May, and I had been living abroad for about five months when I went to see *As You Like It* at the Globe in London. To say that I was geeking out would be an understatement. By that point, I had spent a fair amount of time in theaters, onstage and behind the scenes. I had even helped re-create the Globe on a smaller scale for a production of *Taming of the Shrew*. However, what surprised me most about being at the London Globe was that, even though it was grand and impressive, and in an entirely different country, I felt strangely at home there.

It is this sense of ritual, of homecoming, that I most wish to convey in this book. There are new faces, and new scenes, but the heart, I hope, is the same. I hope you feel as much at home in the world of Bea and Ben as I do.

–Olivia Taylor

THE PERSONS OF THIS PLAY

(In order of appearance)

BEA BRIGHT, our heroine, a journalist from *The Paradise Post*.

ELAINE EVANS, Bea's mentor, editor-in-chief at *The Paradise Post*.

JOHNNY DONAHUE, a journalist from *The Paradise Post*, half-brother of Peter Prince.

HONEY NOBLE, Bea's best friend.

LEONATA NOBLE, Honey's mother, owner of The Paradise Motel.

PEARL PITTMAN, head of the Historical Society, grumpy buzzkill.

DIANA PITTMAN, Pearl's granddaughter.

PETER PRINCE IV, C.E.O. of Buccaneer Trail Productions, everyone's friend.

BEN CONSTANT, Creative Design Manager of Buccaneer Trail Productions, annoyance.

CHARLIE LOVE, Honey's boyfriend, Story Manager of Buccaneer Trail Productions.

MEG SMITH, a cosmetologist, sometime ally.

EMMA BEATRICE, Bea's small niece.

PASTOR AUGUST CONSTANT, Ben's father, pastor of First Non-Denominational Church.

OPHELIA PRINCE, historian, owner of Beau's Bridal and the mermaid lagoon, distant relative of Peter.

CRYSTAL PITTMAN, Mrs. Pittman's other granddaughter.

DOUG BERRY, head of security at the Kissimmee Renaissance Faire and Fandom Convention.

VERGE S., Doug's assistant.

Assorted FRIENDS, FAMILY, TOWNSPEOPLE, and CO-WORKERS.

ACT ONE

ONE FOOT IN SEA AND ONE ON SHORE

CHAPTER ONE

Here, There Be Pirates

Video Game Creators to Appear in Pirate Parade

Beatrice Bright
Wednesday, August 30, 2017

This year's Pirate Fest will be even more swashbuckling than usual. Peter Prince IV, Ben Constant and Charlie Love, creators of the wildly successful video game, *Swashbuckleriad,* and owners of the video game company, Buccaneer Trail Productions, will appear in the Pirate Parade tomorrow night. The trio, who grew up in here in Paradise Fla., are promoting the latest edition of the game and the relocation of their gaming company of the same name, which will open its new headquarters here in June. *Swashbuckleriad* is an action-RPG set in a Golden Age of Piracy redolent of dime novels and vintage action films. Ben Constant, the company's spokesman, said, "Paradise's colorful pirate history was a huge influence on the game."

Constant, the son of First Non-Denominational Church Pastor August Constant, means this literally: several years ago, he discovered that he was a descendant of Paradise's most famous buccaneer, Captain William Constant.

"It really fired my imagination," he said. "I couldn't help but wonder—what would it be like to live back then? I was playing around with some basic coding and animation at the time, and just kept working at it. When Peter and Charlie got involved, I knew it was gonna work, but I never imagined that it would take off the way it has. Anyway, we're proud of our roots, and we hope that bringing our company to Paradise will help us to share our success with the community."

The young entrepreneurs will also be signing autographs at Pirate Fest on Saturday. Prince is the son of FL State Representative Emma Prince, and Love is the son of local attorney Jeff Love.

—from *The Paradise Post.*

Bea scowled at the computer screen. "Do we really need to include the parents? It's kinda clunky."

Elaine Turner, editor-in-chief of *The Paradise Post,* leaned back in her swivel chair at an angle that was especially dangerous for a 70-year-old. "You know our readership of retirees cares much more about the parents than these young upstarts and their infernal devices."

"Okay," said Bea, holding up her hands in a good-natured gesture of surrender as she turned back to her computer. "Anything else?"

"Yeah. That line about the Golden Age is too long. And no one uses the word "redolent."

"Got it."

After Bea's back was turned, Elaine watched her, her leathery face creased with concern. Her young protégé pushed her auburn hair out of her eyes, readjusted the green velvet kimono that hung around her shoulders, then attacked the keyboard with a relish. Her long, stubborn fingers beat out a staccato rhythm that was not at all in tune with the smooth-mannered article she was supposed to be writing. Bea was like electricity, Elaine thought. *The Post* needed her, but there was always a chance that she might set the whole place on fire.

Elaine shook herself abruptly and turned back to the proofs spread out over her wobbly wooden desk. Her immaculately manicured purple fingernails contrasted sharply with her wrinkled hands as she smoothed out the large sheets. "Make sure you get a good image for the cut," she said. "I want it nice and big for the front page."

"Will do," said Bea. She took a long, slow sip from her mug, which was patterned with glittering stars, and pulled up an old snapshot of the subjects of this week's headline. Peter, Ben, and Charlie — three bespectacled teen-age nerds — were sitting at a table scattered with soda cans and tabletop roleplay paraphernalia. Peter, the oldest of the group, was GM by virtue of his theatrical experience. Shy, watchful Charlie had his arm around Bea's best friend, Honey, a lovely girl with bubblegum-pink hair. Bea had been behind the camera, as always. Now, she zoomed in on the nerdiest of the three guys, the one with the piratical grin. Ben.

It was too bad, she thought, that she couldn't use this picture instead of the glossy publicity photo he'd sent her — a photo of ridiculously stylish 20-somethings air-brushed to the point where they were almost unrecogniz-able. Almost.

So. After seven years away, the guys were coming home for good.

Her gray eyes were glassy with memory and computer fatigue as she stared at Ben's digitized, mocking face. It was one thing, she thought, to deal with him over holidays and occasional weekends. But now things were going to change. The newsroom was crackling with rumor and possibility. Buccaneer Trail Productions would revolutionize the small island city's limping economy. But Bea remembered only too well what had happened the last time that the brilliant minds behind Buccaneer Trail—in particular, the brilliant mind of Ben Constant—had taken their small town by storm.

• • •

Until their senior year of high school, Bea and Ben had been close friends engaged in a good-natured rivalry to see who could shine the brightest in school, at work, and in battles of wits. Video games were the only thing they didn't compete in. Bea thought they were too lowbrow and mind-melting (and she knew Ben would win).

Scholarships were the only way she'd be able to afford college since her parents had taken a serious hit during the recession. She'd applied diligently to everything she could find—but the scholarships kept fizzling out. This one, however, she'd worked hard on and been sure of. The night before the deadline, giddy with excitement, she had recounted her plans to Ben. The scholarship was for a private college near Orlando. Exciting things were always happening there, and she would be on the scene to report its wonders to the world. Ben acted like he wasn't going to apply—he was hoping for another school close to Orlando's fast-growing gaming industry. For once, they went a whole evening without bickering, caught up in their daydreams of the future. Bea went home in a happy daze, wondering if she might have feelings for him.

The next morning, Ben submitted a last-minute scholarship entry that had blown everyone else out of the water.

It would later go on to revolutionize the video game industry as *Swashbuckleriad*.

Even then, it wasn't so much what he'd done as what he'd said afterward. Bea had stormed into the video game store where Ben worked to demand an explanation.

"I can't believe I was stupid enough to trust you!" she'd said. "I can't believe I thought that you cared about what I was doing and not just sizing up the competition! I thought—I thought we were friends, Ben." She could feel tears burning in the back of her throat.

"Friends compete!" said Ben. "Hey, I can't help it if I'm smart enough to pull together something overnight that's brilliantly prizewinning." He turned away and began coolly tacking a poster for the latest first-person shooter game to the wall behind the desk.

Undaunted, she stormed around to his side of the counter. "Well, I hope that's a consolation when you're rolling in money and don't have any friends because you trampled on all their dreams!"

"Hey, I'm not exactly rolling in it over here," Ben snapped, turning around to face her. "Preacher's kid, remember? What do you want me to do anyway, give you the money?"

"No!" she cried, throwing up her hands in exasperation and knocking over a stack of old game cartridges in the process.

This time, Ben held his ground. "What then? Say, 'Gee, Bea, I'm so sorry I entered a scholarship that literally anyone could enter?' I'm sorry that I just happen to be smarter and more likable than you!"

Her hands shook. "All you care about are rules and numbers and—video games! You don't have a heart, just a circuit board."

"Well at least I'm not like you!" he said, "I love books and newspapers as much as anyone, but there's no future in the past, Bea. That's why you can't get any money. You couldn't change with the times if your life depended on it!"

Bea backed away from the counter in disbelief. "I can't believe I almost—if you can't see what's wrong, then we can't be friends anymore."

"Frankly, I can't," he said. "And really, I'm fine with that."

"Well, so am I!" she said. "So. Am. I!"

Then she had walked out of the game store and slammed the door behind her.

• • •

"Beatrice!" cut in Elaine's sharp, high voice, startling Bea out of her reverie. "Mrs. Pittman and her minions are going to be out in full force tomorrow afternoon. Under no circumstances do I want another incident like last time, understand? You're the best reporter I've got, but don't think that's going to save you if you can't maintain some professionalism. Calling one of the most respected citizens in town the 'anointed sovereign of idiotic bylaws' to her face—while entirely accurate—is far from professional."

Bea winced. "Yes ma'am. It won't happen again."

"Good." said Elaine. "Johnny's good for a bit of color, but I'm counting on you for the facts. And don't call me ma'am. It makes me feel old."

Bea frowned slightly at the mention of Johnny Donahue. He was the older half-brother of Bea and Ben's friend Peter Prince (Johnny had taken his mother's maiden name when his father, Peter Prince III, remarried). He had only been on staff for about a year, but had already managed to charm his way into a full-time reporting position, covering the crime beat.

At that moment, Honey burst through the office door carrying a box of doughnuts. Her long hair was still the same cheery shade of pink. Honey was the sort of person who had a dress for every occasion, although most of them were thrifted. Today she wore a primly-cut, almost 50's style dress in a floral sunrise pattern — her "Friday dress," as she called it. "I've come to barter for Bea's release with these," she announced, depositing the box of doughnuts on Elaine's desk. Behind Honey's crisp teacher voice, there were still hints of her Florida-cracker drawl.

Elaine pretended to scowl. "Sorry to inconvenience you, but this is the first real news we've had since the beginning of summer — are those the cream-filled ones?"

Honey danced over to Bea. "Quick, while she's distracted," she stage-whispered, motioning for the door.

Bea laughed, and began packing up her stuff.

Honey started to laugh with her — but she fell silent when she saw Johnny coming into the newsroom.

"Did you get any of the pink lemonade doughnuts?" he asked. He was good looking, in a greasy sort of way — tall and muscular, with large features and thick dark hair that was a little too long to be professional. He always dressed like he came from money, (which he did) — polos and pastel pants and boat shoes.

Honey stiffened. "I'm afraid not."

Bea gave her a quizzical look. She was not fond of Johnny — she didn't trust men who wore orange pants — but his questionable clothing choices didn't seem like sufficient grounds for the fear in her friend's face.

Johnny's dark eyes gazed hungrily at Honey over his too-wide smile. "That's too bad," he said, ignoring the doughnuts completely and stepping closer to her. "They're my favorite."

When she saw Honey shrink away from him, Bea instinctively put herself between Honey and Johnny. Deliberately ignoring Johnny, she turned to Honey and said, "Are you and Charlie doing anything later?" In addition to being one of the founders of Buccaneer Trail Productions, Charlie Love was still Honey's long-distance boyfriend.

"Yes," said Honey, brightening. "We're going to some kind of fancy charity gala." This was not strictly true — Charlie wasn't coming in until the next day, and the gala wasn't until the day after that, but it was, technically, "later."

"We'd better get going, then," said Bea, shouldering her camera bag and leveling a threatening glance at Johnny. Bea was short, but she could still be intimidating when she wanted.

Johnny took the hint — along with a fistful of doughnuts — and left.

Elaine, preoccupied with the proofs, was oblivious. "Don't forget, you're reporting on the parade tomorrow night," she called as Bea and Honey left. "You know the drill. Photographs and a real interview, not another canned publicity statement from Ben."

Bea made a face. She and Honey fled out the door and into the Florida sunshine.

• • •

Honey wrapped her hair up into a messy bun as they

walked, desperate to get the weight off her neck. It was almost dinnertime, but it was still smothering. Slack tide. Summer in Florida was shipped fresh from Hell by way of Death Valley, and it stayed longer than an unwanted guest. The walk to their apartments at the Paradise Motel wasn't long, but it would feel longer in this heat. Honey just wanted to be back home and safe in the air conditioning.

The motel was owned and run by her mom, Leonata Noble, who had converted it into an apartment complex during the recession. It was a dysfunctional and decrepit relic of the 1950's, but it was across the street from the beach, and it was the only apartment complex on the island that straddled the fine line between cheap and (mostly) safe.

The shortest way home was through the small picturesque downtown where *The Paradise Post* was located. Their route wound past the heavenly-scented confectionary wonderland of the ice cream store where Honey had worked in high school and the tacky neon-and-graffiti video game shop where Ben used to work.

Bea strode along beside her, her velvety green kimono hanging limply on her shoulders. Honey was a little envious of Bea's ability to pull off comfy professional outfits. "Thanks for getting me out of there," said Bea.

Honey gave her friend a grateful smile. "I was about to say the same thing." She tried not to think about the lingering, hungry look on Johnny's face. It was Friday, she was off from work, and tomorrow was the biggest party of the year, and, best of all, Charlie was coming back. She peeled off her Paradise Elementary teacher ID, crumpled it up, and shoved it in her pocket.

They passed The Lazy Fisherman, the main bar in town; Shredders, the surf shop where Peter and Charlie had worked; Jitterbug Coffee; and Ye Olde Paradyse Tea Companye (bitter rivals with Jitterbug). The historic courthouse with its moon-like clock tower and large Italianate fountain came into view. Honey's ancestors had helped build it in eighteen-something. "Wait—" she said, stopping in front of the fountain. "Let's make a wish!"

Bea started to dig in her purse for change, but Honey stopped her. "I got this," she said, handing Bea a shiny new penny. "I found two of them on the way to work this morning. Figured it was a sign."

"Thanks," said Bea.

Honey closed her eyes. *I hope Charlie proposes to me soon*, she wished. Then she murmured, "For fair winds and following seas," and tossed the coin in the fountain. It landed in the topmost bowl with a small splash.

"Fair winds and following seas," repeated Bea. Her coin landed in the largest bowl at the bottom. Honey was pretty sure she wished that she would make it through the year without getting fired.

Having completed the ritual, they walked on, past the yellow cinderblock used bookshop where Bea had worked in high school, and the high school itself, with its sprawling football field. Johnny had been the star quarterback there. This must have reminded Bea of the unsettling episode with Johnny. "Guess Johnny's still salty about you turning down his date," she said.

"Yeah," said Honey, grimacing. "I tried to be as nice as I could. I don't see how he couldn't have known that I'm dating Charlie."

Bea shrugged. "It's not your fault that he can't get over himself. But let me know if he gives you any more trouble. How are things with you and Charlie, by the way?"

Honey hugged herself and looked away. "Fine, I guess."

Bea raised her eyebrows in query.

"I'm just nervous," said Honey. "Every time we see each other, it's a weekend or a holiday or something like that. What if, when he's around me all the time, he realizes he doesn't actually like me?"

"Well, then he's obviously an idiot who doesn't deserve you," Bea replied. "Besides, you guys have been dating for ages. Surely you would have figured out by now if either of you wasn't interested."

As they walked on, the bunches of cute pastel Victorian houses and storefronts gave way to small and brightly colored vacation cottages, and then to glossy new condos and vast beachfront mansions. Finally, the pink cinderblock walls of the Paradise Motel came into view — the last holdout of a bygone age sandwiched between two condos.

As they stopped at the crosswalk in front of Tropical Bob's Beach Diner, Bea said, "It'll be fun to have the guys around again. Almost like old times."

Honey caught the note of false bravado in her friend's voice. "What about Ben?"

Bea looked away, out at the slim ribbon of ocean visible over the tops of the dunes. "I'm going to have a hell of a time interviewing him. He wouldn't answer a direct question if his life depended on it. But at least it'll be interesting."

As they crossed the street and went into the parking lot of the motel, they talked over Bea's photography business, which she had run on the side since she was fifteen, and Honey's latest teaching adventures. Today a kid had asked their phone for the answer to a question on a test — out loud. Aside from that, it had been a good day. Honey had designed the school's float for the Pirate Parade, and she had just put the finishing touches on this afternoon with the help of some of the older students.

"By the way," said Honey as they climbed up the concrete steps to their rooms on the second floor of the Paradise Motel, "Mom just told me that Charlie and Peter and Ben are renting out the three big rooms here! You know, for old times' sake." She gestured across the way to what Leonata referred to as the "executive suites." "Isn't that great? I'll be able to see Charlie every day!"

Bea glanced over in dismay at the rooms. "Oh, that's fantastic," she said sarcastically. "Just what I wanted. I can see Ben's stupid face out the window every day."

Honey laughed. "Oh, come on. It'll be fun! Just like old times."

"Yeah," said Bea, her voice oozing with sarcasm. "An absolute blast."

CHAPTER TWO

Loved of All Ladies

The Origins of Pirate Fest

Beatrice Bright
Friday, September 1, 2017

Three hundred years ago, Captain William Constant, terror
of the seven seas, sailed into the harbor of Paradise, then
known as the Spanish town of Cielo, terrorized the residents,
and spent a king's ransom in treasure. According to local
historian Ophelia Prince, he wasn't the first pirate to visit the
island, but he ensured that the residents would be obsessed
with pirates for centuries after. Rumors of sunken ships and
buried treasure abounded, but the Chamber of Commerce
quickly discovered that the real treasure, of course, was pirate
tourism. And thus, Pirate Fest was born.

—from *The Paradise Post.*

The next afternoon, Bea arrived at the parade route armed
with her camera and ready for action. Since it was an out-
door event, she'd dressed casually to blend in—a Pirate
Fest t-shirt with her nametag pinned on one side; mint-
green shorts; chunky, practical sandals; aviator sunglasses
perched on her head; camera bag slung over her shoulder.
The historic district was already teeming with people.

There were parade marshals, volunteers, security officers, business owners, festival vendors—and obsessively early parade watchers. Some families staked out their ideal vantage point when they first moved to the island and would chase off anyone who invaded their territory.

Bea staked her claim on a low brick wall between the ice cream store and the video game shop. It was a great vantage point, but today it reminded her unpleasantly of her long-ago confrontation with Ben. Now she would have him for a neighbor again. She wondered if he remembered that the nostalgia of the Paradise Motel came with persistent mold, immortal flying roaches, and spotty hot water.

She hadn't really expected to avoid Ben. But he could have at least had the decency to move into some other apartment complex. It was kind of humiliating, if she was being honest. After all, *she* wasn't exactly living there for the nostalgia...

But if things went well, all that would change soon. Elaine was retiring at the end of the year, and she had hinted that she would like Bea to take over as editor-in-chief. She wouldn't be video-game rich, but she'd be able to save up enough for a nice little house or an apartment built within the last decade. Unless she let her temper get the better of her again and Johnny sweet-talked his way into the editor's chair.

Sweet-talking was not Bea's specialty.

She made a face and looked back over her notes. The trouble with small towns was that time was circular, really. Sooner or later, everything that happened would come around again. Especially your mistakes.

She leaned back on her hands and closed her eyes,

determined to savor the few moments of relative peace before her family arrived. The onshore breeze came billowing down the street, and she basked in the sharp, living smell of the blue salt sea.

An irritated squawk attracted her attention. To her dismay, she spotted Mrs. Pittman (Anointed Sovereign of Idiotic Bylaws) approaching from eleven o'clock. She was wearing a neon green Pirate Festival T-Shirt and bedecked in enough plastic beads to outfit all of Mardi Gras.

Mrs. Pittman was the chair of the Historical Society. Bea had first run afoul of her a few years ago, when Bea, Honey, and Honey's mother Leonata had asked the Hysterical Society (as they were locally known) to help them raise enough money to renovate and restore the Paradise Motel to its former glory. Mrs. Pittman had scoffed at the idea and bullied the rest of the society into renovating the Old Post Office instead. Bea had the nerve to protest against the way they were treated and beg them to reconsider. This quickly earned her the old lady's hatred. Today, Mrs. Pittman was followed by a small entourage of fellow retired ladies who resembled a flock of tropical birds, as well as some sweaty and sullen teenage girls from cotillion.

"Beatrice! You're out early today," shrilled Mrs. Pittman.

"Yes ma'am, I am out early," Bea replied. Her Southern accent always got a little thicker when she was making an effort to be polite. *Keep it together,* she ordered herself. She instinctively reached for her enormous camera, which had been sitting on the ledge. There was something comforting about the heft of it.

Mrs. Pittman looked Bea over disapprovingly. "I see Elaine has relaxed the dress code."

Bea felt her smile grow stiff. "She prefers that we blend in, to make people more comfortable."

"I don't think she needs to worry about that," said Mrs. Pittman. "No one would mistake *you* for anybody important."

A snarky reply tingled on the edge of Bea's tongue. She wondered if Johnny had paid Mrs. Pittman to be unusually nasty to her to clear his way to the editor's chair, or if she was just like that naturally. As Mrs. Pittman went on talking, Bea nodded politely and concentrated on imagining a house of her own. She would paint the kitchen mint green, and hang Honey's painting of the bookstore in the living room, which would also be the library…

"We've just finished putting up barricades around the Old Post Office," said Mrs. Pittman. "You would not believe what people did to the steps last year. There was trash everywhere."

You called? Bea thought wryly. She had tried to watch the parade from the steps of the Old Post Office last year. The post office was a hideous relic of Brutalist architecture that was built sometime in the 1970s. The Hysterical Society's renovations had not improved it much, but it did have convenient parade-watching steps. That year, just as the parade was about to start, the Society came and chased everyone off to keep them from "damaging" the steps, leading to the "anointed sovereign of idiotic bylaws" episode.

Good lord, the woman was still speaking. "Make sure you get some photos of the theater's float," Mrs. Pittman ordered. "My granddaughter, Diana, is the lead in *Pirates of Penzance* this year, and she looks simply stunning. Although really, they should have had their own float instead of sharing the limelight with that upstart gamer company that's coming in to tear up all the buildings."

"Yes ma'am," Bea replied, bracing for the next onslaught.

Mrs. Pittman gave her a toothy grin. "Oh yes. Diana's really carrying the production. Much better than the one they did a few years ago. I've heard that the girl who played Mabel then couldn't act if her life depended on it."

Bea bit her lip, knowing full well that Mrs. Pittman knew Bea had been Mabel in the last production. "I've heard good things about this one," she managed.

She would bring back the "Arts and Culture" section of the paper, and redesign the website, and start an apprenticeship for aspiring journalists in high school…

Much to Bea's relief, Mrs. Pittman, having failed to get a reaction, had already turned away to issue orders to her entourage. "Let's get back to our float, everyone."

With that, she and the others departed.

Thank goodness. Bea smoothed back her escaping hair, and then got back to work. She snapped a few practice shots with her camera—the wizened crepe myrtles; the Georgia-clay brick stores with their pastel, gingerbread facades; the expectant shopkeepers gearing up for the busiest weekend in the entire year. But she was not to be left in peace for long.

As she looked over the test shots on the viewscreen, Johnny sidled up to her and peered over her shoulder. "Looking good," he purred. "You really do have a gift. The one you got of the manatee rescue last week was incredible."

She gave an exasperated sigh and turned so that she had the length of the big camera lens between them. "What do you want, Johnny?"

"Just trying to establish a little workplace camaraderie," said Johnny. "And, you know, I was hoping, since you and Honey are close, that you might give me some tips to get on her good side."

"You could start by taking 'no' for an answer," said Bea. "You know she and Charlie have been in love with each other since high school."

Johnny shrugged. "People don't marry their high school sweethearts, Bea. Maybe I'll catch her on the rebound." He licked his lips.

"Or maybe you should do your job instead of being a creep," said Bea. "Don't you have to interview the sheriff or something?"

"That's not a very professional tone to take," chided Johnny. "After all, Elaine hasn't mentioned who she's naming as the new editor-in-chief. Rumor has it we're the top two contenders. So, you'd better step up your game, sweetheart."

It took every ounce of professionalism Bea possessed not to knock him into the middle of next week's edition. Instead, she gave him a level glare that would have withered lesser mortals on the spot. Johnny sauntered away.

Muttering things under her breath, Bea got back to work. Soon, more families appeared. She snapped a few obligatory photos of adorable children in pirate costumes and got their parents' permission to include them in the paper. Her own family arrived, followed by Ben's family, the Constants; Honey's extended family, the Nobles; Charlie's parents, the Loves; and Peter's enormous family, the Princes. The Nobles had been around since the time of the first Spanish settlement, while the Princes had simply crawled out of the swamp sometime after the Jurassic period. As the two oldest families on the island, the Princes and the Nobles maintained an uneasy alliance against the invading snowbirds and adopted newcomers they deemed tolerable, like the Loves, Constants, and Brights.

"Alright, everyone, I need you to look respectable," said Bea to the assembling clans, who were busy scolding small children, setting up folding chairs, and passing around beverages. "Elaine wants some pictures of 'the excited family members gathering to witness their sons' triumph.'"

"Triumph my foot," grumbled Grandma Constant as she settled cautiously into her lawn chair. "Benny should get a real job instead of playing video games all day."

Honey arrived wearing a shimmery sea-green dress that made her look like a mermaid. Everyone at school had wanted her to ride on the float. She had politely, but firmly, refused. She hated being in front of a crowd. She was soon surrounded by a cluster of adoring little cousins and was tasked with keeping them from getting in the way of the parade.

After snapping a few frozen and unnatural-looking group shots, Bea decided to just sneak in some candids later, because the first parade floats had started making their way up the street.

While anyone who came from Orlando, Louisiana, or New York would have found the Pirate Parade lackluster, it was still the most lavish spectacle that Paradise could possibly afford, resplendent in all its kitschy glory. Despite being technically "at work," Bea reveled in the glittering mess of off-key marching bands, obnoxiously loud classic cars, bad dance routines, canned rock music, boats, floats, and of course, pirates. The float Honey had designed for the school looked spectacular. A colorful cardboard submarine traversed a fantastical underwater landscape complete with umbrella jellyfish, pool-noodle coral, and a refrigerator box treasure chest. The float was populated with a "school" of small children wearing t-shirts with fish on them. Even though Bea knew what the various components were made of, it still looked real, somehow. She believed in the world Honey created, and so did the children.

The cannon from the Buccaneers float could be heard from a mile away. When the float finally rolled into view, the sound was deafening. The ship, really an ancient and elaborate float pulled by a pickup truck, came sailing down the street in full regalia. It was manned with pirates from the community theater's production of *Pirates of Penzance*, who were flinging candy and beads to small children to make up for terrifying them with the cannon.

At first, all Bea could do was stare. If the publicity photos had rendered Peter, Ben, and Charlie unrecognizable, it was nothing compared to this. They were lounging in massive captain's chairs towards the stern of the ship, looking impossibly suave, beaming with million-dollar smiles. They were surrounded by the women of *Pirates of Penzance*, including Diana Pittman and some other questionably dressed "wenches," some of whom had been pageant contestants in high school. Diana, had, as usual, managed to look a little more extra than the others — an elaborate, low-cut period gown, her hair an ostentatious pile of golden ringlets, dark, dramatic eye makeup, and bold lips and cheeks. There was a part of Bea that admired how over-the-top Diana was, but mostly she just got on her nerves.

There was Charlie, dressed in the latest beach hipster fashion—light wash skinny jeans, a weirdly striped button-up shirt, and aviator sunglasses. His artfully shaggy brown hair made him look like a 2005 heartthrob. When Charlie saw Honey, he pushed his sunglasses on top of his head and rushed to the side of the ship to stare at her with burning blue eyes.

And there was Peter, standing tall and strong in a blue fishing shirt and khaki shorts. Really, Peter didn't look that different. He always reminded Bea of a golden retriever, with his sandy surfer hair and perpetually friendly demeanor. He spotted her and waved, and she waved back. Thank goodness for Peter. He was like a big brother, but more fun.

And, last, there was Ben, sporting his trademark black leather jacket over a graphic t-shirt and black skinny jeans, gleefully throwing candy and cheat codes to the crowd. He was also tall, but slighter and paler than Peter and Charlie. He made up for it with a piratical demeanor, a strong jawline, and a head full of dark curly hair he kept a little over-grown to make himself look taller. He was the only one of the three who hadn't swapped out his glasses for contacts. The dark, square frames reflected his intelligence but couldn't mask the mischief.

He has no business looking that good, Bea thought. She raised her camera and squinted through the shutter, scolding herself mentally for letting surprise get the better of her. Now she'd only have a few moments to get the needed shots. Without really thinking about it, she zoomed in on Ben, who was now standing at the wheel of the boat looking as if he owned the damn thing.

As the camera shutter clicked, Diana grabbed Ben and

kissed him firmly on the lips.

"What the—" Bea muttered, lowering her camera in disbelief. Then, remembering herself, she quickly snapped shots of the less-occupied Peter and Charlie, making sure to include the logo of both Buccaneer Trail Productions and the Paradise Community Theater. Then she turned her lens to the Hysterical Society's float, a garish model of the Old Post Office.

She did not see Ben frantically disentangling himself from Diana, or the panicked look he shot in her direction.

The clustered family members around Bea immediately broke into a buzz of gossip and speculation:

"Isn't that Diana Pittman?"

"Oh, she'll do anything to get attention. Last year at the—"

"As if Benny wasn't the biggest attention hog in all of Volusia County. Of course he did it on purpose."

"Don't you dare talk about my son that way—"

Bea swallowed, trying to banish the sharp, nasty feeling that had risen in her chest. Photographed or not, that was an image she wasn't going to get out of her mind for a while. He had a right to kiss whoever he wanted, but...

• • •

As Peter gazed out on the crowd from his vantage point on the parade float, smiling and waving to his friends and neighbors, he wondered if it really had been a good idea to move the company back to Paradise. He had been wondering this ever since he'd spotted Honey in the crowd, waving up at his float with an incandescent smile. It wasn't so much her appearance, although to him it seemed as if she always walked in the golden light of the afternoon sun.

It was the sudden, terrible joy of her presence that pierced his heart. *Home* was the only word he had for it. And she gazed up lovingly — not at Peter.

At Charlie.

That was how it had always been, and that was how it should be. Peter hated himself for resenting it. There was no reason he should. He glanced at Charlie, who was leaning out over the railing of the boat, looking back at Honey, enthralled. Ever since they had decided to move back home, Charlie had talked of nothing except wanting to marry her.

As the float began to roll away, Honey spotted Peter, and waved at him with all the ease of someone greeting an old friend, and he hated how he could feel the light spread through his whole being as he smiled back at her. He'd get over it. He would. He would learn to be normal around her.

He stood there, gripping the railing so tightly that his knuckles turned white, smiling his frozen smile. He was home for good. Not just for Christmases and Thanksgivings and weekends.

There was Bea, little and fierce, wielding a camera that, from this angle, looked almost bigger than she was. She was staring at Ben with a mixture of contempt and fascination. Peter shook himself from his reverie and waved at her. The genuine, ordinary delight of finding a friend in the crowd pulled him back from the brink. She grinned and waved back at him enthusiastically. Bea was the only one who knew how he felt about Honey.

As the parade traveled on, he saw his parents beaming with pride. He would be able to go fishing with his dad again and play guitar with his mom. There was his younger cousin Dave, who was gazing up at him as if he were a superhero, and there was Mrs. Johnson, his music teacher, who he'd been able to hire to work at Buccaneer Trail after the music program had been cut from Paradise Elementary.

When he had passed by the entire clan, he climbed up into the bow of the boat, clinging to the side so that he didn't tumble off, so that he could peer over the tops of the hotels and see the ocean—his ocean, a perfectly luminous blue in the last rays of the setting sun.

● ● ●

Meanwhile, Bea had spotted Mrs. Pittman coming her way like an angry goose. "You photographed them! You're worse than the paparazzi!"

"Please, Mrs. Pittman, I wasn't trying to—I wasn't expecting that to happen,"

"Delete that photo of my granddaughter and Benny Constant this instant!" said Mrs. Pittman. "I will not have her reputation ruined by you writing up some trashy story about her! Or selling it to the tabloids or splashing it all over the internet!"

"The *Post* is a respectable paper, not a tabloid," said Bea, straightening up. "And nothing trashy happened. Just a fan getting overexcited...I guess."

Her hesitation was fatal. Mrs. Pittman turned purple. "Don't you dare insinuate such things to me!" she shrieked. "I'll have your job for this!"

Bea was beginning to wonder if it would really be such a tragedy to lose this job. Except for, of course, inconvenient demands such as rent and food.

"Please, I didn't mean anything," she said, raising her

hands in a palliative gesture.

"Don't think you can fool me! You've been nothing but rude to me from day one!"

Then a big, soothing voice boomed, "Whoa, whoa, whoa, Mrs. P." It was Peter. He came striding in to intervene, with Ben close behind him. "It was just a little misunderstanding, that's all. I can vouch for Bea. So can Ben." He gave Ben a significant look.

"Uh, yes," said Ben, who suddenly didn't know what to do with his hands. "I didn't encourage—I don't think she meant anything by it. Diana, that is. Just got caught up in the excitement. And Bea would never take advantage of anyone like that—" His dark curly hair was plastered to his forehead with sweat, and his pale cheeks were reddened from the sun. Or embarrassment. Or both.

Mrs. Pittman scowled and folded her arms.

Diana sashayed up to them and said, "Grandma, chill out. Any publicity is good publicity. Gotta do something to get out of community theater and into the big time." She winked at Ben, who involuntarily took a step back to hide behind Peter as Diana ushered Mrs. Pittman away.

Bea took a deep breath. Her job was still intact. For now. "Thank you," she said, mostly to Peter.

His brown eyes crinkled up into a gentle smile. "Don't mention it."

Then Bea rounded on Ben. "Look, I don't know how you do it, but you just *had* to pick the granddaughter of the person who's hell-bent on getting me fired, so could you just—"

"I didn't pick her!" he said. "You heard her. I was just a convenient prop. Besides," he added, slicking back his hair in an attempt to recover his composure, "I can't help it if the ladies can't resist me."

Bea rolled her eyes. "Well, we all know your mouth is your defining characteristic."

"And all live in fear of your dagger-like tongue," he said, giving her a mocking bow. "You are the one and only Queen of Sass. How can such a humble subject as myself ever be worthy of your notice?"

"You're not," said Bea. "You just keep getting in the way of my shots."

"Then maybe you should get a different lens," he said, gesturing to her camera.

"A different lens makes no difference if there's a big smudge of dirt on it," she said.

Ben put on his best imitation of his preacher dad: "Is it dirt, or the plank in your own eye?" he asked, raising his eyebrows. "But I thought you would have left this dump long ago?"

"Well, they started paying me to talk to the garbage, so I had to stick around," she replied.

He grinned. "You were destined for the profession."

"And you're destined for the obituaries if you screw up my job again," said Bea, shaking her fist at him.

"Well, at least I wouldn't have to talk to you again," he replied.

"Oh, don't tempt me," she said, getting up in his face.

Peter gently but firmly put his hands on their shoulders to part them. "As entertaining as that would be, Mrs. Leonata wants to know if you guys are coming to dinner or not. Dad's making shrimp boil."

"Wouldn't miss it," said Bea, turning to Peter. "Sorry." She gave him a quick hug. "Hope you weren't counting on a peaceful existence."

"What fun would that be?" Peter replied. "But Ben, really, if you could try to control your fangirls, it would make all of our lives a little more peaceful."

Ben gave him a mock salute. "I shall do my best, Captain."

Peter just shook his head and smiled. "C'mon, I'm starving."

As he steered them down the street towards the Paradise Motel, he could almost smell the spicy, buttery aroma of shrimp and sausage and corn on the cob billowing up in clouds of steam from an enormous pot. Lights flickered off in shop windows and glimmered on in house windows. Overhead, a few stars were beginning to emerge from behind the gauzy blue screen of sky as it deepened into dark.

• • •

Charlie had stayed behind to talk to Honey, but he was finding it more difficult than he expected. She was currently surrounded by a large crowd of Paradise Elementary children, who had come to announce that the school had won first place in the float decorating contest. Honey caught Charlie's eye and smiled apologetically, but she couldn't seem to extricate herself. He folded his arms and leaned against the wall to wait. It was cute that she was great with kids and everything, but he thought that he, her boyfriend, should be a little bit more of a priority than a bunch of snotty first graders. Especially since this was his big homecoming.

Eventually, the mob dispersed and Honey came over to him, flushed and breathless with excitement.

"Congratulations," he said, although he didn't sound

as enthusiastic as he'd intended.

A streetlamp flickered on, casting a wan yellow glow over them both.

Honey started to move towards him, and then stopped. He looked so different. It wasn't just the hipster clothes. Something else. Confidence, maybe? The way he carried himself. That seemed like a good change. He'd always been so shy. So why was she so painfully conscious of the difference?

"Sorry to keep you waiting so long," she said, brushing a strand of hair back behind her ear. "They just...came out of nowhere. I had no idea it would be such a success."

"You designed it," he said. "Of course it was a success."

Charlie's face had become more structured in the years that she had known him, the round boyish face straightening into defined lines, sharper points. She wanted to draw him, to re-create each feature and see if she could find by searching what so unsettled her.

"I'm sorry I didn't get to see your float," he was saying. "It was too far ahead of ours."

"I know," she said. She began picking at her glittery nail polish. "I hope you don't think I was trying to upstage you or anything. They just asked me to help and I—"

"Did what you do best," said Charlie. His smile did not quite reach his eyes. At any rate, they would have to make sure they got Honey to do *his* float next year. Surely someone else could do the school's. Then, seeing the worried look on her face, he added, "Besides we, uh, had enough excitement of our own."

"Ugh, I know," Honey said, covering her face with her hand. "I don't know what Diana was thinking. I'm just glad it wasn't you." She kissed him on the cheek, which took more nerve than it normally did. What was the matter with her? She had seen him in Orlando last weekend. Why should he be any different now?

And suddenly, as if by magic, he was her own darling Charlie again, a smile spreading over his face as he looked at her. "So am I," he said, putting his arms around her.

When he leaned in and kissed her, everything was exactly as she had remembered.

CHAPTER THREE

Conflict of Interest

We've Seen the Last of Irma

Beatrice Bright
Wednesday, September 13, 2017

Hurricane Irma made landfall near Marco Island last Sunday, September 10, as a Category 4 hurricane. The storm made its way up the west coast of Florida, leaving a trail of devastation in its wake. It finally stalled out in Valdosta, Georgia, and dissipated yesterday. The Keys and the Gulf Coast bore the brunt of the destruction. The effects of the hurricane were less severe for Paradise and Volusia County than for the south and west coasts. Wind speeds here were less than those of Hurricane Matthew last year, but hundreds of county residents are still without power. There was severe flooding in nearby Daytona Beach. A flood watch remains in effect, but the bridges are open, and curfew has been lifted. Volusia County schools will be closed through today.

—from *The Paradise Post.*

Hurricanes were one of the occupational hazards of living in Florida, along with alligators, giant pythons, sinkholes, and snowbirds. Around the beginning of August, the TV news would begin threatening apocalyptic devastation, but nine times out of ten it never materialized. Sometimes, one would make landfall close by. Residents would hunker down in their homes for a day or two, or evacuate, and then go out to clean up the mess and get on with their lives. If it was a particularly bad year, they might have to do this several times.

Paradise was a barrier island, which meant it ran parallel to the coast and bore the brunt of storm surges, thereby protecting the mainland. If people had any sense, Bea thought, they would have settled on the mainland and left the island as a barrier. But people possess very little common sense where beachfront property is concerned. Besides, it was hard to blame them. The island was very beautiful.

Even though the danger was not as severe as it was made out to be, it was still present. The year before, Hurricane Matthew had inflicted some serious damage. Paradise had just about put itself back together from Matthew when Irma hit. Most hurricanes contented themselves with a small part of Florida, or, if they were really ambitious, with either the east or the west coast. In that case, people would evacuate to the other coast, or just go inland. But Irma somehow managed to make itself felt over the entire peninsula. By the time the official evacuation order went out, the roads were gridlocked, and it was impossible to get out of the state.

Elaine had ordered her staff to the mainland a few days before it hit. "What those idiots in broadcast journalism do is up to them, but I'm not having you risk your lives just to tell people that they can't go outside yet."

Bea had agreed — on the condition that her crusty boss evacuated to her granddaughter's house in DeLand.

Most of the islanders were able to get to the mainland or hole up with one of their neighbors who lived on higher ground — the gigantic, overgrown sand dunes in the middle of the island. Bea hunkered down with her family at a cousin's house in Daytona. She spent the next few days frantically texting Honey, Peter, and Elaine (and even, occasionally, Ben) to make sure that everyone was still safe. It happened every year, and every year she came back to find everything still standing, but there was always the chance that this year would be the one that wiped her beloved city off the map.

The storm came, and the storm went. They lost power for a few days. Bea was able to get back to Paradise by Tuesday and help those who had started cleaning up the island. The fishing pier and the marina had been destroyed. Some of the streets had flooded, but none of the houses. The Paradise Motel was old, but it had been built by people who knew about hurricanes, and it had once again withstood the test. The not-quite finished Buccaneer Trail headquarters had lost a few windows, some shingles, and most of its landscaping, but was otherwise fine. The biggest problems were the trees. Massive live oaks and tall, spindly palm trees had fallen in roads and yards, stripping up the earth and baring their roots to the sky. Every available inch of ground was covered with Spanish moss. It would be months before all the debris was cleared away. For days, the island buzzed with the sounds of chainsaws.

By Wednesday, the *Post* was up and running, albeit off a generator. By the next week, everyone had regained power and things were more or less back to normal.

Two weeks later, Elaine started demanding that Bea get an interview with Ben. "Lord knows there's enough hurricane news to last us through the end of this year, but no one wants to read that," said Elaine. "We need something different."

But somehow, Bea still couldn't get an interview with Ben. At first, she'd chalked it up to the hurricane — after finishing cleanup in Paradise, he and Peter had gone over to the Gulf Coast to help with disaster relief efforts for a week. She had been able to placate Elaine with a story about Peter and Ben's heroic relief work in between helping Honey and Leonata patch up the motel and doing cleanup in her parents' neighborhood.

After Peter and Ben returned, four weeks went by, and Ben still hadn't bothered to show up for an interview. Bea sent unusually polite emails, called, sent ruder emails, asked Peter to intervene, and yet somehow Ben kept canceling at the last minute or coming up with convenient excuses. At first, she'd kept busy with other news stories. There was plenty with the hurricane, and then there was the shark-fishing tournament, and the cotillion dance, and a reenactment at the old fort. But four weeks went by, and the Post found itself once again in a news slump. And still, nothing from Ben. Bea was annoyed, and so was Elaine.

"He has to be hiding something," said Elaine.

Bea thought he was probably just avoiding her, but she kept this thought to herself. Still, it was out of character — Ben had no problem with flaunting his success.

Sensing a scoop, Elaine told Bea that the time for politeness was over. "You live in the same apartment complex. Figure it out. I want that interview on Monday, or I won't give you a bonus for the extra copyediting."

With that, Elaine bustled out of the room.

Johnny, who had been pretending to work at the next

desk over, looked up and smirked at Bea. "Too bad your personal life's getting in the way of your career. If only there was someone more competent around who could do the job..." He slicked back his hair and puffed out his chest.

"Too bad there isn't," said Bea.

• • •

Bea was still fuming later that night as she carried her laundry basket down the stairs from Room 204 towards the communal laundry room. She'd found a mushroom growing out of the bathroom wall after coming back from work and had been deep cleaning furiously ever since. She was exhausted and hungry, and her hands were slightly burned because the bleach had somehow soaked into her gloves, but the laundry wasn't going to do itself. The island was getting rain bands from yet another tropical storm off the coast, so it was pouring. She hunched over the basket, trying to shield her clothes from the rain as she crossed the motel courtyard. The last thing she wanted right now was to have to listen to just how fabulously well things were going for Ben. But she needed that bonus for her house fund.

Still, taking advantage of his proximity felt like a low move. Really, though, he was the one who had invaded the space she'd carved for herself out of the moldy cinderblock walls of the Paradise Motel.

Ugh, finally. She ducked inside, breathless, and shook herself like a wet cat.

The laundry room reeked of mold and mildew and abandoned socks, and it flooded when it rained. There was a perpetual puddle near the entrance from a leaky A/C window unit. Usually, a pile of someone else's laundry sat on top of the only working dryer, unless someone was feeling particularly vengeful and had tossed it into the floor. Tonight, however, Ben was sitting on top of the dryer and looking at his phone. He was wearing a tuxedo shirt over a pair of especially hideous swim trunks. Clearly, laundry day was long overdue.

"Evening, hot stuff," said Bea, setting her basket down on a mostly dry patch of floor. To her chagrin, she noticed that the washer was already running. "Are you starting a fashion line in addition to the tech accessories?"

Ben started, then said, "Oh I could, but I think that our target audience would find my devilish good looks too disheartening."

"You do look like you could use an exorcist," Bea replied.

"Only for my inner demons," he said with a crooked smile.

He glanced at Bea's bleach-stained cleaning clothes and wild, streaming hair. "I see you're going as yourself for Halloween. Excellent. You're the scariest thing I know."

Bea had had enough. "Good," she growled, stalking towards him with such ferocity that he yelped and scooted to the very far back of the dryer. "Now, if you'd be so kind, perhaps you'll tell me why you can't be bothered to give me an interview."

"Okay, fine," he said, raising his hands in defense as if he thought she would strike him. "I can tell you why, but only if you promise you won't put it in the *Post*."

Then, instead of settling down for an explanation, he jumped down from the dryer and made a break for the door. But Bea was faster than him. She cornered him between the wall and the washer and stood on her toes so that she could yell in his face.

"Benedict Dante Constant, you better give me some answers, or so help me I will take your designer laundry and throw it out into the rain!" At this moment, there was an exquisitely timed flash of lightning, followed by a rumble of thunder that sounded like the heavens were about to collapse on their heads.

"Okay," he yelped. Up close, Bea noticed that Ben's dark eyes were wide with fear and luminous with reflected lightning. A few beads of rainwater still clung to his glasses. For a while, he simply stared at her without saying anything, his lips slightly parted. She was suddenly less comfortable with the fact that she was this close to his face, close enough to —

It was at that moment that Peter entered the laundry room. He blinked in surprise. "Hope I'm not interrupting anything. Just came to get my laundry."

Bea sprang away from Ben. "No! We were just, uh — "

"Bea's holding me hostage," said Ben as Peter began pulling his laundry out of the dryer. The dazed note in his voice only confirmed Peter's suspicions.

"I told you that you needed to get back to her," said Peter, smirking. He opened up the dryer and began loading his laundry into the basket. Bea was apparently absorbed in watching the ever-increasing puddle by the front door. Ben opened his mouth as if he were going to say something, and then closed it again without speaking. Still smirking, Peter picked up his laundry basket and walked out, closing the door behind him.

Studiously avoiding her gaze, Ben took his laundry out of the washer and began moving it to the dryer.

Bea pulled an abandoned laundry basket in front of

the door, turned it upside down, and sat on it. "Look," she said, "I don't like this any more than you do, but people are starting to think you guys are hiding something. It would probably be in your best interest if you stopped acting so suspicious and answered my questions. I'll let you out when your laundry's done."

Ben raised his hands in surrender. "Okay." He ruffled up his hair, and then leaned against the dryer. "So, about two years ago, Johnny asked Peter if he could work part-time at the company to make some extra cash. It was a terrible idea, and I told Peter so, but I didn't have the heart to tell him that his own brother hates his guts."

Bea couldn't resist interjecting, "Wait, you have a heart?"

"Shocking, I know. It was my fault, really. Peter wanted to put him on cyber security, but I convinced him that it would be better if he worked in the graphics department with me. I tried to keep an eye on him, but then we went big—really big, and it was all I could do to keep up with the demand. We were riding high after that, and I didn't pay as much attention—"

Suddenly, the door was thrust open, knocking Bea off her seat. She hit the concrete floor with a painful thud. When she looked up, Johnny was standing in the doorway, scowling. "What the hell are you doing in the middle of the walkway?"

She was surprised to find that Ben was at her side, helping her to her feet. "It's called having a polite conversation," Ben said, glowering at Johnny. "You should try it sometime."

Johnny gave the laundry room a disparaging look. "Most people would find somewhere more comfortable for a polite conversation." He picked up his laundry basket, muttered something under his breath, and left.

"This journalism stuff is dangerous business," said Ben, turning back to her. "Are you ok?" For once, he sounded genuinely concerned.

Bea dusted herself off. "I'm fine. You'd better go on with your story before someone else comes in."

"Just a minute," said Ben. He waited a few moments, listening. The noise of the rain made it impossible to tell if Johnny was still nearby.

Bea leaned against the washer, checking her scraped hands to make sure they weren't bleeding. Her leg stung with the beginnings of a nasty bruise.

Ben shot her a worried look. He was pretty sure Bea would rather die than admit to him that she had a serious injury. But she seemed fine. It took him a moment to remember why she was staring at him with a look of growing impatience. Then he retreated back to his seat on the dryer and resumed his story. "The storm wreaked havoc on a bunch of the company computers, so Charlie and I went through everything to see what all needed fixing. Well, a few weeks ago, Charlie figured out that Johnny had been embezzling money from the company." He drew a deep breath and looked down at the floor. "It broke Peter's heart."

For a moment, there was only the dull roar of the washer and the dryer and the rain. It took Bea a few minutes to sort out her thoughts. There was a certain amount of poetic justice in the pirate video game company getting robbed. And she wasn't exactly surprised that Johnny would do something like that. But even so, what a nightmare.

"What did you do?" she asked finally.

He gave a slight shrug. "We fired him. Peter didn't want to press charges, but I kept Johnny from finding that out until we got the money back. Peter's been trying to keep it a secret, because he knew Johnny would never be able to get any more work once people around here knew. But he told his parents, because they needed to know, and it's only a matter of time before word gets around. But not through the *Post*. Please."

He stood there, dripping, in the last of his clothes, looking completely desperate.

"Not through the *Post*," she agreed. "But I have to tell Elaine. She's thinking of making him editor-in-chief!"

"I thought she was going to make you editor-in-chief," said Ben.

"Depends on the day," said Bea. "She's playing us against each other. Keeps us from getting careless—What if she thinks I'm just saying it to get him fired?"

"I guess Peter and I will have to tell her," said Ben with a grimace. "I'd like to see Johnny talk his way out of that one. But please. No one else. For Peter's sake. He's having a hard time as it is."

Bea gave him a quizzical look, wondering how much he knew or guessed about Peter's feelings for Honey. She was tempted to ask him; but decided against it. "Of course I won't. Ugh. The thought of anyone doing anything so horrible to Peter just makes me want to—" She raised her hands, then let them fall abruptly. "He's such a sunshiny person."

Ben sat up straighter, surprised. He was so used to thinking of Bea as an angry rage monster that he had almost forgotten how much she cared about people. "He's a tough guy," he said gently. "He'll get through it."

Bea leaned against the washer, thinking. "Things have never been good between them."

"That's the reason we came back," said Ben. "One of them, anyway. Peter thought that maybe, if he moved back, he could undo some of the damage." He stared, unseeing, at the abandoned sock in the middle of the floor. He should have paid more attention. And now it was going to get out, one way or another. He couldn't ask Bea to protect Johnny. They would have to relive that ugly scene all over again, Johnny all smooth words and plausible explanations, Peter wanting so badly to believe him and knowing it wasn't true.

Bea tried to process the news, wondering if there was any way she could help Peter. Suddenly she wanted nothing more than to leave the whole mess alone. Johnny was dangerous. But she couldn't do that. Not to Elaine. Not to herself.

Ben slid off the washer. "Well, since that's all you wanted to know, I'll just be going," he said, edging towards the door.

"Not so fast!" said Bea. "I still need an interview I can publish."

"Oh, come on!" said Ben. "I told you our deepest darkest secret. What more do you want from me?"

"I just need you to answer some boring questions about how things are going with the new headquarters and the ethics of video games. If you keep being so difficult, I'm going to start thinking you're hiding something else."

"No, I just enjoy being difficult," he said with a smirk. "Oh, what the hell. Fire away."

• • •

Transcript of an interview with Ben Constant, Wednesday, October 24, 2017 (unedited, but annotated by Beatrice Bright)

Bea: What's your name?

Ben: You know my name!

Bea: They make us do it.

Ben: [sighs dramatically] Benedict Dante Constant. Benedict with a T.

Bea: I'll start with a softball. What's your vision for the future of Buccaneer Trail?

Ben: [cleaning his glasses on his shirttail] Blurry.

Bea: If you keep being snarky, I'll include that in the article.

Ben: Is that a threat or a bribe?

Bea: What is the company's stance on the shift from multiplayer to single-player gaming?

Ben: [impressed] You have done your research.

Bea: It's what they pay me to do.

Ben: [clears throat pompously] Community is a huge part of the company vision. Without multiplayer games, this company would never have existed. We wanted a better way to play together in a world that we loved. We are exploring more single-player options, because not everybody has the luxury of a gaming community. However, I believe that the current focus on single-player games is a trend, not a paradigm, and Buccaneer Trail will continue to be primarily oriented towards a multiplayer format.

Bea: Several parents have raised concerns about the possibility that *Swashbuckleriad* encourages violence in children and teenagers. What would you say to them?

Ben: First of all, there are several studies that show no

correlation between video games and later acts of violence — I'll email them to you when I get back upstairs. Video games, like many other things in life, are pieces of art, and like all art, it's designed to move you, and you have to be aware of —

[At 0:45 we were interrupted by Honey, who left her beach towel in here earlier. Conversation resumes at 1:25]

Ben: Anyway, part of the reason we promote multiplayer gaming is that being around other players keeps the individual player focused on their relationship with the other players, rather than on violence for its own sake. That being said, the game is rated T for Teen for a reason. As fun as it is to romanticize pirates, violence is an inherent part of the landscape. Parents who are concerned that their children will not react well to violence should stick to E games. We currently have a *Treasure Island*-based E game in the works and are taking pains to ensure that it's wholesome and fun.

Bea: So you're saying that there's such a thing as too much video games?

Ben: As someone who works on them way more than 9 to 5 — absolutely. But that doesn't mean they're bad in and of themselves.

Bea: All right. Last question. How would you respond to reviewers who claim that the game's portrayal of women contributes to the ongoing trend of sexism in the gaming industry?

Ben: [raises an eyebrow] Is this a *Post* question or a you question?

Bea: Both.

Ben: All the characters in the game are meant to be larger-than-life because that's part of the appeal of the genres that inspired it. Sexism is, regrettably, just as much a part of the history that inspired the storylines as violence is.

Bea: It isn't just that. Most of your women characters are either [pause] temptresses or saints.

Ben: Temptresses? [smiles] That's a bit archaic for reviewers, don't you think?

Bea: [resists the urge to slap him]. You know what I mean. None of them look or act like real people.

Ben: [shrugs] What can I say? We were teenagers when we started created the original game. Like most teenage guys, our perception of women was pretty limited. And after that, we didn't want to change too much for fear of alienating our audience. [pause] Then again, there's always room for improvement.

Bea: [snorts]

[At 3:24 the dryer went off and Ben got his clothes out of the dryer. Conversation resumes at 3:30]

Ben: Well, does that satisfy you?

Bea: Yes. Thank you.

****

Bea stopped the recording, and then closed out the app on her phone.

Ben shifted uncomfortably, and added, "Off the record, Charlie actually wrote and designed most of the girls. I got bogged down in the research and the overall visual design of the game."

Bea folded her arms and jutted out her chin. "Well, off the record, the big draw of your game is that you get to see the story from all these different perspectives. Think about how much better it would be if you actually delivered on that."

He didn't look at her. He appeared to be making a thorough investigation of his sandals. Then he scraped the lint off the filter and tossed it in the trash can. "Just please, don't tell anyone besides Elaine about Johnny."

"I won't," she said. She began moving her clothes from the washer to the dryer. "You know, you're actually a pretty good interviewee when you're not being a jerk."

"Only the best for you," said Ben, picking up his basket and heading out the door. "Enjoy your evening, psychopath journalist."

• • •

Ben's head was spinning as he carried his laundry up the slippery concrete steps. The rain had slowed to a light drizzle, but it was still thundering like the world was going to end. *She's crazy.* But Bea's last question had given him more food for thought than he wanted to admit. From a certain point of view, he had inadvertently written himself into that fiasco with Diana. She had just played the part that was expected of her a little too literally. Not that she was a bad kisser but—God, no. Without warning, it had been kind of awful, in front of everybody like that. In front of Bea.

Bea.

Just a few moments ago—it had been the last thing on his mind—and then suddenly there she was, a few inches from his face, and then all he could think about was how much better it would have been if—

He was so absorbed in this "if" that he didn't see Charlie sitting on the steps until it was too late. Ben tripped over him and went sprawling.

"Are you trying to kill me?" Ben hissed as he frantically

scooped his wet laundry into the basket. Then he did a double take. "What are you doing out here anyway?"

"I went for a walk," said Charlie dreamily.

The world lit up for an instant like a searchlight being turned on, and then plunged back into darkness. Thunder rumbled in the distance. Ben rolled his eyes. "What is *wrong* with you?"

"I'm in love," he said.

"Well, I knew that," said Ben, picking up his basket and continuing up the steps. "Anything else?"

"I want to ask Honey to marry me, but I need your help."

Ben came to a full stop a few steps above Charlie. He turned back to him and raised his eyebrows. "*My* help?"

Charlie got up to follow him. "Peter's busy."

Ben ducked under the wide concrete awning that protected the second-floor balcony from the rain. "C'mon then, I'm going to need a drink."

He ducked into his room for a change of clothes and left the door open for Charlie, wondering if he was in some weird video game where everyone around him goes crazy until he was the only one left. But in those games, of course, it would turn out that he was the crazy one the whole time. It wouldn't exactly fly for the *Treasure Island* game but maybe it would work later on. He scribbled the idea on a sticky note, added the title *Welcome to the Paradise Motel*, and stuck it on the wall next to a small cloud of sticky notes filled with cryptic memoranda:

Fairbanks plot circle X
Bermuda triangle level 2??
Space pirates a go for november
Definitely NO space pirates — Peter

Use snorkel gear to simulate ghosts
ALL the space pirates — Ben
Vampire pirates? — Honey

When Ben returned to the living room in his (some-what) dry pajamas and the big fuzzy bathrobe that his grandma gave him for Christmas, the front door was still wide open. "Charlie?" Ben called as he pulled a beer out of the fridge.

"Out here."

"And this is how you get killed in the game," Ben muttered under his breath as he went out the door. "Charlie, you're letting out all the air conditioning." *I really am becoming my dad.*

He found Charlie leaning on the metal balcony railing, gazing dreamily at Honey. She was standing in front of Bea's room on the opposite side of the motel, giggling at something. Ben saw Bea, silhouetted in the warm light of the doorway in the shimmering rain. *Crazy,* he thought again. Something uncomfortable twisted inside him, and he pushed it away.

"Get away from there, you idiot," he said to Charlie. "You'll get electrocuted."

Ben sank down into one of the faded beach chairs that sat against the cement-block wall of his apartment. It occurred to him that the chair was also made of metal, and therefore the possibility of getting struck by lightning was just as great as it would be leaning on the railing, but he was too tired to get up. At least he wouldn't get wet. He said, "Man, you will not believe what just happened — I was doing laundry, minding my own business, and Bea just appears, out of nowhere, looking like something out of a Gothic novel — "

"A what?" said Charlie as he sat down in the chair next to Ben's.

"It's from—oh, never mind." Ben looked over at his friend, suddenly remembering the reason they were out there. "So. You want to propose to Honey."

"Yes," said Charlie, with a fatuous smile.

Ben waited for Charlie to elaborate. He did not.

Apparently, Bea and Honey also thought this was the perfect evening to chat outside. They sat down in the beach chairs in front of Bea's apartment. A strand of colored Christmas lights framed the window behind them. Bea insisted that they could be used as decoration all year round. Ben thought this was ridiculous, but they did look cheerful against the never-ending rain.

Charlie sighed. "Isn't she the most beautiful woman you've ever seen?"

"I mean, she's okay I guess," said Ben. "Bea's much prettier."

Over the sound of the rain, they heard Peter's big, familiar voice echoing up the stairs. He was singing some old jazz song absently, which was not unusual for him. He appeared at the stop of the stairs, dripping wet, and shook himself off. When he saw Ben, he stopped singing and said, "Hey, Charlie, you'll never guess who I saw looking *very* cozy in the laundry room!"

Ben went scarlet. "Shh!" he said, frantically gesturing in the direction of Bea. "It wasn't like that!

Peter grinned.

"It wasn't like that," Ben repeated. "She was just mad at me for putting her off about the interview." He took a deep breath. "Peter, I had to—"

Charlie interrupted him. "Peter, I've just had the most

amazing idea about how to propose to Honey — "

The frozen expression on Peter's face made Ben decide to go get him a beer.

When he returned, Charlie was babbling about the Halloween party and candles and rose petals, and Peter was listening with pristine cheerfulness. It reminded Ben vaguely of some play Peter had been in.

Charlie was still talking: "But I need one of you to decoy her out there, and I need to figure out a way to get Bea to do the pictures without her knowing what it's for, because she'll totally tell Honey."

"Well, that's easy enough," said Peter. "I can keep Honey distracted while you get ready, and Ben can manage Bea."

Ben ignored him. "But like, where are you going to get all this stuff?"

The swashbuckling trio put their three collective brain cells together to work out the details.

• • •

Meanwhile, Johnny was fuming outside his own apartment, which was directly beneath Ben's. He had locked himself out and was waiting on Leonata to bring him the keys. When he heard Charlie's plans, he began listening intently. Perhaps this dump did have some advantages after all...

• • •

After what seemed like an eternity, Charlie finally departed in a haze of anticipation, mumbling trite cliches about his own unworthiness of the angelic Honey. Across the way, the girls had gone inside.

"We're getting old, Benny," said Peter, taking a sip of his beer.

Ben snorted. "You're 27. Besides, I'm two years younger than you, so there's no 'we' in this business."

"Our friends are starting to get married," said Peter. "Before you know it, we'll be the only ones left."

Ben stared at the chair where Charlie had been. "Is everyone this much of an idiot when they're in love?"

"'Fraid so," said Peter.

"I just won't fall in love then," declared Ben.

"Sure," said Peter.

Ben sighed. "I had to tell her, Pete."

"About Johnny?"

"Yeah."

Peter sighed. "Figured you would have to, sooner or later."

Ben covered his face with his hands. "What are we gonna do?"

"The right thing, Benny."

The rain continued to pour ceaselessly from the rooftop into the courtyard below, where Johnny was still listening.

• • •

When Bea arrived at work the next morning, Elaine was waiting for her with her arms folded. "Beatrice," she said. "Would you mind stepping into my office?"

Bea swore silently. Of course Johnny had overheard. It was 8:00 a.m. Peter and Ben weren't supposed to be there until 9. She squared her shoulders. "Yes, as a matter of fact I have something I'd like to discuss with you."

Sure enough, Johnny was sitting in Elaine's office, looking responsible and serious. He had even used hair gel.

Bea decided to shoot first. "My interview with Mr. Constant revealed some very interesting information."

"Yes," said Elaine. "Johnny has just told me that he was in fact fired from the company for embezzlement."

Bea rounded on him warily. "He did?"

Johnny, eyes downcast, looked like a repentant child.

"Yes," said Elaine. "He said that you got the information out of Ben in a highly unprofessional manner."

Bea flung up her hands in exasperation. "I asked him why he'd been avoiding an interview, and he told me. I lost my temper, certainly, but that doesn't bother Ben—he's used to it."

"That isn't the issue," said Elaine, regarding Bea steadily over the top of her glasses. "To put it bluntly, Johnny says you were flirting with Ben in order to get information out of him."

"Oh, for the love of—I can't believe you think I'd stoop that low for the pathetic secrets of an eight-bit programmer." If Ben found out about this, she'd never hear the end of it.

"Bea, I know the two of you have a history," said Elaine, in an unusually maternal voice that made Bea nauseous.

"We do not have a 'history!'" said Bea. "We were friends once, and then we had a falling out over something that was purely academic. There has not been, and will never be, anything between us."

Ben walked into the newsroom just in time to overhear Elaine's statement, and Bea's reply. He stopped just before he reached the almost-closed door to Elaine's office. He had said the same thing to Peter, of course. There was no reason it should bother him. But his hands were shaking as he reached for the doorknob. Then he felt Peter's big hand on his shoulder.

Ben cleared his throat, and then opened the door. "She's quite correct, Elaine," he said. His voice was about half an octave higher than he would like, but otherwise his entrance had the desired effect. Of course, that may have had something to do with the way Peter's massive frame filled the entire doorway behind him. Ben went on, "Sorry to barge in on y'all like this, but Peter and I talked it over and thought that the sooner we came over here, the better."

Bea put a hand on the back of a chair to steady herself, and then turned towards them. But she couldn't bring herself to look at Ben.

In his smoothest voice, Ben said, "Bea's persistent, but no more so than the average journalist. There was no cause for concern. We've known each other far too long for that."

Bea tightened her grip on the chair and wished she were in another country. Like New Zealand.

Peter closed the door behind him. "Johnny has a way of getting people off-topic," he said.

Johnny was doing his best to make himself invisible, which is not an easy thing to do when you're six feet tall.

Elaine scowled. "I did wonder why you declined to give a letter of reference for him," she said.

"I'm sorry," said Peter, with the same disturbingly pristine composure that Ben had seen the night before. "I was trying to let him have a second chance."

"I've had it with all of you," said Elaine, stomping back behind her desk and sitting down. "Johnny, you're going to take a month of unpaid leave. Your return will be conditional on your conduct during that period. Bea, you're going to cover Johnny's beat as well as your own until I decide what to do with him. Please refrain from any more unorthodox journalism, or so help me I will fire you."

Johnny started to protest, but Peter took him firmly by the arm and escorted him out of the building.

Bea risked a quick look at Ben. His eyes met hers for an instant, dark and enigmatic.

"Don't you have an interview to type up?" growled Elaine.

Bea and Ben took the hint, and escaped from the office.

No one else was in the newsroom. "Thank you," said Bea coldly. She went back towards her desk without stopping to look at him. With sharp, violent movements, she whipped out her laptop, opened it up, and began typing furiously.

Ben sauntered over to her and leaned against her desk. "Wow," he said, his voice oozing with sarcasm. "I had no idea you would risk your professional reputation for a scoop."

She stopped typing and slammed the laptop closed. Her eyes were smoldering with rage. "Just once, just *once*, could you not make my life any more difficult than it already is?"

"Oh, don't worry, I won't compromise you any further," he said. He turned on his heel and stalked out of the room.

Coward, she thought. He always left before she could get in the last word.

CHAPTER FOUR

To One Thing Constant Never

Local Historian Reveals the Origins of the Masquerade in Paradise

Beatrice Bright
Friday, October 27, 2017

The Legend of the Masked Pirate: It sounds like something out of the latest Hollywood blockbuster, but, according to local historian Ophelia Prince, the legends surrounding the exploits of Paradise's very own historical pirate, Captain Constant, may in fact be true. While going through a box of papers from one of Constant's descendants, Prince discovered an 18th century letter from John Hedges, the British governor of what was then known as East Florida. Hedges is locally known as the man who turned the Spanish town of Cielo into the English town of Paradise.

In the letter, written to his brother in England, Hedges describes how Constant was captured by the governor's troops shortly after Hedges assumed control from the Spanish. Due to a technicality, the governor could not directly try the pirate for his crimes. Because Constant was a gentleman, the governor placed him under house arrest in his own mansion, which stood where the Prince House stands today. Hedges, sensibly enough, did not trust the pirate, but he was impressed by his "excellent manners" and "intelligent discourse." As time went on, Hedges found that he enjoyed the company of this educated English pirate more than that of the local or Spanish leaders. This was partly due to the language barrier and mostly due to prejudice. He gradually began allowing Constant a little more freedom in the house. He was still surprised that the pirate did not seem inclined to escape. When he asked Constant about this, the pirate replied, "My dear sir, better to serve in Heaven than to reign in Hell. I live better under your guard than I do as captain of a rotting vessel on the godforsaken ocean."

Their friendship came to a sudden end on the evening of Governor Hedges' masquerade ball...

(Continued on 3A)

— from *The Paradise Post*

Halloween dawned in a suitably ominous fashion. It was hotter than ever, but everyone was frantically busy. There was candy to buy, food to prepare, music to arrange, tents to raise, tourists to chase off the beach, and, most importantly, costumes to assemble. Everyone in Paradise dressed up for the Masquerade. Half-hearted attempts at costumes were scorned. Bea and Honey's friend Meg had set up a pop-up costume shop for the occasion in the salon where she worked. She agreed to do Bea and Honey's hair and makeup just before closing to pay them back for helping her set up.

Bea was happily humming musical theater tunes off-key as she swept up the last of the glitter. Meg was in the process of sweeping Honey's hair into an elaborate updo. Bea and Honey had both known Meg for ages, but weren't especially close to her. Meg was the daughter of Tropical Bob (of beach diner fame). She had grown up in Paradise, but had run with a much cooler crowd in high school. She only kept up with the Nerd Squad, as she thought of them, because they shared her secret passion for cosplay. Meg's in-crowd had dispersed after high school, so she'd been spending more time with the nerds, especially since she lived a few doors down at the Motel. Tonight, she was dressed as Aphrodite in a foamy aquamarine gown, and her golden hair was wreathed with real roses.

"I'm so glad you've kept your hair like this," said Meg, pinning another pink curl into Honey's hair. "I was worried they would make you change it when you started teaching."

"They wanted to, but I showed them how much the kids liked it," said Honey, who was wearing the sparkliest and poufiest pink prom dress that could be found in the thrift stores of Volusia County. "Most of the first graders are still convinced I'm a fairy. Or a mermaid."

"It always makes me sad when women come into the salon and tell me they want a natural look because they have to get a real job now," said Meg. "I mean, who decided that being an adult had to be boring?"

She pinned the last curl in place and sprayed a cloud of hairspray over the finished work. Then she gingerly placed an ornate, glittering crown on Honey's head and began anchoring it with hairpins. Meg had been Miss Paradise several years back and had been allowed to keep the crown after a new one was donated.

"Are you a good witch or a bad witch?" asked Bea, laughing.

"I'm a princess," declared Honey. "Thanks for letting me borrow this, Meg. What was it like, being Miss Paradise?"

"Boring," she said as she tied on Honey's mask, a

custom one from Meg that somehow managed to render the whole outrageous outfit classy. "We got to ride in the parade, but we didn't have any hot celebrities to kiss like Diana did. Although I can't say Benny would be my first choice."

Bea and Honey laughed uncomfortably.

On the other side of the island, preparations of a different sort were going on. Peter was helping Charlie set out what felt like a million candles and at least forty pounds of rose petals for his proposal, and seriously questioning his life choices. *How did I get roped into this? Why do I have to be so damn nice to people? Why didn't I just tell him to set out his own damn candles?*

Then he thought about how happy Honey would be when she saw all this. It would kill him a little less to know he'd been part of it.

Charlie lit several of the candles to test them out in the gathering dusk. The scent of cheap candles wafted over to Peter. They smelled exactly like the ones that filled the middle school auditorium two years ago, when he'd come down to help Honey build the set for *Romeo and Juliet...*

• • •

Honey had been asked to take over the production after the original director got sick. It was flu season, and a bunch of people were under the weather, including Charlie. She'd sent out a panicked SOS to her friends, explaining that she would be building and painting the set all by herself. Everyone but Peter and Ben had previous commitments. Since Peter was the handier of the two, he went back to Paradise for the weekend to help her while Ben kept the company afloat.

When he arrived at the middle school auditorium, Honey ran up and gave him a fierce hug. "You're a life-saver," she said. "Thank you so much!"

She had hugged him before, and hadn't meant anything unusual by it, but it threw him, for some reason. "Don't thank me yet," he'd said, feeling like he should disentangle himself, and not wanting to. He pulled away. "My shop skills are a little rusty."

"Mine too," she said, with a grim smile. She was dressed in work clothes, and her pink hair was tied in a messy bun, but she still looked lovely. "I've lit some candles to help us get in the spirit—and to ward off the smell of unwashed middle-schoolers," she added. "I guess we'll have to put them out when we start building, though."

"Some" was a bit of an understatement. There were clusters of strategically placed candles at the four corners of the stage, making it look like some kind of occult ritual.

"They're beautiful," said Peter. "But you're right." He turned to survey the rest of the stage, which was empty save for a few lonely-looking folding chairs, and some large dust bunnies. "'In fair Verona, where we lay our scene,'" he murmured to himself. Then he turned to Honey and said, "I'm sorry Charlie couldn't make it."

"Yeah," she said, with a small sigh. "Hopefully he'll come as soon as he gets better."

"I'll make sure to give him some time off," said Peter, smiling. "So, how are we going to 'lay our scene?'"

"Well," said Honey. "We need to build a staircase for the balcony, because according to school regulations, ladders aren't safe enough." As she spoke, she walked upstage to point out where it would go.

"And they're trusting *our* carpentry skills?" said Peter.

"Apparently. And then we need several flats for the different scenes."

"What about this back wall here?" asked Peter.

"We'll do something like a stone wall covered with vines," she said. "Tan stone, not gray stone."

Then they blew out the candles, got down from the stage, and started unrolling a gigantic orange tarp to mark their workspace. The school didn't have a wood shop, so they set up an impromptu one in the auditorium. Peter brought in his power tools, and they set to work. Soon the air was filled with the earthy, promising smell of fresh sawdust.

They spent the afternoon constructing the staircase, which somehow turned into a full-fledged balcony (Peter's carpentry skills were better than he let on). It had been a while since he'd been alone with Honey, and he was surprised by how easy and natural it felt. To get them in the spirit, he found himself reciting the Prologue from *Henry V* as a kind of blessing over their work. Then he and Honey swapped theater stories. Honey was terrified of being onstage, but she loved the haphazard, many-layered world behind the scenes. She had a gift for managing large groups of children that many of the community theater directors envied. Her eyes shone as she talked about a shy, lonely child who had come to life because of the last play, and Peter thought, as he often did, how much better the world was with someone like Honey in it.

"I don't know why they put the middle school kids through this," he said as he laid a 2x4 on the sawhorse. "*Romeo and Juliet* is just about the worst possible play for middle schoolers."

"I know, but it's public domain, so they don't have to

pay for the rights," she said in between attaching some of the already-cut pieces together with a nail gun. "And it's educational."

"I'll say," he said. "Ours was a nightmare, do you remember?" He began sawing through the wood—he was making do with a slightly-dull handsaw until the electric one finished charging.

"I do," she said, laughing. "Poor Benny. He really hated being—"

Peter cried out. The saw blade had slipped and sliced into his palm.

"Oh my God!" said Honey, dropping the frame and rushing over. "Are you okay?"

"'Tis but a scratch," said Peter through gritted teeth, clenching his hand and holding it to his chest.

"Here, let me see," she commanded.

Wincing, he held out his hand. She grimaced. "That's gonna need stitches. Hold on. I've got a first aid kit in my purse." She sprinted backstage.

He stood there helplessly, still holding his hand to his chest. It didn't hurt as bad as it looked, but it certainly wasn't pleasant.

Honey returned a few moments later with the kit, set it on a chair, and began rifling through it. "Here we go. This should keep it from getting infected. Here, let me see it." She took his hand and turned it upwards so that she could see the palm, and then sprayed something on it.

"Damn!" he cried out. "What's in there? Demon spit?"

"Basically," she said, turning back to the kit to grab a bandage.

"It's a good thing you're prepared," he said, gritting his teeth as the disinfectant continued to burn.

"Well, when you work with kids all day, you gotta be ready for anything," she said. She patted away some of the blood with gauze. The she began wrapping some thicker gauze around his huge hand, going slowly and carefully to keep it from hurting too much. He gradually forgot about the pain as he saw and felt her smaller, strong hands move over his. He was suddenly aware that his heart was pounding, the blood rushing through his chest and down his arm and out of the gash in his hand, some of it escaping the gauze and staining Honey's fingers. What was wrong with him? She finished off her first aid with a gigantic bandage and smoothed it out with the same tenderness she bestowed upon everybody. He felt as if the ground had dropped from underneath him.

Oh God. Honey was taken. Or practically taken, anyway. It wouldn't be fair to either of them. He sat there as the realization crashed down on him, horrified that he was capable of wanting someone like this, knowing it was wrong.

"How does that feel?" she asked, looking up from his hands to his eyes.

It felt, he thought, as if the world had suddenly filled with golden light, flowing from her face, her hands, into him.

• • •

A castaway who happened to wash up on the beach on the evening of the 2017 Masquerade in Paradise would have probably thought that he hadn't survived at all and had instead ended up in some very weird version of Purgatory. The beach in front of the Paradise Motel was dotted with tiki torches and huge bonfires. Costumed revelers with glittering masks were dancing around them with frenzied abandon. Up in the deeper sand, there was the usual melee of freestyle dancers and middle schoolers flossing. Closer towards the water, there was an unusually large cluster of ballroom dancers on the hard-packed wet sand, thanks to a dance studio that was popular with most of the older people in Paradise.

Somewhere in the center of all this madness, Bea was leaning against a picnic table and watching the dancers swirl around her. She was dressed as Athena in a shimmering, pale-gold tunic, armed with a plastic sword and a shield emblazoned with the head of Medusa. The night was humid as usual, so she'd taken off her helmet-like mask and her tall warrior sandals — they tripped her up while dancing. Her hair was bound up in intricate battle braids. Charlie, dressed as Honey's knight in cardboard armor, had just swept her off into the dance, and Bea felt strangely bereft.

She had just made up her mind to go get some more candy when a pirate clad all in black tapped on Bea's shoulder with a gloved hand. "Arr! Dance with me, love, or I'll make you walk the plank," he said. The top half of his face was covered by a black leather mask. He sounded suspiciously like Ben doing a bad pirate accent.

"Only if you can best me in single combat," Bea replied, leveling her plastic sword at him.

"With pleasure," he replied, bowing, and drawing his own flimsy plastic sword with a flourish. A short and surprisingly skillful skirmish began, complete with the cheering and applause of Peter and his companions.

"You're good at this," the pirate gasped, sounding a little alarmed as their battle advanced across the sand.

It was definitely Ben, she decided. He was using the same moves his self-insert character, Captain Constant, used in *Swashbuckleriad*. Bea had been quietly playing through the first level of the game, purely for research purposes.

"All thanks to you," she said. "The community college laid off their fitness teacher, so they let me take stage combat instead." She delivered him a stinging blow on the hand.

He winced. "That would explain why you're so dramatic all the time."

"Really, that's the best you can come up with?" she asked, going for another slash from the shoulder.

"Well then," he said, advancing on her again with an impressive counterattack she'd forgotten about, "it's just a question of whose choreography is better."

"No," she said, striking at the hilt of his sword—"it's just a question of who's better at improvising." As the blow connected, Ben's flimsy blade snapped, and flopped unceremoniously into the sand. Ben stared at it, stunned. Then he dropped the hilt and held up his hands as if in surrender. "All right, all right. You win."

She sheathed her sword with a triumphant smile. "Sorry about your sword."

"Oh, don't mention it," he said. Then, his eyes kindled with mischief, and he caught her in his arms and swept her off into the dance—specifically, into the ballroom dance side of things. "This wasn't part of the deal!" she exclaimed, finding herself somehow in the middle of a lively waltz.

"If you really can't stand to be near me for a three-minute song, feel free to leave," he said, relaxing his hold.

She thought about telling him that the song was really

more like five minutes, but decided against it. "We're in the dance traffic now. May as well stick it out."

"Wouldn't want to upset the old people," he said. He resumed his firm lead, trying to conceal his delight that she seemed in no mood to let go of him.

"Never thought of you as much of a ballroom guy," said Bea. She tried to think of the situation in technical terms like *closed position* and *ballroom hold* instead of —

"Well, if I wanted to go over to the freestyle side, I wouldn't have bothered asking for a partner," he said. "Ballroom allows me to be unpredictably predictable."

"You call this asking?"

"Well, I suppose there are other words one could use if we're going to quibble about semantics. Abducting. Absconding. Kidnapping." With each word, his voice grew deeper and slower, making her feel increasingly uncomfortable—but not necessarily in an unpleasant way. He went on: "Enticing. Carrying off. Sweeping you off your feet—" With that, he brought her into a short, close dip.

She was definitely out of practice—she felt much dizzier and more disoriented than she should for such a short dip. His eyes were...almost hypnotic, deep and dark as outer space...and just as unsettling. He smelled faintly of rum and strongly of campfire. He'd been put in charge of making (and tasting) s'mores. There was a tiny bit of marshmallow trailing from the corner of his mouth.

For whatever reason, she was finding it difficult to get her breath in this position. She was about to tell him about the marshmallow when he set her back on her feet. They resumed a more standard traveling box step, oblivious to the glares of the couple who'd nearly run into them when they stopped.

"Semantics?" she repeated, in an attempt to conceal whatever effect he was having on her. "Absconding? Where did you learn such big words?" She decided not to tell him about the marshmallow.

The coarse, brown-sugary sand was now filled with more footprints than a dance instruction diagram. Or a crime scene.

"Is it so impossible to believe I just came across it while reading?" he asked. They dodged around a breakdancing competition that had somehow ended up in the middle of the dance floor.

"Yes, actually."

She was amused at how genuinely offended he looked. They danced down almost to the water's edge, where the sand was wet and soft. They both stumbled a few times, when their feet had sunk down further than anticipated. Over Ben's shoulder, Bea caught a glimpse of the moon's smooth reflecting path along the glassy ocean.

"Shocking as it may seem, I actually read quite a lot," he said, steering them back towards firmer ground. "Where do you think all my brilliant ideas come from?"

"From other people, I assumed," she said.

"Well, even Shakespeare wasn't above a little creative borrowing," he said, twirling her around. Then he realized what she'd implied. "You don't seriously think I'm dishonest, do you?"

"I can think of an occasion that might cause me to believe that," she said bitterly.

They followed the dance traffic to the circle around the big bonfire, which was far too hot for an October night in Florida.

Ben groaned in exasperation. "C'mon, Bea. It's been

years since that stupid scholarship thing. You're not seriously still mad about it?"

"Well, yeah," she said. "It's not like the effects of it just went away while you went off and became successful. Do you really expect me to not resent it when you show up rolling in riches?"

"You were a humanities student," he said. "You wouldn't have been any richer if you'd gotten it."

He felt her body tense with anger, and knew he'd made a grave mistake.

Someone tossed another log on the bonfire, and it blazed up behind Bea. "I know you think I'm overreacting. And maybe I am. But people were lining up to throw money at any idiot studying something with 'science' in the title. Even computer science. And you knew it. And you knew that I didn't have a long list of people wanting to help me out. It was all I had, Ben. And you took it. I didn't think that you would go that far, but I always knew the only person you cared about was yourself."

She waited, breathless with a fierce, grim pleasure, to see how he would reply.

For once, he didn't say anything, just directed her silently through the next turn. Suddenly she wished he wasn't wearing a mask, wished she could search his face to see if there was any trace of regret on it, if she'd made any kind of impression at all. She couldn't tell anything from his smile. Was there a suddenly frozen quality to it?

"You didn't always think that," he said quietly. "That day — after I won the scholarship — you said you thought I was different."

"Well, that was my mistake, wasn't it?" said Bea.

They danced in silence as the alt-rock waltz chorus

continued ad nauseum.

Bea said, "You remembered me saying that?"

"It wasn't exactly easy to forget," said Ben. He gazed down at her with a weird, intense look as they rose and fell in time to the music, until Bea's anger had to vie with some other sensation that she couldn't quite identify. Then, mercifully, the song ended. Ben released her almost at once, and made a stiff, theatrical bow.

"Just in time," said Peter. He came clattering up to them in his tinfoil space cowboy costume with a beer in hand. Bea turned towards him in evident relief—and then realized that he looked red and a little unsteady. Peter saw her concern and forced a smile. "I think Charlie's about ready to—for you to take some photos."

"Crap, I almost forgot!" she said, checking her watch. "I'll never hear the end of it if I'm late." She darted off into the night.

Peter took a long sip of his beer and did his best to ignore the hollow ache in his chest. It took him a few minutes to realize that the always-talkative Ben was still staring after Bea in dazed silence.

"She did a number on you, didn't she?" said Peter.

"Hmm?" said Ben. "Must have been the punch from earlier. Leonata makes it pretty strong."

"Oh, definitely," said Peter, with a small smile. "Nothing to do with Bea."

"Course not," said Ben, a little too quickly. After a long pause, he added, "You would not believe what she said to me! She said that I—"

As he half-listened to his friend rant and splutter, the beginnings of an idea began to form in Peter's mind, a welcome distraction from the events at hand. One night,

Honey had gleefully informed them all that there was a lot of *Swashbuckleriad* fanfiction and shipping. And fanart. The most popular ship was Captain Kate x Captain Constant, "Katestant" for short. Kate's character was loosely based off of Bea, and Captain Constant was basically Ben. There were also a host of other, weirder ships. Honey had told him not to read any of it under any circumstances. Naturally, Peter's curiosity got the better of him—and then he quickly wished it hadn't. Still, shipping was a useful concept. Especially when your two best friends don't seem like they're ever going to get out of a state of violent denial about their feelings without some outside intervention...

As Ben wandered off to splutter somewhere else, Peter began humming an 80's song quietly to himself.

"I like your costume," said Honey, coming up beside him, radiant in her sparkly princess dress.

"Thanks," said Peter. "It was Ben's idea." He bowed low and put on his best theater voice. "You look lovely, Your Highness."

"Thanks," she said, curtsying with a grin. "Likewise, good sir."

He held out his hand—the one with a faint scar on the palm. "May I have this next dance?"

"Of course," she said, taking his hand.

With a grave tenderness, he led her over to the circle of dancers. He knew the song well.

He took her in his arms, and they began to dance, rising and falling with the melody of the song, with the inhale and exhale of the waves crashing on the shore.

Peter was smiling, but something about the way he held her made Honey sense that something was wrong. "What is it?" she asked.

"Nothing," said Peter, too quickly. His brown eyes were soft and sad.

"Come on, you can tell me," she said. The gentleness in her voice was almost more than he could stand.

For a moment, he considered it. *I love you. Run away with me. Let's get off this godforsaken island and forget everyone else.*

• • •

Johnny readjusted his carnival mask as he strode down the beach towards Charlie. Peter was playing into his plan beautifully. If Johnny could spin this correctly, there would be no engagement tonight. Of course, he would still have to compete with Peter after that. But Peter could be dealt with. Still, Johnny was nervous. He had just barely talked his way out of getting fired yesterday. Then again, Elaine was a lot sharper than Charlie.

• • •

Charlie was beginning to worry. At least he looked good, he thought, flexing in his cardboard-and-tinfoil armor. And Honey looked stunning. Thank goodness Bea was such a good photographer. The engagement photos would definitely go viral. He could just imagine the comments from his fangirls. They would be heartbroken. Honey would make a good wife. Not like Meg. What a bitch she had been. But Honey was a perfect angel. He checked his watch. Only three minutes had passed. There was still a good ten minutes to when Peter promised he would bring Honey over. But where was Bea? He sank down into the sand in exasperation — then stood up almost at once when he saw a dark, cloaked figure coming his way. Could it be

Peter? Cautiously, Charlie approached the apparition.

The man took off his mask to reveal Johnny's face. He looked unusually kind and concerned. "There you are! I've been looking all over for you."

"What's up?" said Charlie, hoping Johnny couldn't see the large "Will You Marry Me" spelled out in rose petals behind him. (It was, in fact, visible from space).

"There's, uh, something I think you should see," said Johnny, waving him forward. "I mean, I could be misreading the situation entirely, but I think Peter's about to put a wrench in your whole proposal plan."

Charlie tensed. "What do you mean?"

"Well…" Johnny avoided his gaze. "I'll show you."

He took Charlie by the arm and led him to the outskirts of the party. "See?" he said, pointing.

And there they were, Peter and Honey, slow dancing. They were far too close together for Charlie's comfort. He could only stare, speechless, as they swayed in front of the bonfire. He was so transfixed that he didn't notice when Johnny slipped away. Well. That explained Peter's eagerness to help him out by distracting Honey. And who could compete with Peter?

"So much for bros before hoes," said Charlie.

• • •

But Peter didn't say any of the things that he wanted to say to Honey. Instead, he told her, "I'm just worried about Johnny. I keep trying to help him, and he just pushes me away."

He had to let her go, but he would fix this night in his mind: the cadence of her voice; the firelight flickering in her hair, on her face; her glittering dress; the soft pressure of her left hand on his shoulder, her right hand holding his.

"You can only do so much," said Honey. "It's not your fault he's a trashbag."

Peter smiled. "You sound like Bea."

"Mom always said she'd be a bad influence on me," said Honey, returning his smile. "You can't let Johnny get you down, because that's what he wants — to make everyone as miserable as he is."

It had been a while since she danced with Peter. It was nice. Comfortable. He led with a quiet confidence. Ben was always a little too extra, and Charlie was still a little tentative. But Charlie was getting better. She wondered if Bea was right, if Charlie was planning to propose tonight.

Peter said, "You're probably right." He twirled her around. "Our best defense is to enjoy ourselves." The firelight flickered on his blond hair, making it look almost golden.

"It's a good night for dancing," she said, spinning back into him. "And a good song."

"Yeah," said Peter. The song washed over him, soothing the sharp ache in his heart as Honey smiled up at him, her thoughts clearly on Charlie. It was from the first show he'd ever done, he remembered suddenly. It felt like a lifetime since then.

Then Honey said, "I've got this funny feeling, like something important is going to happen."

"Once again, you're probably right."

"Okay," she said, feeling her heart begin to race. *I knew it. Oh my God. It's finally happening.*

The song wasn't even about love, really, at least, not the kind that was currently putting Peter through hell. It was about vocation, about doing something purely for the love of it. But like most good songs, that was just the first layer.

When the song ended, the music gave him the strength to let go of her.

• • •

They had danced out of sight. Charlie turned to leave in despair, and almost collided with Bea.

"I swear, Charlie, if you break my camera, I'll break your face," said Bea. But she softened instantly when she saw his tragic expression. "What's wrong?"

"It wasn't really a family photoshoot," he said. Tears were streaming down his face. "I was going to propose to Honey."

"Was?" said Bea. "And you were going to do what now?"

To say that Bea had been suspicious of Charlie's request that she do the Love family's Christmas card photos at Halloween was an understatement. But the Loves had always been a little weird. At least it was better than the usual white-shirt-khaki-pants routine. But this—?

"Peter stole Honey from me," said Charlie. "Johnny told me, and I saw."

"Bullshit," said Bea. "Peter would never do something like that. And even if he did, were you just going to let him? Grow some backbone. Besides, Honey's crazy about you, and I know her better than anyone. If you believe Johnny, then you're an even bigger idiot than I thought." She dug a packet of tissues out of her bag and shoved them at him. "Now, pull yourself together—they're coming down the beach."

She then darted away to survey the site. "This is pretty decent, actually." Charlie had even piled up extra sand to create a fake set of "dunes" for her to hide behind. She promptly did so, and started setting up for her first shot.

Charlie was too bewildered to be entirely convinced, but he took a deep breath and pulled out the ring. Bea snapped a few test photos of him waiting. She hoped the pictures wouldn't end up in an internet article titled "Pictures Taken Seconds Before Disaster."

There was Honey, looking amazing as always, walking slowly towards Charlie as if in a dream. There was Charlie, getting down on one knee, and Honey clapping her hands over her mouth in surprise. Good grief. They all did that. Bea hoped she wouldn't do that when someone proposed to her. Anyway, Charlie's tears looked pretty groundless, because Honey had thrown her arms around his neck and kissed him.

The shutter snapped and chittered like some metallic insect as she continued taking photos. She fell into the world of angles and lighting and composition and framing, faces, everything clearly aligned in the small luminous box. It was amazing, how short these apparently defining moments were. She was grateful that technology could keep up with the blinding speed of time. Only when Honey and Charlie had walked off, hand in hand, captured in a final frame, did she allow herself to realize that it was her best friend's face that was so radiant. The wind off the water made her shiver.

"Well," she said quietly. "That's that."

She walked back alone to the outskirts of the party. She sat down in the sand, not really caring if her costume got dirty, and looked out at the white rolls of foam on the dark water. She heard the sound of footsteps crunching through the sand, and saw Peter coming up to her.

There was a soft *thump* as he sat down beside her. "How'd it go?"

"It went great," she said tonelessly. "I'm happy for them," she added. There was a pause. "At least, I will be, when I get used to the idea."

"You really are a pro," said Peter. "I'm sorry we had to spring it on you, but we knew you'd tell Honey if you knew."

She opened her mouth to protest, then realized that this was, in fact, true, and closed it again. "Well," she said again. "And so it goes. They'll get married, Meg will catch the bouquet, and we'll dance." She laughed, but there was a note of sadness in it. Then she looked over at Peter. He was sprawled out in the sand and looking out at the ocean with a glassy stare. "Are you surviving?"

"Yeah," he said.

She put a hand on his shoulder. "You're a good man, Peter."

The goddess and the space cowboy returned to the party.

MASQUERADE IN PARADISE (continued from 1A)

In England, Governor Hedges had made a tradition of hosting a masquerade ball every Halloween. He decided to continue the tradition in the New World at the request of his eldest daughter, Minerva. She was reported to be very beautiful. Hedges gave special orders to make sure Captain Constant was closely watched that evening, to prevent him from escaping under cover of the party. However, with the help of his first mate, who had gained access to the house disguised as a servant, Constant was able to disguise himself as one of the masquerade guests.

Instead of escaping immediately, he snuck into the party

and persuaded Minerva to elope with him. Hedges later learned that they had fallen for each other over the course of the pirate's imprisonment. The next morning, the governor awoke to find that his daughter, half his treasury, and several cases of his best wine had vanished. The pirate also left a note: "I could have easily taken all, but I leave half your goods in recognition of your most excellent hospitality." In response, Hedges wrote, "Now I may truly say with Shylock, 'my daughter and my ducats! O my ducats and my daughter!'" He concluded the letter by urging his brother to use his influence with the Royal Navy to find the couple and make sure "that abominable pirate" was destroyed.

According to our historian, the fates of Captain Constant and Minerva Hedges remain unknown. There is no record of his ever having been executed, but if Hedges' brother followed the instructions in the letter, there would not be.

"Local legends differ on what exactly happened," said Ophelia Prince, "but all agree that this was the end of Captain Constant as we know him. Some say he was found and killed, either by the governor, his brother, or one of his men. Some say he abandoned Minerva. Most, however, say that the reason we hear no more of Captain Constant after this is that he settled down quietly with Minerva and enjoy his ill-gotten gains."

About a century later, some young women of the Prince family discovered this happier version of the legend. Delighted by its romantic possibilities, they decided to stage their own version of the masquerade, which eventually evolved into what we now know as the Masquerade in Paradise Charity Ball.

--From *The Paradise Post.*

CHAPTER FIVE

Plotting

Noble-Love

Leonata Noble announces the engagement of her daughter, Honey Cecelia Noble, of Paradise, Florida, to Charles Andrew Love, also of Paradise. He is the son of Jeff and Andrea Love. Honey teaches first grade at Paradise Elementary. Charlie is the Story Department Manager at Buccaneer Trail Productions. They plan to be married near the end of January.

—from *The Paradise Post*

"January!" shrieked Bea, who had been checking the announcement for typos. "You mean 2019, right?" Honey had brought her draft of the engagement announcement over. The internet had gone out at the *Post*, so Bea was working at the kitchen table in her small apartment. Bea did not believe in minimalism. Her apartment was filled with books, Honey's paintings, film posters (mostly rom-coms and 80s fantasy films), a CD shelf (cheaper than vinyl) and a jumble of castoff furniture from relatives and thrift stores. She had attempted to impose some order on the incongruous conglomeration of furniture by painting the pieces in harmonious shades of green. It sort of worked. The ceiling was festooned with Christmas lights, and an assortment of half-dead plants crowded the windowsill. Honey was sitting across from Bea at the kitchen table. She had on a pastel-striped sweater, tall boots, and a scarf. Even though it was only about 60 degrees outside, it was unseasonably cold for this time of year in Paradise. Honey was practically sparkling with excitement.

Bea, on the other hand, was in shorts and an old tie-dye t-shirt, and her face was crumpled in dismay. She closed her laptop and looked across at her friend in disbelief. "You do realize that it's November, right?"

"I know—there's a lot to do in a short amount of time, but I don't see any point in waiting," said Honey, with a cheerful shrug.

"He's barely been home for two months."

"I've known him practically my whole life, Bea. You're acting like he's some stranger I met online."

"You can know someone for a long time without really knowing them. You said yourself that you were worried about what things would be like now that you're not long distance." Bea heard her voice rising and stopped, trying to get a grip. She took a sip of her coffee. It was stone cold.

Honey said, "And you said that there was nothing to worry about! And you were right! Him being here is even better than I hoped it would be. We don't need a fancy wedding. Charlie's going to make me happy. Even my mom is happy. So why aren't you?"

"You don't need a man to make you happy! You're a whole, amazing person all by yourself," said Bea. She got up to reheat her coffee, as if the discussion were over.

Honey followed her. "Yeah, I'm all by myself. *You* don't need a man to make you happy. But I do." This morning was not going the way she'd anticipated. Bea was supposed to be just as excited as she was.

Bea punched the numbers into the microwave with too much force. "I just don't see why you want to rush into it when—"

"Okay, then, I'll spell it out for you. I don't want to live in my mom's apartment complex for the rest of my life while babysitting other people's children to make a living! I want to live in my own house and raise my own family and teach my own children. Maybe you can live with work being the most important thing in your life, but I can't!"

Bea sighed, and shut the door of the microwave slowly. "You really think that my job is the most important thing in my life?"

Honey felt a stab of guilt when she saw her friend's expression. "I'm sorry. I didn't mean that. I just don't see why you're unhappy."

Bea took a deep breath. "Everything's changing faster than I can keep up with, that's all." But it wasn't just that, she realized. For some reason, she had never really liked Charlie. She couldn't put her finger on it exactly. Some of it was just not wanting to let go of her friend. That was probably most of it. Still, there was something about him that she didn't like...

The microwave emitted an ear-piercing shriek, startling both of them. Bea took her coffee out, took a sip, and cried out in pain—now it was too hot. It wasn't like she could say anything about Charlie. She didn't have anything real against him. Besides, she wasn't exactly an expert on relationships.

"It is a big change," said Honey. *A wonderful change*, she thought to herself. Charlie, all hers, every day. Waking up to his beautiful face, the sun streaming through the windows of their own house. Doing laundry and cooking and laughing and just existing together. No more waking up alone in that dank and drafty apartment...

Bea leaned against the weathered pink Formica countertop and blew on her coffee, trying to process it all. In January, Honey would move out, and the next-door apartment would be vacant. There would be no more knocks on the door followed by, "Do you want to go on an adventure?" No more wandering in and out of each other's apartments, impromptu dinner experiments, or late-night gossip sessions. They'd stay friends, of course. But marriage changed people. That much Bea knew. And then some cranky old couple or pot-smoking beach bum (or worse, Ben) would move in next door...

"Bea!" said Honey. "Did you hear any of what I just said?"

"Sorry," said Bea. "Zoned out. I really need this. What did I miss?" She took a tentative sip. It was drinkable now, thank goodness. Out of habit, Bea pulled out Honey's favorite mug (the rose gold one) and poured her a cup of coffee.

Honey twisted a dishtowel in her hands, "Well, this probably isn't a great time to bring it up, but the real reason I came over was to ask if you wanted to be the maid of honor."

Bea smiled (it was only a little bit forced) as she poured in the cream and sugar. Honey's coffee was mostly just cream and sugar. "Of course I will!" said Bea. She handed Honey the mug, went back into the living room, and sat down on the couch.

"Thank you!" said Honey, putting down the coffee and hugging her fiercely.

"Of course," said Bea again, and, to her alarm, found that there were tears starting in her eyes. She blinked them away fiercely. Fortunately, Honey was busy enjoying her coffee and didn't notice. Bea took a deep breath, and, out of habit, pulled out a notepad. "Okay. Tell me everything. Who are the other bridesmaids going to be?"

"I'm going to ask Meg," said Honey. "I'd love to have her do hair and makeup for us, but I'm worried it might be too much. And Christine and Eva—I don't know if they'll come or not, it's a long way to fly."

Bea jotted this down on her notepad. "Have you thought about the venue?"

"Oh, yes, Charlie and I talked about that already. We want to have it on the beach! Since it's where we, uh, met." She sipped her coffee with a faraway look in her eyes.

"It was certainly memorable," said Bea, her restless hands tightening around the coffee cup.

If not for Charlie, Honey might have died that day.

• • •

It was summer, during high school. Honey was seventeen, and Bea was eighteen. They were at the beach with Peter and Ben, as they were almost every week that summer. Bea was lying on a towel, reading *The Mysterious Island*. It was slow going. Honey, Peter, and Ben were surfing. It was just after lunch, and the sun was beginning to feel truly oppressive, even to a seasoned Floridian. Bea sat up and squinted at the ocean, trying to decide if she wanted to go in and join them. The water was unusually rough. There was a tropical storm not too far from the coast, which was great for surfing, but less great for the casual swimmer. Honey had drifted far away from Peter and Ben and was paddling out towards the next line of swells. Bea squinted at her anxiously. Even though she knew her friends could handle themselves, she did not trust the deep water.

Honey attempted to catch an unusually large wave, and wiped out. Bea didn't think much of it at first. But after a few minutes, the foam had subsided, and her friend had not reappeared. Bea sat up straighter and took off her sunglasses. There was Honey's pink and yellow board—but no Honey. Bea scrambled to her feet, frantically scanning the water—and then she saw Honey being dragged out to sea. *Rip current.* Bea started running towards the ocean. The tide was going out, and it seemed like ages before she reached the water. She had just opened her mouth to cry out to Peter—he was a lifeguard; he'd know what to do—when she heard the thud of footsteps on the sand behind her. A tall, bronzed lifeguard that she did not recognize sprinted past her and dove into the water. Bea went in anyway, screaming for Peter and Ben. It took them a few minutes to figure out what was wrong—then Peter took off after the other lifeguard.

• • •

Honey's giddy voice cut through Bea's thoughts: "You know, that day, on the beach, I never would have dreamed—" She giggled. "I can't believe I'm marrying that hot lifeguard who saved my life."

"Neither can I," said Bea. She hugged her friend tightly. *Thank God for Charlie.*

Honey smiled at her. Her memories of that fateful day were a little different than Bea's.

• • •

Honey knew about rip tides, knew that you were supposed to wait until the escape point so that you could swim around and out, but she was going out so far and so fast that she began to panic. She tried to at least swim sideways, as she'd been told to do, but she was worn out from surfing and couldn't break free of the rip. Waves washed over her, and she kept struggling up for air. Her strength had almost given out, and she was terrified. She went under. This time, no matter how hard she tried, she couldn't seem to claw her way back to the surface of the water.

Then suddenly she felt strong arms pulling her up to the surface. She coughed up what felt like a bucket of seawater, gasping, feeling the air rushing through her lungs, dimly aware of a young man's voice going, "You're all right. It's going to be okay," as he pushed her onto the rescue board and began pulling them both back to shore. After that, she was mostly preoccupied with how awful it felt to have her lungs washed out with seawater. She remembered Peter's voice, desperate, urgent: "Is she okay? Tell me she's okay."

Then the lifeguard had picked her up and carried her from the shallows onto the beach. She still felt waterlogged and exhausted, but she was now conscious enough to be embarrassed. He set her down gently in the sand and knelt down beside her. She coughed up more water, and someone handed her a towel. Gasping, she looked up into the face of her rescuer. He was dazzlingly attractive.

"How are you feeling?" he asked, his burning blue eyes fixed on her face. Was there a hint of something besides professional concern in his voice?

"Like a drowned rat," she replied. *I probably look like one too,* she thought miserably. She sat up. "The rip—I'm sorry—I tried to—"

"It's all right," he said gently. "It's my job."

He started giving first aid instructions—partly to her and partly to Bea. Her friends clustered around and thanked him profusely. Then Peter introduced him: "Guys, this is Charlie—we were on Station 13 together last summer."

Charlie. Over the years, his name had taken on an enchanted sound.

Charlie waved awkwardly in greeting. "Peter's always telling me how awesome you guys are," he said. He gave her another dazzling smile. "You must be Honey."

Honey didn't believe in love at first sight, not really, but this was pretty darn close.

Charlie had stayed, chatting animatedly with Peter and Ben about surfing and video games, but his attention was never far from Honey. Much later, he had told her, "When I first saw you, it was like...I don't know, I had seen an angel or something." That first day, Honey had watched him and listened, spellbound. Bea caught her friend's eye and smiled knowingly, and Honey couldn't stop from grinning. Somehow, Charlie ended up being invited to the Friday campaign. Honey was worried that he would write them all off as hopelessly nerdy, but he turned out to be just as nerdy as the rest under all those muscles. And a little shy. It took him a while to get up the nerve to ask her out.

The rest, as they say, is history. That was how she would tell it.

• • •

At 5:00, Johnny came into the Windswept Salon for a haircut. The air was so thick with the smell of hairspray, shampoo, cheap perfume, and essential oils that it made him cough. The salon was deserted except for him and Meg.

"Thinking of trying a shorter style?" she asked hopefully.

"Yeah," he said, scowling. "Something more professional. I need to smooth things over with Elaine."

"You better let me wash it," she said. "It looks like you use motor oil for hair gel."

"Okay," he said.

He swathed himself in a black styling cape and followed her back to the washing station.

"When do you get to go back to work?" she asked.

"Beginning of December," he said, sitting down in the shampoo chair as if it were a throne. "Remind me to schedule another appointment for January."

"I take it you want to look nice for the wedding?" Meg asked as she started to wash his hair.

Johnny stiffened. "Something like that." He closed his eyes as she began massaging the shampoo into his scalp.

Meg was used to dealing with people's hair on a regular basis within the context of the shop. Normally she didn't think about it at all. But as his hair started to feel cleaner, she found herself thinking that she would like to be more familiar with Johnny's thick, dark hair *outside* of the salon. She wondered if he knew. He usually did.

"You seem…very relaxed about the whole thing," she said.

"What? Letting you loose on my luscious locks?" he asked, looking up at her with an unsettling grin.

Snap out of it, she thought, forcing herself back into service mode. *Honey's the only one he cares about.* "About Honey getting married," she said, rinsing the shampoo out of his hair.

"Well, I always was a good liar," he said. For a moment,

he let his guard drop, and his face darkened. "God. At least it's not Peter."

"I wish it were Peter," said Meg, rubbing his hair vigorously with a towel. "I wouldn't wish Charlie on anybody." Her hand rose automatically towards her cheek.

"He hurt you that bad, huh?" said Johnny. His voice was dangerously gentle.

Meg dried her hands and moved towards the salon chair. "It was a long time ago."

"Time's tricky like that." He followed her again and sat down in the salon chair.

She began combing out his hair. "I've thought about telling her, but I don't think—"

"She wouldn't believe you," he said bitterly as he watched her get out her scissors. "She's completely infatuated."

Meg sighed and began cutting his hair. "Yeah. I can't see it lasting long. That's some consolation for you, at least."

"I've got a more direct form of consolation in mind," he said.

Her busy hands stopped, and she stared at his face in the mirror. "What do you mean?"

"I think I know a way for both of us to get what we want," he said, his dark eyes holding her gaze in the mirror. "Something that requires your particular expertise."

She frowned. "What makes you think you know what I want?"

He reached up, took her free hand, and kissed it. She was so surprised that the scissors fell from her other hand, but she did not pull away. "I know what everyone wants," he said.

• • •

Friday was campaign night, when Peter and his friends

crowded around the elaborate gaming/dining table in his apartment. They laughed and argued as Peter, the GM, spun their choices into increasingly improbable adventures.

"What is taking Bea and Ben so long?" Peter grumbled, rolling a handful of dice absently on the table, which was covered with an assortment of makeshift paraphernalia that marked the boundaries of their imaginary world.

Honey glanced up from where she and Charlie were cuddling in the corner. "Looks like they're fighting again." She waved vaguely towards the dining room window. Peter looked out just in time to see Bea push Ben, who was fully clothed, into the swimming pool.

"Oof," said Peter, darting to the window for a better look. "That water's cold."

"Wonder what he said this time?" said Honey as she and Charlie crammed in next to Peter to get a better view from the small window. This resulted in Honey getting squashed against Peter's shoulder, causing him to momentarily short-circuit.

He pulled away and tried to get himself back into GM mode. "I'm definitely incorporating that into the game tonight." He headed towards the kitchen. "Does anyone want more wine? It looks like they're going to be a while."

Honey shook her head in mock exasperation as she watched. Bea was standing at the edge of the pool, laughing at Ben as he floundered in the deep end. "And this is why she's still single," said Honey, waving one of the enormous sleeves of her lilac velvet gown for emphasis. She was the only one who dressed up for the game. She was also a surprisingly ruthless player.

"I got the impression that she's single because she likes being single," said Peter from the kitchen.

"Sure," said Honey.

"What's that supposed to mean?" said Charlie, following her.

Honey hesitated, wondering how much to share of what she knew — and guessed.

Peter caught Honey's eye as he filled up her glass and gave her a conspiratorial smile. "You know, she and Ben would make a great couple."

"Did I miss something?" said Charlie, as Peter filled his glass. "Because last time I checked, they hate each other's guts."

Peter shrugged. "There are worse places to start."

"Heck yes," said Honey. "Katestant all the way."

Peter suddenly wondered if Honey was in fact behind some of those *Swashbuckleriad* fanfics. He picked up the small red and blue figurines that served as the markers for Bea and Ben's characters in the game, and then spoke in his GM voice: "I've got an idea that should bring Beatrice the Bold" — here he waved the red piece aloft — "and Benedict the Grandiloquent" — here he brandished the blue piece — "from the Swamps of Loathing" — represented on the board by a mildewed dish sponge — "to the top of the Mountain of Affection." He placed the two figurines on the top of an upside-down plastic cup. "But I'll need your help to do it. Will you join me on this quest?"

"Roll for it," said Honey.

"Okay, rolling for bluff," said Peter, shaking the dice vigorously and throwing them on the table.

"20," said Honey. "Beatrice x Benedict, enemies to lovers, 20,000 words."

Peter's eyes glittered with mischief. "Oh, I think we can do it in less than that.

CHAPTER SIX

Unnecessary Complications

The Three Best Pirate Books, According to Me

By Bandersnatch Crinklefries
November 22, 2017

Hi everyone! In this post, I'll be dispelling an urban legend and introducing you to some of my favorite pirate books. Contrary to some rumors circulating around on the internet, I actually can read, and do so on a fairly regular basis. It's a great way to get inspiration for your creative projects, and tons of fun, especially if you need a break from the screen (or if your parents set screen time limits). As many of you know, I'm kind of obsessed with pirates, so I'll read just about anything with pirates in it, but let me tell you — there's a reason these are classics. I've ranked them from worst to best to force you to keep reading. Also, I recently discovered that my grandma reads these posts, so that's why the language is so... PG. Love you, Grandma.

3. *20,000 Leagues Under the Sea* by Jules Verne

So, the only reason this one isn't higher on my list is that technically there aren't any pirates. But come on, Captain Nemo is pretty darn close. He engages in illegal seafaring activities, has an awesome ship, a loyal crew, and a crap ton of treasure that he gives to help people suffering under British imperialism, and considers drowning people who get on his nerves. No pointless romantic drama. Beautiful. The only downside is...Jules. Just because you're going 20,000 leagues under the sea, it doesn't mean you have to describe *all* 20,000 species of fish under the sea.

2. *Captain Blood* by Rafael Sabatini

Speaking of ridiculous names...This one's got it all. Swordfights, romance, adventure, swashbuckling, and, above all, a tragically wronged main character whose real name is literally Peter Blood (s/o to my man Peter). This is the stuff that *The Princess Bride* was made of. It's basically nonstop action from page 1. Sabatini was also really interested in historical accuracy, so you might even learn something (the white slavery thing is kind of iffy, though). Read this on the beach or on a long sea voyage. Also featuring an annoying and stuck-up love interest, Arabella, who just can't forgive Captain Blood for being a pirate. Let it *go*, lady. You know you want to.

1. *Treasure Island* by Robert Louis Stevenson

There's just something so comforting in reading about blood-thirsty drunken pirates stabbing each other in the back. The older you get, the more relatable it becomes. Also, this seems to be one of the few stories where the treasure is actually the main point of the book, which is kinda great. Sometimes the real treasure isn't the friends we've made along the way, guys. It's just the treasure. It also doesn't have any lame romantic drama, which is awesome. While I realize that stories thrive off unnecessary complications, romance just always seems. So. Unnecessarily. Complicated.

—From the blog *BandersnatchCrinklefries*

The next day, Ben went to the pool. The heat had returned with a vengeance as Thanksgiving drew nigh. On the way, he passed Charlie's window. He caught a glimpse of his friend holding up different suits in the mirror while smooth jazz crooned through a Bluetooth speaker. Ben made a face and hurried down the steps. If love destroys your taste in music, Ben was having none of it. Charlie used to listen to punk and alternative and rock (and combinations thereof) but now—dear God. He had even talked Ben and Peter into watching a chick flick when Honey had to go away for a weekend trip.

That was the trouble with love, Ben thought as he splashed into the water and flopped onto an enormous peacock-shaped pool float. It turned perfectly normal guys into immature idiots. He opened the latest issue of *Space Opera Monthly* with a flourish and began to read. Soon, he was deep into the details of the highly anticipated new film and all speculations, gossip, and conspiracy theories pertaining thereto. He had floated into the deep end of the pool when Peter's voice came booming across the courtyard:

"What do you mean, Bea is in love with Ben?"

Ben sat up so quickly that he upset the peacock's delicate balance—it dumped him unceremoniously into the water. It took him longer to get back to the surface than he'd expected, and he came up gasping. Peter and Charlie were coming down the stairs, so he ducked under the float, trying to slow his breathing down so he could listen. His breathing seemed to echo through the pool float as he inhaled the smell of sun-baked latex and chlorine.

Meanwhile, Charlie shrugged in response to Peter's question as he sat down on the lounge chair. "Isn't it crazy? Honey just told me, but she made me swear not to tell Ben."

"Why?" Peter asked as he knelt down and started waxing his surfboard with an almost-worn-out bar of wax. The coconutty smell wafted across to Ben, who was trying to make his way slowly and silently to the shallow end of the pool without being noticed so that he could stand and listen.

"Because if he found out, he'd just make fun of her," said Charlie.

"But how does Honey know that Bea's in love?" asked Peter, apparently completely absorbed with his surfboard. At this moment, Ben slipped, and went under again with a loud splash.

Taking advantage of the distraction, Peter leaned over and whispered, "Make it good! He's totally falling for it."

Charlie grinned and sprawled out in the lounge chair. When Ben came up spluttering again, he went on: "Well… she's been going through the photos of the last few parties, and she'll sit and stare at the pictures with Ben in them for hours."

"No!" gasped Peter, in what might have been the most overacted moment of his life. "Although…" he unwrapped a new bar of wax, "now that you mention it, she has been a little more obsessive over the photos than usual. Still, that could be coincidence. But she has seemed to be a little more spacey lately."

"Oh, that's not all," said Charlie, stretching out in the lounge chair. "She's started writing poetry again."

Peter made a face. "Well, maybe that will cure her."

"Nah. It's just made her worse. She scowls and swears when she can't come up with the perfect word — she's thrown away dozens of half-finished poems; but can't seem to stop writing them. Honey salvaged one of them — there was a line about 'the complicated magnetism of a *constant* crooked smile'."

From the general direction of the peacock pool float, there came a surprised yelp.

"Now that you mention it," said Peter, "I do remember Honey saying that she and Bea had a sleepover, and that she heard Bea murmuring his name in her sleep." Peter had a sudden fear that Bea would find out about this and strangle him on the spot, but he forged ahead. "I still don't see why she can't just tell him."

"Honey says that she'd rather die than tell him. It would be too humiliating," said Charlie.

"Maybe you're right," said Peter. "Ben's a good guy, but sometimes he can be pretty callous. You know he's never apologized to Bea about that whole scholarship fiasco."

"Really?" said Charlie. "It's been years, and they still haven't worked that out?"

"They're both stubborn as hell," said Peter. He was sorely tempted to turn and look at Ben to see how he was reacting to all this, but he knew it would be ruined if they did.

Charlie said, "You know, I remember Honey mentioning that Bea once told her that she was starting to have feelings for Ben right before he won the scholarship."

Peter pretended to be absorbed in putting the finishing touches on his board. "Yeah, it's too bad. But she's way too good for him, anyway. She's gorgeous, and fun to be around, and incredibly smart."

"Except for being in love with Ben," said Charlie.

Peter sighed. "True. If only Ben could get over his giant ego—then maybe. Just maybe."

"Well," said Charlie, coming over to inspect Peter's progress on the board. "Are we gonna go surfing, or not?"

Peter gave the board one last swipe with the wax and

wiped his hands on his board shorts. "That should do it." He stood up, stretched, and sauntered off in the general direction of the beach. Once out of sight, they fist-bumped each other in celebration. Part 1 of Operation Cupid was complete. (Honey had tried to come up with a ship name, but nothing quite worked: Benetrice? Bean? Bronstant? Yikes.)

• • •

As soon as he was sure that they had gone, Ben crawled out of the pool, soaked and utterly flabbergasted. He looked down in dismay at the soggy, pulpy mass that had been *Space Opera Monthly,* and then tossed it aside.

Bea was in love with him? Was that even possible?

He pushed his hair out of his eyes and flopped into a pool chair. Fragments of Peter and Charlie's conversation reeled through his mind. The guys weren't above a good prank, but Peter, at least, had been serious. He strained his memory, trying to think of anything that might— Halloween, surely. Bea wouldn't have felt any qualms about leaving him in the middle of the dance floor, what-ever she said about dance traffic. She had enjoyed it—at least until...

If she was determined to hide how she felt there wouldn't be a lot, but then again, Bea wasn't particularly good at hiding her emotions. And if she was in love with him, of course she wouldn't show it directly, since they roasted each other mercilessly on a daily basis...

He jumped up and started towards the beach. This was too much to process sitting down. He needed to go for a walk.

The walk did not make matters any clearer. Days later,

he still couldn't get her off his mind. He kept trying to run into her, to gather some data, but apparently, she and Honey had gone off on a spontaneous camping trip. He found himself trying to sort out his bewilderment at the most inopportune times, like in the middle of a presentation on the new edition of *Swashbuckleriad,* or in the checkout line at the grocery store. He hadn't realized he'd told the cashier "Love you too" and completely forgotten his groceries until he'd gotten back to his apartment.

When he realized that he'd left the groceries, he leaned back against the concrete wall of the motel and covered his face with his hands. He was such an idiot.

The truth was, there was more than part of him that wanted it to be true, wanted her attention to be more than just irritation, wanted Bea to see him as more than just a friend, or an enemy. Exasperating as she was, he was fascinated by her, had always been drawn to her. Whenever she was around, the world seemed more alive.

His mind circled around again to Halloween. He'd been such a jerk. Somehow, he'd never thought that anything he said actually mattered to her—it was just part of the game—but when he'd made that dig about her not being successful, he'd seen how much it hurt. Worst of all, he'd been happy about it—happy that he'd made her feel *something,* at least. Come to think of it…maybe she wasn't the only one using insults to hide her feelings.

He ran his hands through his hair in exasperation. How could he have been so stupid? How long, exactly, had he been antagonizing her because he wanted her attention, because he was—*Frick! There she is!*

Sure enough, Bea was climbing up the stairs on the opposite side of the courtyard—apparently back from camping. Ben was suddenly possessed by a desperate need to be seen by her and a completely opposite but equally desperate desire to disappear entirely and never be found. Paralyzed, he stayed where he was, against the wall, his heart racing as if he'd just run a mile—*how embarrassing*—straining to catch every detail of her across the courtyard. She saw him, and waved awkwardly, her face and hands and hair illuminated by the autumn morning light. He waved back, and realized his hands were trembling.

In that moment, one thing, the thing that he'd been trying to avoid for years, became inescapably clear.

The questions that had been swirling around in his head for the past few days fell abruptly into place as he watched her disappear into her apartment. He gave up, let the thing he'd been running from, the terrible vulnerability, wash over him, coursing through every fiber of his spirit.

Bea emerged from her apartment and began carrying something down the stairs and out of sight. Even though she wasn't looking at him, he felt naked, weak, exposed. It was horrible.

And then it wasn't. He felt as if a great weight had settled on him, and yet he was light, light enough to fly.

He had to believe Peter and Charlie were right about her loving him, in spite of how crazy it seemed. Because he loved her.

The sudden clarity sent a jolt of adrenaline through him. He began to pace up and down the walkway. He needed to—what should he do? What should he say? How would he even act around her knowing this?—Did he actually know anything?

At this point, he turned a corner and almost collided with Bea. This was too much for his brain to process, and he uttered a noise that sounded like a strangled pterodactyl.

"Where are you going?" she demanded, brandishing an enormous glass casserole dish like a weapon. "We're supposed to be going to the Princes' house to set up for Thanksgiving, remember?"

"I, uh…" His brain refused to provide him with an appropriate response, and he just stood there, panicking. She was so beautiful.

She looked him over with apparent disapproval. "You forgot, didn't you?" To his horror, he realized that he was in his sloppy weekend clothes — practically his pajamas.

"Uh…yeah. Sorry," he managed. *Don't just stand there, idiot.* Was it his imagination, or did she look a little flustered?

She tilted her head a little to the side. "You do remember that today is Thanksgiving, right?"

"Yeah," he said. "Definitely remembered." *Well, that would explain why the store was so crowded.*

"C'mon, there's no time to stand around and look pretty," she ordered. "Get changed and meet us at the car in five minutes. I am *not* putting those tables up by myself again this year." She turned and strode off towards the parking lot.

She thinks I'm pretty? He brushed back his hair, which had the unfortunate effect of making it poof out to twice its usual volume in the humidity.

I swear, I think he HAS forgotten it's Thanksgiving, thought Bea as she wedged the casserole dish into the backseat.

She's definitely in love with me, thought Ben triumphantly as he hurried off to get cleaned up for Yet Another Stressful Family Gathering.

• • •

The Princes were so excited to have Peter home again that they decided to invite Ben, Bea, Charlie, and Honey's families over for Thanksgiving dinner. The Princes believed that if anything was worth doing, it was worth overdoing, but mostly in the best way possible. Their house was massive, and they loved filling it with people, so the invitation got extended to their friends' disgruntled relatives who'd been banking on a Thanksgiving beach vacation. There were entirely too many people, in Bea's opinion. Vast, fantasy-novel quantities of food had been cooked and consumed. Everyone had gone around the room to say something they were grateful for (with varying degrees of sincerity). Honey and Charlie, of course, joined the ranks of couples who gushed about how thankful they were to have found each other. Bea was thankful that this occurred before they ate and not after, or she would have had to fight the urge to puke, but for once she did not say so aloud. More than once, she caught Ben staring at her in the strangest way. She wondered if she had lipstick on her teeth or something.

Sometime after dinner, Bea sank onto the couch in the designated "children's room" to watch one of the parades on television, surrounded by assorted cousins, friend's cousins, and her two-year-old niece, Emma Beatrice. Children were always a bit strange to be around, but at least they didn't expect a reasonable answer to the question "What are you going to do when you grow up?" And, comparatively, they were relatively easy to please—or at least their wishes weren't quite so existential as the adults' wishes.

Peter's sister, Grace, who lived in Oregon and was several years older than Peter, had four small children. Mr.

98

and Mrs. Prince had gone a little overboard in making a fabulous playroom to encourage their children and grandchildren to come and visit. It looked as if it were Christmas morning already. There were dolls, and trains, and plastic spaceships, and building sets, and pillow fort materials, and stuffed animals, as well as all the newest gaming consoles for the older kids, thanks to Uncle Peter. At the moment, two kids were having a serious battle between the knights and the ninjas in one corner, which occasionally intruded into the block engineering or the tea party. One of the smaller kids had fallen asleep in another corner, and three more were constructing a pillow fort around Bea. Emma Beatrice had vouched for her as a nonthreatening Big Person. It was a peaceful sort of chaos.

Bea was daydreaming about the parades. Maybe next year the high school band would be good enough to play in one of them, and she could talk Elaine into sending her up there to report on it. Or maybe she would talk Honey into skipping Thanksgiving and they could rent a hotel room and watch it from the balcony—except that Honey would be married by then. She would, she realized grimly, have to be on the lookout for a new adventure buddy. She could always go alone, but that seemed a bit weird for this particular trip. Perhaps Mom. Or Emma Beatrice. In a few years, she could take her to some of the epic toy stores there. Or the art museums, she thought, watching her niece working intently on her crayon drawing. Bea closed her eyes as the commercials blared. Maybe Peter had some connections...

"Are you sure that Ben really is that much in love with Bea?" came Honey's voice through the door...

• • •

Bea leaned back against the wall outside the children's room, with a blanket over her head, dazed and utterly discombobulated. She wondered how much (if any) of what she'd heard was true. Could it really be possible that Ben was in love with her? That would explain why he'd been acting so weird lately...but there had to be a more reasonable explanation...

Emma Beatrice, who had just noticed that Bea was missing, came out of the children's room to investigate. "Are you playing hide and seek?" she stage-whispered, causing Bea to jump.

"Yes—no. I don't know," said Bea, standing up and disentangling herself from the blanket. She had scrambled into the hall, desperate to catch all that she could of Honey and Meg's conversation before they got too far away to hear.

"Can we use your blanket for our fort?" asked Emma Beatrice.

"Yeah," she replied, handing it to her. Satisfied, Emma Beatrice threw it around her shoulders and strode off like a queen.

As Bea dusted herself off, she caught sight of Ben at the far end of the hallway. He was carrying a giant crock pot towards the garage door. His face was contorted into a look of goofy-but-earnest determination as he tried to keep the soup from sloshing onto the pristine carpet. He looked so awkward and human that she felt a surprising rush of something — softness? Affection? — towards him.

It would be worth the risk to find out, she decided. After all, it was her business to find stuff out.

CHAPTER SEVEN

The Wedding

Entertainment: Deck the Halls with the Jolly Roger

Beatrice Bright
Friday, December 1, 2017

Swashbuckleriad, the bestselling multiplayer pirate video game, may soon be coming to a big screen near you. Several production companies have contacted the company about optioning production rights for either a feature film or a television series. "We're so stoked about the possibility of a new way to share our story," said Ben Constant, the company's attractive spokesman, in a confusing interview with the *Post.* "But we want to make sure that any adaptations stay true to the spirit of the game." Constant says that he and C.E.O. Peter Prince will fly out to California to begin negotiations. If all goes well, a film may appear in theaters in late 2020.

Meanwhile, gamers young and old are eagerly hoping to receive awaiting one of the most asked-for Christmas gifts this year — the company's new family-friendly offering, *Jim Hawkins Sails Again.* Critics have noted the game's surprising incorporation of female characters, a nod to the ever-growing population of "gamer girls." According to Constant, "The original game was more pirate-centric, but with this one's more world-centric — you can play as part of any of the different groups on the island — pirates, sailors, castaways,

mermaids. It gives us more room to offer the player a different story every time." The game will be released on December
10th.

—draft of an article for *The Paradise Post*

The interview with Ben about the *Swashbuckleriad* movie
deal took place in the wee hours of a cold December morning on the way to the big airport in Orlando. Bea's ancient
station wagon was in the shop (again), so Ben had offered to
let her drive his truck while he was gone—if she gave him
and Peter a ride to the airport. Between wedding preparations and the impending launch of the new game, everyone had been insanely busy, so this was the closest Bea and
Ben had come to being alone together. The interview had
occupied most of the drive, but now that it was over, the
awkwardness was so palpable that it had rendered even
Bea and Ben at a loss for words.

In the backseat, Peter was desperately wishing that
he'd thought of a way to get to Orlando by himself. He
didn't think either of them would broach the subject with
him there, but there was always the chance—and then,
good or bad, whatever happened would be even more
uncomfortable. Somehow, when he planned this all out, he
never imagined he'd have a front-row seat to the conse-
quences of his actions.

"This is a nice truck," said Bea, in an attempt to dispel
the awkwardness. "You sure you want to let me borrow it?
If I keep it too long, I might not want to give it back."

"Guess we'll have to come back quickly, then," said
Ben, a little too enthusiastically.

Bea shot him a quizzical look. He *wanted* to come back
early? To see her?

Ben cleared his throat and shifted in the passenger seat. "I mean, wouldn't want you to get too attached to it."

"Oh." Her face fell, and she turned her attention back to the road. She said, "Seriously, though, thanks for helping me out. When they told me it would be at least two weeks before they could fix the Wagon, I almost lost it."

"Well…some of the stuff you said made me realize that I've been…kind of a jerk, and I'm trying to be…less of one," said Ben.

Bea was so surprised that she couldn't think of anything sarcastic to say in response. She risked another quick look at him. He looked serious. More serious than she'd seen him in a long time.

He went on: "And I realized I never really apologized to you for the whole scholarship thing. I should have at least told you what I was planning to do. I knew it was important to you, and it was selfish of me to just forge ahead without considering that. And I shouldn't have been a complete — jerk — to you afterwards."

His apology was met by a stunned silence. "Thank you," she finally managed. "I know it happened a long time ago, but it…means a lot." She looked out at the skyscrapers of Orlando streaming past them and felt much of her bitter resentment dissolve. "Looking back on it, I probably overreacted a little."

"No comment," said Ben, which made her laugh. A lovely sound. Ben leaned back in his seat in relief. Screw Peter. He had to find out how she felt before they left for California.

He was just gathering up the nerve to ask her when Peter's phone went off. "Hey guys, apparently they just moved our flight up by about 20 minutes," said Peter.

Bea glanced at the clock on the dashboard. "Crap. We're still about 20 minutes out. That doesn't give you much time to get to the airport, let alone catch your plane. Hold on to your butts — this could get crazy."

She drove off the main lane and onto the shoulder, rattling over the rumble strips at impossible speed until she reached the next exit and began zooming through the streets, oblivious to stoplights. "You know how to get to 417?"

"Sure," squeaked Peter, who was gripping the handle on the roof tightly. "Take a left up on Gator Trail."

"Here?"

"Here!"

The car careened around the corner, taking out a few traffic cones as they went. Two near collisions later, they were zooming down Highway 417, weaving in and out of traffic and off and on the shoulder. A maze of spaghetti-like airport exits and access roads flew by in a blur. Miraculously, they screeched to a halt outside the terminal unscathed and unpursued by police cars.

Even Ben, who was a notoriously reckless driver, was a little shaken. Peter blinked, shook himself, then leaped out and began unloading their luggage.

Ben, however, remained in the car and forced himself to collect his wits. It was now or never. "Bea," he said, and the change in his voice made her look over at him, half surprise, half hope. "There's something else I—"

Her gray eyes looked into his, asking questions. Needing to be answered. Her auburn hair had tumbled down around her shoulders, offset against her Christmas-green sweater and dark red lipstick.

But then Peter's voice cut in: "Benny! The plane leaves

in five minutes! Come on!"

Had he been Captain Blood, or Captain Nemo, or someone cool like that, Ben would have just kissed her then and there and then dashed off to catch his plane— or forgotten California entirely. But he was, unfortunately, just Ben Constant, who was, underneath his swashbuckling and highly fictitious persona, a very ordinary man whose romantic experiences with women had been limited to a few short and ill-fated dates (and overeager fangirls). So instead, he mumbled, "tellyouwhenIgetback," jumped out of the car, and ran after Peter to catch the plane to California.

Bea was left alone and confused. And irritated.

She had half a mind to call Ben when he got to California and demand an explanation, but decided she'd rather wait and have the satisfaction of demanding it in person. So, she drove back to Paradise and tried to banish the incident from her mind. She had promised to meet up with Honey and her mother to go wedding-dress shopping. Ben had said they would be back in time for Christmas.

Paradise had exactly one bridal store, and even that one was on shaky ground. There were a lot more funerals than weddings in Paradise. But Honey's mom, Leonata, was close friends with the owner of Beau's Bridal, Mrs. Ophelia, (who was also the town's chief historian and a distant relative of Peter's), so getting a dress anywhere else was not an option. Beau's was in the same shopping center as the salon where Meg worked. The small shop was stuffed to the gills with an overwhelming array of dresses (new and vintage, mostly vintage). With the exception of several floor-length mirrors, every available inch of wall space was occupied by bridal gowns, which made it seem like the customers were inside a cloud of silk, satin, and tulle.

When Bea arrived a few minutes late, Mrs. Ophelia had already swooped down upon Honey in an ecstasy of lace and rhinestones and bustled her off to the dressing room. Canned music groaned faintly from a speaker that was muffled behind a wall of gowns. The shop smelled of mildew, coffee, and fresh flowers, with a dash of Eau de Thrift Store.

Bea sat down on a pink shag-carpet ottoman that had seen better days to watch the weird spectacle unfold, rubbing at a smudge on one of her tall black boots with the edge of her sleeve. She had dressed up to take the guys to the airport, since she was technically "working," but she still felt underdressed amidst all this bridal splendor.

Honey's mom, Leonata, was pacing up and down, jittery with excitement. Even on a day like this, her tanned, weathered face had stern, hard lines in it, but there was a warm glow in her brown eyes that reminded Bea of Honey. Leonata dressed simply and carried herself with the athletic, no-nonsense grace of a local. Her thick, dark hair was streaked with gray, and was braided into a neat bun.

At first, they were the only ones in the shop. It looked like it would be a while before Honey emerged, so Bea hummed "Deck the Halls" absentmindedly as she pulled out her ancient, enormous laptop and began typing up Ben's interview, trying not to yawn. She was technically off today, but Elaine had insisted she get the scoop on the movie deal. Bea would have to remember to double-check for any accidental gushing references to Ben. Last week, she had failed to catch a line that described him as "the game's dashing creative heart." Elaine was never going to let her live that down. At least she would be too busy to make much of a fuss about it. Paradise's eventful Christmas season made the fall seem tame by comparison. There was the Christmas tree lighting, the Dickens festival, the toy drive, three concerts that had been deemed newsworthy because somebody's cousin was the fourth chair in the orchestra, the office Christmas party, the family Christmas party, volunteering at the nursing home… And then there was the bridal shower, which Bea was hosting. She thrived on the continuous excitement, but it was 10 a.m., and her adrenaline and first cup of coffee were quickly wearing off.

She was about to risk some of Mrs. Ophelia's coffee when the bell over the shop door tinkled and Mrs. Pittman entered. She was followed by her other granddaughter, Crystal, and a sulky-looking Diana. It was hard to say who looked more triumphant—Crystal, with her blindingly enormous engagement ring, or Mrs. Pittman.

"Oh-pheel-li-aa!" sang out Mrs. Pittman, "We're here for our appointment!"

"In a minute!" came Mrs. Ophelia's muffled voice from the dressing room.

"Hmph," said Mrs. Pittman. She turned to survey the room and raised her eyebrows when she saw Bea. "*You* can't possibly be here for a wedding dress," she said.

Bea steeled herself. *The Wagon's not going to last forever. I need that promotion so I can get a new car.* She sat up straighter and said, "I'm Honey Noble's maid of honor."

"Aha," said Mrs. Pittman. "Always the bridesmaid, I see."

"This will be my first time, actually," said Bea, turning to Crystal with a desperate smile. She was tall and slender, with straight, shoulder-length blonde hair, and was dressed immaculately in pearls, heels, and an expensive, tropical-print sheath dress in cheerful highlighter colors. Bea didn't know Crystal well—Bea had never really gotten along with the pageant-and-cotillion crowd—but she had to be more pleasant than her grandma. "Congratulations, Crystal. Who's the lucky man?"

Mrs. Pittman answered for her. "Everett Prince, the mill manager."

"Assistant manager," said Crystal, clearly embarrassed. "His dad's still the manager."

Bea nodded in recognition. "Oh, he's Peter's cousin." Even before the success of Buccaneer Trail Productions, Peter had always been a celebrity to the people of Paradise. It was kind of weird, but for once she was thankful that she could throw his name around so easily and still be polite. His cousins, including Everett Prince V, had run the paper mill, Paradise's main source of industry outside of tourism, for generations. Everett was a little stuck-up, but otherwise a decent guy.

"Yes. I've always liked *that* side of the Princes," said Mrs. Pittman. "Peter the third, on the other hand, really had terrible judgement when it comes to women."

It was widely known that Mrs. Pittman was still bitter that she hadn't been the one to snag Peter's father, Peter Prince III, before (or after) his first marriage.

Bea was saved from having to reply by Honey, who emerged from the dressing room in a gown so fluffy that it seemed to fill the entire square footage of the tiny shop—with puffy sleeves to match. It looked like it was straight from 1980. She was trying her best to keep from giggling. "How do I look?"

"Like a cloud," said Bea.

"It's lovely!" cooed Leonata.

Mrs. Ophelia followed after her. She was the quintessential hippie grandma, with a loose, patchwork blue dress, bifocal rose-colored glasses, a crystal amulet around her neck, and flowers plaited into her long silvery hair. She folded her arms and looked Honey over. "Well, now that you've got it on, I'm not so sure."

Honey nodded in agreement. "I think it's a little much for the beach."

As Mrs. Ophelia dove into one of the racks to search for another dress, Bea had the weird sensation that she was in one of those reality TV shows about weddings. Mrs. Pittman butted in: "Ophelia, can't you see we're waiting?"

Mrs. Ophelia resurfaced from the sea of white with a dress on each arm, handed one to Honey, and ushered Crystal into the other dressing room with the other. Fortunately, Mrs. Pittman went back with them. Unfortunately, this left Bea alone with Diana Pittman.

Bea couldn't resist asking, "So, Diana, how's your theatrical career coming along?"

Diana sat on the pouf across from her. "Great, actually! One of my friends got a video of my little parade stunt, and it went viral. I got a job as an extra in a big-name movie they're shooting in Georgia. Can't say which one, of course." She took out a small makeup bag and began reapplying lipstick in one of the big mirrors.

"Congratulations," muttered Bea, shifting in her seat. "I'm sure they'll appreciate your improv skills and respect for other people's boundaries." She must have missed Diana's viral phenomenon in the hurricane excitement.

Deciding she'd had enough, she got up. She was about to make a beeline for Mrs. Ophelia's coffee, when Diana said, "You know, the first thing Benny did once he got free of me was look at you."

Bea froze, but she did not give Diana the satisfaction of seeing her face. Then, as if sleepwalking, she went over to the coffee. Her hands went through the motions with the ancient percolator and cracked vintage china.

She turned again when she heard Honey come out of the dressing room. This particular wedding dress looked more like it was destined for a boudoir session. Honey's face was pinker than her hair.

Mrs. Ophelia was saying, "You know, I thought since you're having a beach weddin' you might want something with a little more freedom of movement..." Her voice died away under Leonata's scowl. Bea gave a gentle but decisive shake of her head, and Honey retreated, clearly relieved.

Crystal emerged as Honey was going out. "Ugh, I hate lace," she said. "I look like you, Grandma."

Bea covered her mouth with her hand to keep from laughing. Leonata sidled up to her and whispered, "The apple don't fall far from the tree."

Mrs. Pittman scowled when she saw them laughing.

Leonata said, "Why don't you give Ophelia a hand with pulling dresses, Bea? You know what Honey likes. I'll hold your coffee." Bea was about to protest—but seeing Mrs. Pittman's death glare made her change her mind. Bea strode off into the racks to see if she could find anything suitable.

As she worked her way through the racks, examining dress after dress, she remembered late-night giggling conversations with Honey on the deep philosophy of wedding dresses. Was it acceptable for them to be any color besides white? (Both were on the fence about this—there's just only so much you can do with white, but the symbolism was so messy.) Why were both royal wedding gowns were so terribly boring, and when did it became illegal for dresses to have sleeves?

Anyway, Honey needed something that was both practical and whimsical. There, yes, this one should do nicely. This one might also work. As she reached the end of the row, weighed down by armfuls of dresses, she had the feeling that she was being stalked. Sure enough, there was Mrs. Pittman. This time, there was no escape.

"I guess Elaine doesn't need you as much at the *Post* now that she's got Johnny," said Mrs. Pittman. "From what I've heard, he's really top-notch."

"He's an individual with unique talents," said Bea. *Particularly when it comes to breaking the law.* "But I've actually been quite busy. Just sent Elaine an exclusive article about the *Swashbuckleriad* movie deal."

"Dear Elaine," said Mrs. Pittman. "She was always so good about humoring young people's delusions of grandeur."

As she pulled another dress, Bea thought that if Johnny had hired Mrs. Pittman to antagonize her, he really should have given her some lessons in subtlety. She wasn't going to rise to anything that obvious.

But Mrs. Pittman was still at her heels. "You know, when I heard that Honey was engaged to Charlie Love, I was really kind of shocked. Couldn't believe he'd commit to someone like her."

Bea stiffened. Her stressed, sleep-deprived brain was fighting a losing battle to maintain her composure. She shifted into her theater voice, each word clearly and crisply enunciated so that it carried through the shop: "I beg your pardon?"

Mrs. Pittman gave her a nasty smile and said, so loudly that Honey could hear: "I always thought that Honey was the sort of girl he'd fool around with until he found someone better."

Bea deposited the dresses on the mobile rack. She saw the shock and hurt on Honey's face. Then she turned to face the sneering old lady. Bea's whole body was taut with rage. "Take that back, you withered old bitch."

Mrs. Pittman recoiled as if she'd been struck. She turned without a word and strode out of the building, slamming the door behind her with such force that a dozen rhinestone tiaras fell off the wall behind the front desk.

"Thank the Lord," said Mrs. Ophelia, watching her go. "I thought she was gonna be here all day."

Crystal appeared in a dip-dyed dress, looking impressed. "I've always wanted to say that to her."

Bea stammered an apology.

Honey still looked shaken. "What would make her say something like that about me and Charlie?"

"She just can't stand to see people happy," said Mrs. Ophelia in a soothing voice. "Bea, why don't you help her with those gowns while I make a fresh pot of coffee?"

The shop soon resumed its bustling, cheery atmosphere, but Bea had failed, and she knew it. When she got home, she sent Elaine a brief, clear email explaining what had happened, and braced for impact.

The next day, Bea was called into Elaine's office. Elaine was checking off the days until her retirement on a gigantic calendar behind her desk. She did not turn around to look at Bea. "Now, I don't believe half of what Pearl tells me, but I'm only going to say this one more time. It's hard enough to keep the paper running in this day and time without your chief reporter insulting everyone in sight. If I hear of anything like this happening again, you're fired."

"I understand," said Bea. She felt bad for causing her mentor so much stress, but she still seethed against the unfairness of the situation.

• • •

Fortunately, the Christmas chaos kept Bea busy enough to stay out of trouble. December washed through her in a shower of tinsel and sparkling lights. Even so, to her deep embarrassment, Bea found herself pining — looking through old photos, trying to reconstruct her memories through this new lens of possible romance, counting down the days till Ben's return. Unfortunately, the guys didn't come home for Christmas. *Jim Hawkins Sails Again* was a bigger hit than anyone expected. Buccaneer Trail Productions was celebrated throughout Silicon Valley. They found themselves swimming in offers for collaborations with companies they used to dream of working for. The Princes and the Constants jumped at the opportunity to break tradition and celebrate Christmas in California with their brilliant sons. Then it was January.

Honey had been so busy with speed-planning her wedding that Bea didn't have a chance to fish for more information about Ben until the night before the wedding. Honey had planned to host a casual bachelorette party at her house that night before, but early in the afternoon, she knocked on Bea's door. "Hey, Meg's out with a cold, and Christine and Eva's flight got delayed, and if I have to be around any more people before tomorrow, I think I'll die."

"So, no bachelorette party," concluded Bea

sympathetically.

"But you don't count as people," added Honey. "Do you want to come over and bake cookies and watch Christmas movies instead?"

It was the best compliment Bea had ever received. "Of course!" she said, her eyes shining. Then she thought about it for a minute. "Isn't it January?"

Honey shrugged. "Well, we didn't have time to watch them last month."

Until recently, Honey's apartment had been covered in even more Christmas lights than usual and festooned with cheery signs, glittering pink-and-gold ribbon garlands, comfy hand-me-down furniture, old blankets, paintings, movies, and stuffed animals, and was chaotic with Christmas and wedding presents. Each room had been painted in a different pastel hue.

Now, most of her furniture had been moved to her and Charlie's new house, and what remained had been packed away neatly, leaving a bare room with only the dilapidated couch and a battered coffee table. All the rooms had been repainted in the same dreary beige.

"We'll probably order better furniture for the new place," said Honey as she nestled into the couch with her favorite stuffed animal, a corgi named Mr. Bingley. "But I just couldn't plan the wedding and decorate the house at the same time. Besides," she patted the couch affectionately and dust poufed out, "I'm kind of attached to the old stuff."

Bea put the cookies in the oven, trying hard not to think about how this would be the last time she'd ever do so in this apartment, trying hard not to think about how empty the room was. "Well, at least we won't go hungry."

As Bea came back into the living area and sat down on the couch, Honey handed her a box of chocolates. "I snagged these from Mom's apartment. I found them on the counter where she puts all the stuff she doesn't really want, and I thought, 'no reason to waste perfectly good chocolate."

"Mmm. These are really good!"

Bea munched thoughtfully, wondering how to bring up the subject of Ben without giving herself away. "So, uh, I heard Ben is interested in somebody?" she said.

Honey acted very preoccupied with arranging her blanket. "Oh? Where'd you hear that?"

"Uh…y'know, through the grapevine," said Bea. She didn't dare look Honey in the face. This was just as well, since Honey had a terrible poker face.

Honey ate another chocolate to buy herself some time, although she nearly choked from trying not to laugh at Bea's attempts at nonchalance. "Well…" Honey said finally. "I did hear something like that myself."

"Oh?" said Bea, fidgeting.

"Yeah. She's really smart, and beautiful, and super cool," said Honey, who was grinning uncontrollably now.

"Oh," said Bea, her shoulders slumping.

"It's you, moron," said Honey.

"What?" said Bea.

"I mean, it's kind of obvious," said Honey, who by now fervently believed it. "Haven't you noticed the way he gets all flustered around you?"

"That could just be a coincidence."

"Didn't he apologize to you about the whole scholarship fiasco that you guys have been fighting about for literally forever? I thought it was going to be a cold day in hell before Ben actually admitted that he was wrong about something."

Bea rolled her eyes. "Ah yes, basic human decency. So sexy."

"He lets you drive his truck, Bea. He doesn't even let Peter drive his truck. You didn't even have to ask, he was just like—" She put on the silly voice she used whenever she was making fun of people: "Please borrow my truck, Bea. Is there anything else you need? My house, my wallet, my hand in marriage?"

Bea groaned exasperatedly as Honey giggled. "Then *why* hasn't he said anything?" Bea demanded, gesturing dramatically with her hands.

"He's probably afraid you'll just laugh at him," Honey replied.

"I wouldn't!" declared Bea.

Honey raised her eyebrows. "I don't know, Bea, you can be pretty savage." The timer blared. "Ooh! Cookies." She bounced up and went into the kitchen.

Bea picked up Nessie for stability and groaned. "The embarrassing part is that I…" She trailed off, not sure if she was physically capable of saying it out loud.

Honey was trying not to bounce up and down in anticipation.

"I think I do…like him?" said Bea. Then she groaned again. "I do like him, damn it."

"Of course you like him," said Honey as she pried the cookies off the pan with a spatula. "You guys like, sparkle when you're around each other. I mean, sometimes it's more of an 'I'm going to murder you' sparkle. But still." She licked a melted chocolate chip off her fingers in a satisfied way.

"What should I do?"

Honey shrugged. "I don't know. You could always just make out with him and see what happens." Not that she would ever dream of doing such a thing herself, but she firmly believed Bea had the guts to do just about anything.

Bea let out a horrified yelp and dived under Honey's giant pink sparkly couch blanket.

Honey brought the cookies over to the couch. "Oh, come on, Peter said you guys were like, on the brink of it when he walked in on you in the laundry room. Although on the other hand it didn't work out so well for Diana…"

Bea emerged from the blanket. "That was an accident. Besides, I'm certainly not bringing it up." She folded her arms. "I'd never hear the end of it."

Honey sighed in exasperation. Well, this was progress. She'd never really thought Bea would admit that she had feelings for Ben, even to her. Now if only she could convince them to actually admit it to each other…She'd have to reconvene with Peter and Charlie for further plotting. For now, she rested smugly on her laurels.

Bea inhaled the delicious aroma of chocolate chip cookies and once again cursed Ben silently for his weirdness. Or cowardice. Or whatever it was. How ridiculous. How mortifying. The worst of it was, she didn't just *like* him. She had known him too long for that. This was different. This was terrifying.

"Which one do you want to watch first?" asked Honey, holding up DVDs like they were a magician's cards.

Her words brought Bea back to earth. Tonight, she needed to focus on Honey. She offered her a generous portion of the blanket, and Honey burrowed under it.

There had been innumerable nights like this one,

sleepovers at their families' houses when they were younger, giddy celebrations when they'd moved into their own apartments. But as the evening went on, Honey's bubbly, teasing energy faded. At first, Bea put it down to sheer exhaustion. She did her best to refrain from her affectionately sarcastic movie commentary and let her friend recharge. Honey usually came back to life by the end of the first movie. But as the third couple of the evening waltzed off into their happily-ever-after, her friend still had the same frozen look on her face.

"What's wrong?" Bea asked.

Honey pulled her legs up and clasped her hands around her knees. "I'm scared."

"Yeah?"

"What if we've got it all wrong? What if we aren't meant to be together? What if I'm not good enough?"

Bea hugged her. "Hey, listen to me. You're way more than enough, and don't let anyone tell you any different. Especially not crazy old bi—I mean, ladies. Especially not Charlie. If he does, I'll kick his ass."

Honey closed her eyes and leaned against her shoulder. "Okay."

Bea thought about Honey and Charlie. Surely, if they had lasted this long, they'd be fine. Bea had always been a little lukewarm on Charlie, but most of that was just because she resented how much of Honey's time and attention he got. Of course, there was always the chance that maybe Peter's feelings weren't as one-sided as he thought…

"Why do you ask, though? Is there…someone else?"

Honey shook her head and pulled away. "No. It's just— it seems so final. I can't help but second-guess myself."

Bea smoothed out her half of the blanket. "Okay, listen.

I don't know much about love, but this is what I do know. There's no such thing as soulmates. There are people you're drawn to and people you're not, but you're not fated to end up with one person. Love is something you choose. And you've chosen Charlie, and he's chosen you." She began picking up the stuffed animals that had fallen off the couch—Nessie and a polar bear named Marshmallow. "It's normal to be scared. Change is scary."

Honey smiled weakly at her. "Thanks."

Bea handed her the popcorn, and said, "Try not to worry too much. Tomorrow will be amazing. And then you and Charlie can peace out and get away from Gossip City."

This succeeded in making Honey laugh.

• • •

That night, Bea slept like the dead. She didn't wake up the next morning until she heard Meg pounding on her door, shouting, "Beatrice! Do you still want me to do your makeup, or not?"

After that, things were manic. Even though it was a simple wedding, there were somehow still a million things that had to happen, and Bea had volunteered for more than her share. She vowed that, in the unlikely event that she did get married, she was going to elope. At least the guys were moving Honey's couch. If they ever showed up.

Of course, they did show up, at which point Bea blew her cover. Instead of greeting Ben with a customary insult, she had run towards him, beaming, and said, "You're back!"

"I am," he replied, staring at her, dumbfounded. She looked stunning, with full hair and makeup and a shimmery bridesmaid's dress.

Realizing she'd betrayed more of her feelings than she'd wanted, Bea backpedaled furiously. "Uh, how was California?"

He grimaced. "Let's just say it's good to be back. Think we finally got everything taken care of, though."

"Good," said Bea, brushing a stray heat curl behind her ear and staring down at her sandals.

"You look amazing," he said.

Bea did a double take. "Did you just give me a compliment?" As far as she could remember, it was the first time he'd ever done so.

He grinned. "Don't get used to it."

"You clean up pretty nice yourself," she said.

He gave her a look of such genuine happiness that she panicked and ran away.

Finally, finally, it was time for the wedding itself. The afternoon sun began to set, transmuting the sands and the sea into glowing, jewel-like shades of rose and gold and aquamarine. Honey had picked her colors accordingly — rose gold was in that year, and it suited her perfectly. Bea was not a rose gold or pastel person — she preferred her colors to declare themselves openly instead of dithering in the background — but she found herself enjoying the peacefulness and softness of her floaty blush-colored dress. Most importantly, it had pockets.

Ben's dad, Pastor August, had agreed to officiate the ceremony. He stood stalwart in a golf shirt under a plastic vine-covered archway, looking more like a dad than a preacher.

Emma Beatrice was the flower girl. She was wearing a blush-colored tulle dress that was so poufy that it was almost wider than she was tall. She frolicked down the sandy aisle to the only song that Charlie's little brother Dave knew how to play on the guitar.

Then came Mr. and Mrs. Love, proud and pristine.

Next were Meg and Peter. Meg had somehow contrived to make her dress shorter and lower cut than it had been, but that was just Meg, and it suited her. Bea thought that Peter looked handsome but stiff, as if he were making a great effort to look put together. He had so much gel in his blond hair that it looked brown. There were dark circles under his eyes.

Bea was wondering if the weather was going to hold out, when Ben touched her forearm tentatively, as if he was afraid she would bite. She started and turned towards him. He smiled nervously and offered her his arm. She hesitated for a moment before taking it, causing them to miss their cue by a few measures, and felt him tense as she did so. Uneasily linked, a little too conscious of the roughness of the fabric of his suit and the faint weight of her arm, but remembering to smile, they walked down the aisle together. Fortunately — or not — it was a short walk, and they parted, safely outside of the marital arch. Bea looked at him as subtly as she could through a gap in the lattice. Even in beige, he still managed to look roguishly attractive. He caught her watching him and winked. She turned away abruptly, pretending to be fascinated by the audience.

Then, as Dave ground out the last chorus, Charlie appeared, pale and trembling. Bea caught Ben's eye to see if he saw. His brow furrowed, and he gave an almost-imperceptible shrug.

Dave was relieved by a quartet of violinist cousins who called themselves The Four Loves. They began to play an instrumental arrangement of the Canon in D as Honey came down the aisle on her mother's arm. The Four Loves were a bit screechy, but a welcome relief from Dave's full-arm strumming. Leonata looked regally lovely in a pale golden gown, like a queen in an epic poem.

But Honey outshone them all. She came down the aisle in a foam of white lace, like a goddess sprung from the sea.

Bea hadn't expected to cry, but she suddenly felt hot tears streaming down her face. She prayed that her makeup would hold, reached in her pockets for a tissue, and dabbed at her eyes, full of pride and happiness for her magical, incandescent friend. Then they were all assembled. The Four Loves sped to a halt, and a hush fell over the crowd.

All went well until Pastor August concluded the opening portion of the service with: "If any of you show just cause why they may not lawfully be married, speak now, or forever hold your peace."

Then Charlie spoke. "Do you know of any reason, Honey?"

A nervous murmur ran through the audience.

Honey looked up at him, confused. "No."

Pastor August cleared his throat, like a parent who has repeated the question not because he hasn't heard a response, but because he's giving you a chance to say the correct answer. "Do you, Charlie Love, take this woman to be your wife?"

"No," said Charlie. His voice was so loud that it carried to the back row. Peter grabbed his friend's arm. "Charlie, don't," he pleaded. But Charlie shook him off.

Pastor August had witnessed some disaster weddings before, and he realized, with the blank assurance of someone whose car is hurtling across the freeway and into a ditch, that this would be one of them.

Charlie stepped menacingly towards Honey, pointing a condemning finger. "Last night, with my own eyes, I saw you cheating on me with some guy, out on the balcony. You could see it from across the building!" Pastor August and Peter both grabbed Charlie by an arm, pulling him away from Honey.

"What are you saying?" said Honey. She took a step back, frightened. "I love you, Charlie, I would never do anything to hurt you! I would never!" On the last word, her voice began to quiver.

"I saw everything! So did Peter!" he said, struggling to get free.

Bea rounded on Peter—a new and unexpected accomplice to Charlie's madness. "What do you think you saw?" she growled.

Peter could not meet her eyes. "Last night, at the party, Charlie's cousin pulled us aside, and told us there was something we needed to see. He took us down the walkway until we could see Honey's room and said that Honey—" here his voice broke "was...*with* this other guy. I—couldn't be completely certain. I didn't want to believe it. But it did look like—"

Charlie snarled, "Oh, it was her all right. Her face, her hair—"

"No!" cried Honey again.

Through the fog of shock that had descended, Ben realized that this was being filmed—the photographer was still going, and so were a handful of other idiots with their phones. He dashed to the back to take care of it.

"That's impossible," said Bea. "She crashed out at about ten."

"She stayed with you?" asked Charlie, with something

like hope in his face.

Bea replied, "No, she slept in her own apartment like a normal person on the night before her wedding. Be reasonable, Charlie."

Honey went to Charlie and took his hands, tears streaming down her face. "Please, Charlie—whatever you saw—it wasn't me! Please, if you—if you ever loved me, believe me now."

For a moment, it looked as if Charlie had come to his senses. He relaxed, and the two men holding him loosened their grip.

Then Charlie laughed. A terrible sound. "She's convincing, isn't she? So sweet and fragile. Just a mask for the filthy—" he freed himself from the pastor and his friend and started screaming obscenities at his bride. Then, just before they grabbed hold of him again, he struck her. Honey crumpled to the ground and did not rise.

"You—bastard!" screamed Bea. She lunged towards Charlie and punched him, sending him sprawling back into Peter. She felt pain shoot up her arm—it had been a long time since self-defense class. She saw him fall, and then dropped to check on Honey, who was unconscious. Meg was checking her vitals. "Someone call 911!"

Ben came running up the aisle, seeing the whole thing unfold before him like a bad dream. It had taken too long to stop the videos. He couldn't get there fast enough.

Leonata called 911. Charlie fled the scene.

Peter dropped down beside the women clustered around Honey. "I'm so sorry—I didn't know he was going to—I thought they had worked it out—"

"Get out of here!" growled Bea. "You've done enough."

Peter obeyed.

Honey's eyes opened. There was a moment of incomprehension—and then of terrible remembrance. "Where's Charlie?"

Bea and Meg helped her to sit up. "He's gone," said Bea softly. "I'm so sorry."

Honey's eyes were glassy, numb. "I don't understand."

Several long minutes later, sirens wailed, and the ambulance pulled up, unleashing a flurry of paramedics. They administered first aid and carried Honey up to her apartment, assuring her worried friends and family that nothing was seriously wrong. Leonata and Bea went with the paramedics.

Ben and his dad went to chase down Peter and Charlie and try to find out how this had gone so very wrong.

ACT TWO

THEN SIGH NOT SO

CHAPTER EIGHT

In the Wreckage

It was dark when Ben returned to the motel courtyard. The weather had turned depressingly warm for January. The air was wet and heavy. Ben found Bea sitting on top of one of the reception tables in the soulless orange glow of the turtle lights.

Ben moved to speak, but when he saw her, the words

caught in his throat.

Bea was still in her pink, gauzy bridesmaid's dress, but the hem was ragged, and the front was spattered with Charlie's blood. Her auburn hair streamed out in all directions, hanging in tangled tendrils around her face.

She was staring blankly out at the festive streamers and ribbons flapping in the evening breeze, at the half-torn sign that said "Mr. and Mrs. Love" in shimmering letters. The only sounds in the courtyard were the crashing of the waves on the east side of the motel and the buzz of traffic and AC units on the west side. There was an open tub of ice cream beside her, but it was untouched.

Ben cleared his throat. "Uh, I've come to ask for a truce." To his ears, his voice sounded reedy and pathetic.

Bea looked up, startled. "From what?" Her eyes were red, and her eye makeup had blurred in dark rivulets down her cheeks.

Ben approached with caution. "From, uh, us hating each other. Cause I don't...hate you. But that's beside the point. Point is, I know you don't think I care about you — and Honey, but I do. And no one deserves to have — what just happened — happen. Am I making any sense?"

She closed her eyes for a moment. When she spoke, her voice was low and ragged. "I don't...hate you either."

Deciding it was safe to get closer, he cleared away some stray paper plates. She watched him with a faint indication of interest as he climbed up on the table to sit beside her.

"Do you want some?" she asked, pushing the ice cream and a spoon towards him. "It's just going to waste otherwise."

"Sure," said Ben, taking it. Bea reached into a reusable bag beside her and pulled out a packet of makeup wipes and began wiping the mascara off her face.

Ben dipped the spoon into the ice cream and raised it to his lips, then set it down again without tasting it. "How is she?"

"She's resting," she said. "She said she wanted to be alone." Her voice was flat, but her mouth was set in a hard, tight line. "I wrote something to send to Elaine so that the…so that what Charlie said won't be smeared all over the place."

Ben doubted this would be effective, but it didn't seem like the time to say so. Elaine was never one to pass over something this juicy. You never knew, though.

"What happened to the others?" he asked.

Bea shrugged. "They left. Like rats from a sinking ship. Mrs. Leonata's…" She gestured helplessly, her fair, freckled hands looking orange in the artificial light. Honey's mom was never much good in a crisis.

Considering that one person had been left to clean up an entire disaster zone, Bea had made a lot of progress, he thought. Most of the food (except for the ice cream) had been cleared away, and about half the decorations. She had made a start on the tables and chairs.

Ben moistened his lips. His mouth felt inexplicably dry. "I just came back from talking to Charlie and Peter," he said. The words hung like the limp streamers in the humid air.

Bea's face hardened. "I think Charlie's done quite enough talking for one day."

Ben took a deep breath. "I thought…I could get through to him. But it's like he's a different person." He paused, watching the pool lights as they flickered on, remembering Charlie's face, twisted with rage and pride. Was it really

Charlie who had said all those things? None of it seemed real. He tried to think if there was any way he could soften or censor or translate it. No, none of it was really worth repeating. "He's got a nice shiner coming in, though," he added with a faint smile.

Bea rubbed her hand — it was still sore from its collision with Charlie's face. "Good."

From where they were sitting, they could see the light shining from Honey's window. Leonata was pacing back and forth, on the phone with someone. In between gasps of the air conditioning, he could hear her anguished voice. She sounded, Ben realized, just like his mom sounded when Grandad had his stroke. She'd spent hours on the phone with his aunt, hashing and rehashing every terrible moment.

A few minutes later, Meg appeared at the window of her apartment, which was on the other side of Honey's, and turned off her light.

Ben said, "Peter was drinking pretty heavily that night when Charlie — Peter saw — whatever happened, and he — physically could not believe it. Said something felt wrong. He thought he'd talked Charlie into confronting her about it in private. When Peter heard the wedding was still going on, he thought they'd worked it out. He begged me to let him come back and apologize, to help any way he could, but I told him he should probably wait until tomorrow."

Even after the terrible surprises of that day, it had been a shock, seeing kind, always-smiling Peter with his eyes bloodshot, his face haggard and lined with remorse. Ben said, "Whatever he saw, I think....it hurt him more than it hurt Charlie."

"He'll get over it," Bea snapped. "God. If he'd just — "

her hands clenched tightly, and then released. When she spoke again, her voice was calmer. "I guess he told you, then."

"About having feelings for her? Yeah." Ben took off his glasses and tried to clean them with his shirt. Then he remembered that he was still in his wedding clothes and that his shirt was tucked in and made of some useless fabric. "I had already kind of guessed," he added, the old competitive spirit returning. Peter had been wilting steadily ever since Honey got engaged, and it didn't take a genius (which Ben considered himself to be) to put two and two together. He had also felt a little short on pity when Peter told him. It was one thing too many for a day like this.

Bea reached into her bag again, and handed Ben a dust cloth she'd grabbed when she went up to her apartment for supplies. His hands closed over hers briefly as he took it. "Thanks."

As he started cleaning his glasses, Bea slid down off the table. "Well, these chairs aren't going to stack themselves." She began dragging plastic chairs towards a half-finished stack with a horrible scraping sound.

"You know, the more I think about this, the more I think there has to be someone behind all this," she said, slamming a chair emphatically on the pile. "I mean, maybe some guy just *happened* to notice some random couple making out on the balcony next door, and maybe Charlie and Peter just *happened* to get really drunk, and maybe it just *happened* to be the day before the wedding, and maybe it just *happened* to have some very significant benefits for Johnny."

Having finished cleaning his glasses, Ben jumped down and began helping her stack chairs. "I agree with you about the first part, but what does Johnny get out of it? I mean, Charlie blew the whistle on him, but this seems like a really roundabout way to get revenge."

"Well…" Bea went over to start another stack. "He also wants Honey."

"Him too?" Ben tried to pick up a whole stack of chairs by himself. "Good grief. I mean, Honey's great, and all that, but this is getting ridiculous." Seeing Bea about to come over and help him, he said, "No, really, I got this."

She rolled her eyes, then picked up a smaller stack of chairs and followed him as he staggered towards the trailer under the wobbling tower of chairs like a hapless cartoon character. He set them down with a loud thud and leaned against the rough plywood walls to catch his breath. "You know," he panted, "there's someone else we need to consider, too."

Bea set her chairs down firmly. "I was afraid you were going to say that."

He brushed off his hands, afraid to meet her gaze. "Look, I hate even thinking this, but it works out just as well for Peter to wreck the wedding as it does for Johnny. I mean, he *seems* deeply and genuinely upset. But, unlike Honey, he's a good actor."

Bea didn't answer. She walked out of the stuffy trailer and began stacking more chairs together. Peter wouldn't. He was always kind and gentle, always did the right thing. Surely, he wouldn't. But after today she wasn't sure of anything, really. What if he had? How would he have gone about it? She tried to put herself in his shoes as she stacked the chairs. If she was like Peter, desperate, heartbroken, what would she have done? That was no good. She would have been direct about it. None of this sneaking around and skullduggery and beating about the bush. But Peter was dramatic. Creating a scene might appeal to him—but that scene in particular?

Only after she had finished the stack of chairs did she reply: "If Peter had done it, he would have made it look like Charlie was the one who cheated. That way it wouldn't hurt Honey as much." She wished she felt as confident as she sounded.

"That seems logical, my dear Sherlock," said Ben, relieved.

Bea stared at him. The "my dear" had gotten her attention. Sherlock, not Watson. Not the dumb sidekick, not the chronicler of someone else's exploits. She smiled for what felt like the first time in days.

Ben was fighting a losing battle with another enormous stack of chairs. "Well, if anyone is going to figure this out, it's gotta be us, because everyone else is a basket case. I mean, they're individual basket cases. Cases in a communal basket. Whatever."

He really did have a fabulous jawline, Bea thought.

They continued cleaning up the debris, they went back and forth, trying to figure out a plan of investigation, questions to ask, people to talk to. There was, of course, some bickering over who got to do the fun parts of the investigation, like hanging out in bars that Johnny usually frequented, and who got to do the boring parts, like asking the janitor whether he'd seen anything suspicious. There was also a difference of opinion over whether or not hacking into Johnny's computer was illegal and dangerous, and whether or not it was viable to hire a hit man for Charlie. "I don't want to kill him," said Bea unconvincingly. "Just to beat him up a little." Ben suggested they leave the devising of revenge to Honey. Given Honey's disposition, Bea doubted this would be satisfactory. Honey's version of revenge would probably be something boring, like letting go and living well.

•••

By the time they finished cleaning up, it was late. Bea looked up anxiously at Honey's window. It was dark.

"You know," said Ben, "I think Tropical Bob's stays open till midnight now. You wanna get some food?"

She turned to look at him. He was standing on the curb between the courtyard and the parking lot. He stuck his hands in his pockets as if he didn't know what to do with them.

She felt, suddenly, as if there was something strangely momentous about his seemingly casual question. She was too tired to analyze it.

"Sure," she said.

The wet wind sighed against the faded pink concrete walls of the motel, promising rain. The motel's ancient, elaborate neon sign glowed from the edge of the parking lot. The sign currently read, "PARA___ MO___".

"Hold on, I've gotta go smack the sign," said Bea.

The sign was the original one from the 50's. It cost too much money to replace it—it would be corroded almost instantly by the salt wind, anyway—so it was easier to just give it some encouragement when it flickered. Ben followed Bea across the parking lot to the grassy strip on the side of the road where the sign stood. At the moment, there wasn't any traffic. Most of the town's residents were in bed by 9. Except, presumably, for whoever was at Tropical Bob's at midnight. Bea gave the sign a solid and strategic smack, but nothing happened. The rest of the letters stayed cold and dark:

WELCOME TO THE PARADISE MOTEL

NO VACANCY

"We've gotta get that fixed," said Ben. He tapped it a few times, without effect.

Bea turned to look at him. The handful of letters that were still lit cast a rosy glow over them both. He looked different, somehow. Softer. His dark curly hair was plastered against his forehead, and his mouth was partly open, as if he were completely at a loss. Just like that morning when he'd left for California.

"What were you going to tell me, when you left?"

He was thinking that her eyes were like liquid silver, like gray-eyed-Athena, and how do you confess your love to the goddess of war? He pushed his hair back with both hands, nervously. "I uh, I was going to tell you…"

What he'd planned to say had undergone several revisions during his weeks in California, but now all of it seemed pathetically cliché. So, he told her the truth, bare and unvarnished:

"I love you."

The words hovered in the air, in the buzz of the neon sign, in the astonished heart of Beatrice Bright.

So, it was true. All the crazy revelations, the anxious speculations. And suddenly here he was, saying it, clearly terrified. To her. Of all people.

She exhaled softly. "That's crazy."

"Isn't it?" he said. He took her hands in his. "I don't know if it's fair to ask, but do you…"

"Yes," she said, feeling like she had climbed to the top of a hill on a rollercoaster, and was peering down anxiously at the imminent drop. "Yes, I do."

They shared a nervous, relieved laugh. "Of all the impossible things—" she said.

"Just improbable," he replied. His eyes were wide, and his breathing came fast and shallow. "And speaking of probability—" He reached out and brushed her hair away from her face. "How probable is it that you'll let me kiss you?"

Dazed, she replied, "Mmm…I'd say the odds are pretty good."

And he did—with such enthusiasm that they accidentally crashed into the side of the sign. Color and heat and light surged through hollow glass veins, glowing pink and yellow and orange and green, two figures silhouetted against the light.

CHAPTER NINE

Outside of Paradise

Journalist Assaults Millionaire During "Nightmare Wedding"

"I always thought she was a little unstable."

by *donjohn*

Gaming celebrity Charlie Love and his fiancée, Honey Noble, had planned an elaborate wedding bash. Everything was perfect — until Love stopped the wedding to accuse his fiancée of cheating on him. During the shocking scene that followed, Beatrice Bright, a journalist with the local paper and a close friend of Noble, attacked the groom. An ambulance was called to attend to Love's injuries. The bride was also hospitalized due to a concussion she received in the fray. Pearl Pittman, an eyewitness, said, "I've known Bea since she was a little bitty thing. I love her to death, but I always thought she was a little unstable." Love does not plan to press charges.

— from an online news website

The next morning, Bea awoke feeling like it was Christmas. She was eager to be up and about, to see Ben as soon as possible. She bounced out of bed, humming off key as she opened the closet door. Then she saw her bloodstained bridesmaid's dress lying on the floor.

Honey. The wedding.

She sank back down onto the bed. The events of the day before flashed through her mind. When she got up again, her drive to get going came from a very different source.

Honey was normally an early riser, but Bea doubted she would be up early today. She sent an inquiring text to Leonata, and a cautious text to Honey, and went about getting ready. Neither of them responded. She made herself a cup of coffee out of Honey's favorite mug and consoled herself for a few hours by doing some digging about Johnny on the internet. The internet was unhelpful. Then she decided to go check on Honey.

Bea stared at the faded pink door a long time before knocking. She gradually realized that she was cold—the wind blowing off the water was unexpectedly chilly. This gave her the motivation to finally knock. At least it would be warm in there.

Leonata opened the door. She was still in her pajamas. It was the first time in a while that Bea had seen her without any makeup. There were dark circles under her eyes, and the lines around her face made her look harder. Older. She had never really thought of Leonata as old.

"Can I come in?" said Bea.

Leonata shook her head. "She said she wants to be alone today."

Bea swallowed and nodded, trying to ignore the dull ache spreading through her chest. "Please let me do something."

Leonata rubbed her face with her hands. Then she said, "We could use someone to take back the wedding presents. They're over at—the house. Charlie's house. The boys are over there, getting her furniture. They'll give you a hand.

Bring the money by my place this afternoon."

"Thank you," said Bea.

Leonata softened a little. "I don't know how…we would have managed yesterday without you."

Bea shrugged. "It's the least I can do."

Leonata nodded and closed the door. Bea went back to her room for her purse.

• • •

It didn't take long for her to drive to the house. The ritzy suburban neighborhood was coldly pristine in the late-morning light. Ben and Peter were loading Honey's couch into the back of Ben's truck. It was a Florida winter day, which meant that Bea was in her full winter outfit — sweater, evergreen pashmina scarf, jeans, and tall boots — while the guys were wearing t-shirts and sneakers. Across the street, an old man in golf clothes scowled at them as he let out a small white fluffy dog. The air was thick with the scent of freshly cut grass and the rotten-egg smell of sulfur water from the sprinklers next door.

Ben nearly dropped his end of the couch when he saw Bea walking towards them.

"Watch it!" said Peter.

Ben pulled himself together, and they wrestled the couch into the truck.

Then Ben, still breathless, turned toward Bea. He slicked his hair back and swallowed nervously. "It's you," he said.

"Yeah," she said, glancing at his lips and then looking him in the eyes.

He smiled sheepishly.

Peter was sitting on the tailgate, watching, entirely

forgotten. It was at this moment that he realized that his crazy plan had, in fact, worked.

"Did, uh, Honey think we weren't up to the job?" Ben asked.

Bea's face fell. "No. She won't.... see me." To her horror, she felt tears brimming up in her eyes.

"But you're—" he trailed off, with a helpless gesture.

She took a deep breath; and brushed away a stray tear. "Leonata sent me to retrieve the wedding presents."

"I was wondering what we were going to do about those," he said. He glanced back at the house and wrinkled his nose. "You know, given that you and Charlie parted on such friendly terms, maybe we'd better get them for you." He strode off into the house before she had time to refuse.

Bea stared after Ben, her eyes shining.

Peter cleared his throat. Bea turned back to him, startled. He couldn't help but grin as he gave Bea a significant look.

"Shut up," said Bea, turning away to hide her sudden smile.

It didn't take long to load the presents into Bea's car. When they were finished, Peter went inside on the pretext of moving some smaller object.

Bea closed the trunk of her car with a metallic thud. Then Ben leaned against it, trying to look cool and failing. "Do you want to, uh, go somewhere, with me, after we get done with moving?" he asked.

She bit her lip to keep from laughing. "Yes. Definitely yes." She glanced around at the neighborhood in distaste. "As long as it's somewhere outside of Paradise."

The relief was evident in his face. "That can be arranged."

● ● ●

Later that morning, Honey heard a knock on the door. She opened it to find Ben and Peter, who looked unusually sweaty and breathless for a cool winter day.

"We've got a large delivery from uh, Count Charles the Execrable," said Ben, with an awkward half-smile. "Oh, and the…gift refunds, from Bea." He fished in his pockets and handed her a pile of cash, receipts, and gift cards.

Honey looked at the receipts to avoid looking at Peter and Ben. She couldn't stand any more looks of pity. "Wow, this is a lot," she said in a hoarse voice. "Tell her thank you from me."

"I will," he said. "Is it okay if we bring up your stuff?"

"Yes," said Honey, pulling herself together. "Thank you."

Ben turned to go, and then stopped. "Oh—do you just want the couch like it was before?"

Honey was silent for a moment, trying to summon up the emotional energy needed to make a decision. She found herself on the verge of tears again. She had moved the couch over to the window after Charlie started coming over to play video games with her. She drew a deep breath to steady herself. "No. put it against the wall where the TV was."

He nodded, and left, with Peter following after him.

Honey leaned against the doorway and watched as they disappeared down the steps. Her mom had told her they were coming, of course, but she was still surprised. The guys were so inseparable that she had assumed they would take Charlie's side. Peter had taken Charlie's side yesterday, uttering that damning "yes," and a tumble of incoherent qualifying words. And yet here they were. She considered changing into something besides a t-shirt and yoga pants and decided she didn't care enough. Besides, she wanted to paint.

The morning had passed in a dull, aching blur, but the arrival of her belongings stirred her to life. She would almost have preferred to go on living in an empty apartment. Every item would be haunted by Charlie's presence. Damn him. She wasn't going to cry in front of the guys, not if she could help it. She would rearrange everything, make it fresh. She would turn the living area into her studio, with her easel and her paints and her desk at the big window, instead of keeping it in the bedroom, and shove the gaming console in the closet. Or pitch it in the dumpster.

Mechanically, she set the refund money on the counter, and went to open the sliding glass door to make it easier for the guys to maneuver. This wasn't an easy feat, since the door was usually locked and jammed shut with a wooden rod. All the mechanisms and tracks were rusty, corroded by the salty air. She yanked out the wooden dowel with some difficulty, persuaded the lock to open with a few choice words, and began pushing against the door, trying to get it to open. She tried it several times, from several different angles, but it refused to budge.

"Here, let me get that," said a warm, gentle voice. She looked up to see Peter, and her face darkened. She put all her grief and rage into her last attempt, and the door slid open. She looked up at him, breathless, and saw the remorse etched in his face, but she did not soften. He was with Charlie that night. He should have known better.

He bowed his head and turned away.

They brought in the couch and went to get another load. Feeling like she should help, she started to follow, but

Ben raised his hand. "We got this. Just find a good place to give us directions."

Honey sat on the kitchen counter, which overlooked the living area, and plotted out the new arrangement. The guys came and went, pushing furniture around on the ancient tile floors, which were already scarred beyond repair. Then she began unpacking the boxes. The guys helped, hanging pictures and curtains. Ben kept up a constant stream of meaningless chatter, for which she was grateful. Peter, wisely, didn't say much. Her grandmother's cracked but beautiful old china, a delicate rose pattern, was supposed to have been hung as decoration in the dining room. Instead, she stacked it in the kitchen cabinets for everyday use. Her stuffed animals—Mr. Bingley the corgi, Sir Galahad the sheep, and Nessie—had been stowed lovingly away in a cardboard box, where they were to await her future children on a closet shelf. Instead, she fluffed them out and put them on the couch. Her eighty-seven cookbooks returned to their rightful place on the living room shelf (there wasn't enough room in the kitchen). In less time than she would have thought, everything was once again in its place, more or less. Ben didn't linger. He accepted a bottle of water and her thanks, and then darted off with a strange look on his face. Honey devoted her attention to setting up her studio.

But Peter lingered. Ostensibly, he was making sure that one of the pictures was level.

At first, Honey ignored him and continued setting up her easel at the window, determined to paint her way out of her misery, or at least get some good art out of it. Screw Peter.

She began setting out her colors: Midnight Black, Castle Gray, Kelp Green, Ghost White, Five Fathom Blue. Acrylics, because they were cheaper, and because she liked to get messy when she painted. Pre-primed canvas. Something with rocks and cliffs and storms. A shipwreck, maybe.

She realized that Peter was watching her, the level dangling from his hands. He looked disgusting—plastered with sweat, wearing an old ratty theater t-shirt. She looked back at him, and wondered what was going through his mind.

"I know this doesn't make much of a difference," Peter said, his voice thick with emotion, "But I...am deeply sorry for what happened. I should have done more to prevent it. I was too wrapped up in myself to realize what Charlie— was planning to do. I promise, if there's anything I can do, to help you, or to make it right, I'll do it."

She swallowed, and nodded, but said nothing. The old A/C unit hummed loudly in the background.

Peter bowed his head and turned to leave.

But as he reached the door, she said, "Thank you."

They both felt some of the crushing weight lift from them.

• • •

On Monday morning, Elaine called Bea into her office. As soon as she came in, Bea knew something was wrong.

"Tell me what you see," said Elaine, gesturing to the computer monitor.

Bea was confronted by a lurid snapshot of herself punching Charlie. "What the..." With a growing sense of dread, she read through the article. The headline read, "Journalist Assaults Millionaire During 'Nightmare Wedding.'" When she reached the end comment about Charlie not pressing charges, she cursed, then said, "he's lucky Honey's not pressing charges against *him.*"

Elaine had pulled up the article on her massive computer monitor. She turned around to face Bea and adjusted her glittering spectacles. "You do realize I have to fire you, right?"

"You don't understand," said Bea. "They've got it all wrong—Honey got hurt because Charlie *attacked* her! I was trying to protect her! Charlie was completely deranged—I've never seen anything like it, and I hope to God that I never have to see it again. And he didn't have to be hospitalized—the worst he got out of it was a black eye."

"It doesn't matter," said Elaine, folding her arms. "Johnny told me what happened. You knew what you were doing. I told you last time that if you lost it again, you'd be fired, and I'm standing by that."

"I wasn't working at the time!"

Elaine threw up her hands. "I put up with your lack of professionalism in the past because I thought you had promise. But you obviously can't control yourself. You're a liability that I can't afford." She turned away. "Your severance pay is on your desk. Take your stuff and get out."

Bea began to protest. "Elaine, please—"

"I said get out."

And that was it. Bea stared at the dingy beige walls of the office as a soldier might stare at the place where a just-severed limb had been. A strange numbness set in, a vague gray noise in the background. She squared her shoulders and went out of Elaine's office.

Back at her own desk, she took down the travel calendar, the theater and movie ticket stubs, photos of her family and Honey; packed up her coffee mug with the stars on it. She slid her laptop into its sleeve and put it in her bottomless purse and put her precious camera in its case. She deposited the severance check using her phone—the sooner the money came in, the better—and shoved the check in her purse, just in case. The rest they could clean up. She put on her black puffy coat and green pashmina scarf, then shouldered her purse and camera bag. That made her feel more stable.

The door to the office opened, and Johnny sauntered in. "Oh, you're not leaving us, are you?" he said with a smirk.

The numbness vanished. "Listen," she said, summoning up the anger that made even Johnny's hulking six-foot frame seem small by comparison. "I know you're behind all this, and when I find out how and why, I'm gonna—"

"What?" said Johnny, with a smile that did not reach his eyes. "What are you going to do, *ex*-journalist?"

She gave him an icy, smile. Her gray eyes glittered. In her sweetest customer-service voice, she said, "I'm going to destroy you."

Then she shoved him aside and walked out of *The Paradise Post*.

• • •

It felt unnatural, going home at this time of day, but she certainly didn't want to be out in public, and it wasn't like she could go cry to Honey. Running entirely on autopilot, she walked back to her apartment, through the downtown, along the beachfront road, up the concrete stairs. They had gotten into some truly cold weather, with the wind blowing the drizzling rain in her general direction.

"Bea!" Ben's voice echoed down the long concrete walkway as he came running up to her. "I never thought

I'd be this glad to forget my laptop—Bea?"

And that was when she broke down.

"Whoa, whoa," he said in a panicked voice. He hugged her to him, feeling a bit awkward. "What's wrong?"

She was suddenly thankful for Paradise's brief glimpse of winter—there was a comfort in being crushed up against his sweater. Some exterior part of her—a nasty voice—seemed to stand aloof from her in contempt. She should be ashamed for showing such weakness. *Shut up,* Bea ordered. Her own voice was muffled slightly from the sweater when she answered Ben. "Fired," she said, and then tried again: "They fired me."

It took a moment for Ben to process this. There were any number of reasons the *Post* might fire Bea, but nothing recent. "For what?"

"For punching Charlie."

"Fired? They should have promoted you," he said. "It was amazing."

She managed a half smile. "Johnny—"

"Ah," said Ben, soft and grim.

Ben was not the sort of person whose anger burned hot—he usually defused it in some combination of laughter, sarcasm, and apathy, which was part of the reason Bea always baffled him. But suddenly, he felt he understood her a little more, as anger rose up in him against the man who had made Bea—laughing, fiercely proud Bea—cry like this. He held her more tightly to him, grateful, suddenly, for whatever weird miracle had made her trust him, and looked down into the courtyard, hoping against hope that Johnny would round the corner so that he could give him the beating he deserved. But Johnny was probably, at that moment, setting up shop at Bea's desk at the *Post.*

"We're going to fix this," he said. "Using our two collective brain cells — " this got a real laugh from Bea — "we're going to figure this out."

He was entirely uncertain what to do to comfort her other than stand there, but it seemed to be working for the moment. How did one comfort one's girlfriend? Honey would probably know what to do, but he couldn't exactly ask her. He could always ask Bea, of course. *Of course. Idiot.*

"I want to help," he said. "What do you need?"

"Tea," she said.

"Okay. My apartment or yours?"

"Mine, I guess."

However, when they opened the door to Bea's apartment, Honey was in the kitchen. "Sorry!" she cried. "My oven's not working again, and I still had the key from when I took care of your plants, so I came over and — what's wrong?"

Bea hadn't had the chance to tell Honey about Ben, because Honey had been more or less in seclusion. Honey was shocked to see them together like this — Ben's arm around her friend's shoulders, gazing at her with a look of tender concern. She wasn't sure what was more unsettling — that, or the complete look of devastation etched in Bea's face. Dimly, as if from another life, she remembered the plot to trick them into falling in love. She had never really expected it to work. She was torn suddenly between feeling like an intruder and feeling like Ben was the one intruding — she was always the first to know when Bea needed help. Was she really so easily replaced? Both feelings were a welcome distraction from the grief she'd been bogged down in for the last three days.

Bea hesitated, trying to figure out how to explain

without making it sound like she had lost her job because of Honey. She wondered if she should just lie, but she was too upset to think of anything suitable. "I got fired from the *Post,*" she said, praying her friend wouldn't ask for more details. "I would have told you earlier — I just didn't want to bother you."

"Oh, it's *fine,*" said Honey. She knew she wasn't being fair, but it felt so good, after so much helplessness, to be angry, to lash out. "I'll leave you to it, then." She picked up her plate of freshly baked cookies and strode out of the apartment, slamming the door behind her.

Bea made a move to go after her, and then stopped. If she wanted to push her away, then so be it. "*Et tu, Brute?*" she said with a small smile at her own pathetic melodrama and sank down on the couch.

"I'm sorry," said Ben, who felt the awkwardness of the situation deeply.

Bea shrugged. "She's just hurting. I haven't told her about you, or anything, and I guess I should have."

"No," he said, with sudden certainty. "It's not fair. It's only been a few days, and you're doing everything you can for her."

She nodded, looking glassy and defeated. Deciding to leave her alone for a minute, Ben ventured into her tiny, open kitchen. He hoped that locating the tea and the kettle would be intuitive. It was not. He cautiously opened cabinets and drawers, feeling like an intruder, but not finding anything. After banging his head on an open cabinet door, he turned around in defeat to ask for help. She was watching him with a small smile on her lips. The light had returned to her eyes, faint but steady. "It's behind you on the bottom shelf."

"That would have been helpful like twenty minutes ago," he muttered as he dug out the now-obvious sea-green teakettle. An assortment of pots and pans tumbled out of the pantry with it.

"I just thought I'd see how long it took you to figure it out. Aren't you on some kind of list of critical thinking experts?"

"Video games always have a logic to them, so they're easy to navigate. Unlike your kitchen. Do you want Lady Grey, Earl Grey, New Zealand Breakfast, Tiramisu Chai, Champagne Oolong, or the Rootin' Tootin' Highfalutin' Cowboy Gin and Gunpowder Tea?" he asked, deadpan.

"The last one," she said.

"I'm sorry, what did you say?" he said, grinning as he took off his jacket and laid it on the chair.

"The Rootin' Tootin' Highfalutin' Cowboy Gin and Gunpowder Tea," she said, laughing.

"Does it actually have gunpowder in it?"

"Only a little bit," she replied.

He squinted at her suspiciously.

"Not really," she admitted.

She pulled a pillow over and hugged it to her chest. She liked watching the way his hands moved — tense and agile, as he filled up the kettle and set it on the stove, fiddling with the knobs to get it just right, the way he ran his hands through his hair as the stove made strange noises, making his already-wild hair even more bushy, reminding her of the feel of his hands in her hair last night.

She said, "You know, don't take this the wrong way, but if someone had told me a year ago that all my friends from high school had deserted me except for one, you'd be the last one that I guessed."

"Yeah," he agreed. He watched as she burrowed into the couch and pulled a blanket up to her chin, happy that she felt comfortable enough to do that around him. When the kettle started to whistle, he turned back to the stove.

She watched as he peered at the kettle and grimaced at the its dragonish racket. He looked incredibly cozy in his dark blue sweater. "I'm glad it's you," she said.

He turned to look at her. "Me too."

"What kind of tea are you going to have?" she asked him.

"What kind of self-respecting cowboy would I be if I let my — girlfriend — drink gunpowder tea without me?" he asked as he got down the mugs. *Girlfriend.* It was the first time he'd used the word. He froze, wondering how she would take it. Was it too early?

She gave him a conspiratorial smile, and he relaxed.

He took the kettle off the stove and began pouring it into the mugs, remembering from campaign meetings that she liked her tea with an exorbitant amount of honey. "I know you probably don't want to think too far ahead, but I might have a job opportunity for you — but I need to talk it over with Peter first." He brought her cup of tea over and held it out to her. The mug was decorated with a pattern of gilded bees. Some of the gilding was chipping off.

She took it. "Oh?"

"Yeah," he said, going back to retrieve his mug. He did not elaborate.

"All right, keep your secrets," she said as he sat down beside her. She sipped her tea and contemplated her options. "I think I'm going to expand my photography business."

"Sounds like a plan. It's getting close to Valentine's

Day, so there's probably going to be a lot of engagements." He looked down at his steaming mug, which had an octopus on it.

"True," she said, brightening. "I always thought it was kind of a tacky move, but work is work."

Ben filed this information away for future reference. "I can help you out with some of the marketing, if you like," he said. He took a sip of his tea and set down the mug on the battered wooden coffee table, which was stained with little circles from previous mugs. "Speaking of tacky moves, given the way things are going, I think we can safely conclude that Johnny's behind all this." He put his arm around her.

"Oh definitely," said Bea, leaning back against him. "Have you discovered anything from lurking in questionable places?"

"Found out that the bartender at the Angry Lizard makes a mean piña colada," he said, grinning.

"Then you better take me with you, next time," she said.

He laughed. "Word on the street is that Johnny and your friend Meg have been seeing a lot of each other. You might try talking to her."

"Really?" said Bea. Over the years, Meg had dated just about every guy in town—including Charlie (before he met Honey) and Peter (after Charlie met Honey)—but somehow the news was still surprising.

"Apparently."

They continued comparing notes. Bea had tried to track down the random cousin who called Charlie's attention to the encounter, but he had apparently embarked on a research expedition in South America and wouldn't be on the grid for several months. Conveniently enough. One other person at the party had seen Fake Honey and her lover, but they were too drunk to remember much. Bea and Ben had both questioned Peter closely and had been able to get a few details clear—like that it was indeed Honey's apartment and not Meg's, and that whoever Fake Honey was supposedly cheating with was about the same height and build as Johnny.

"Here's the thing," said Ben. "These apartments are tiny. I just don't see how two people could stage something like that without waking the real Honey."

Bea was disturbed by this for a moment. Then she remembered something that made her more disturbed, but in a different direction: "I think…we might have been drugged. Honey found these chocolates at her mom's, and we both crashed out and didn't wake up until way later."

Ben made an alarmed noise and sat up straighter. "You know, I was weirdly tired that night too. Someone brought a plate of cookies to the party—the coconut kind that Peter and Charlie don't like…"

There was an embarrassed pause as both connected the dots.

"Did you eat all of y'alls?" he asked.

She pressed her lips together. "Yep. You?"

He nodded.

Bea buried her head in her hands. "We are such idiots."

Eventually, of course, Ben had to go back to work. Bea busied herself with setting up ads for her business and trying to get in touch with Meg. By the time she was finished, she had two couples wanting engagement photos. She would start applying for more organized jobs tomorrow. She went over to Honey's apartment, wanting to apologize and catch her up on all that had happened, but her friend did not answer the door. She left a candle that she had been saving for Honey's birthday on the doorstep.

At the end of the day, Bea was still alone with the gaping hole inside of herself from losing her job and from alienating Honey. Her apartment felt grim and cold as she got ready for bed. She wouldn't go hungry. Worst came to worst, she could crash with her parents, but she could probably work something out with Leonata. Still, that terrible gnawing sense of failure would not leave her. She turned off the light and lay awake in the darkness for a long time.

• • •

On the other side of the cinderblock wall, Honey also lay awake in the darkness. The events of the past few days played over and over again in her mind. She tried to think of something other than that one horrible day, but all that came to mind was the stricken look in Bea's face when Honey had snapped at her. She threw off the covers, got up, and went into the kitchen to get a drink of water. When she returned, she was carrying the candle that Bea had left on the doorstep as a peace offering, and a lighter. She cleared off her nightstand, set the candle on it, and lit it. The scent of smoke and flame dissolved into the overwhelming sweetness of Cotton Candy Celebration. It was too much, but she didn't mind.

She lay back down and watched the flame flickering in the darkness. The cloying atmosphere triggered a half-forgotten memory: the day she'd lit all those candles in the middle school auditorium when they were doing *Romeo and Juliet*. A lifetime ago, it seemed, but suddenly it stood out quite clearly. The smell of the sawdust, the sound of Peter's rich, theatrical voice reciting a monologue from another play—she forgot which—reverberating through the auditorium as he helped her clear the stage:

Oh for a Muse of fire, that would ascend
the brightest heaven of invention!
a kingdom for a stage, princes to act,
and monarchs to behold the swelling scene!

He had been so kind. And then the cry, and the blood spilling from his hands. That she remembered all too clearly, the slipperiness, the sharp metallic scent. She had been afraid, though she hadn't let him see it. It was a lot of blood. She should have done a better job fixing the cut. It had left a scar.

She should have talked to Bea when she came over. But she didn't really want to talk to anyone. There was too much.

• • •

Twisted versions of what had happened between Honey and Charlie had spread around town like wildfire. There were as many opinions as there were people in Paradise. *The Post* refrained from publishing any official account of the wedding disaster. Sensing foul play, Elaine stubbornly refused to retire and leave things in Johnny's hands, but she was just as adamant about not allowing Bea to return to the *Post*. Most of the Nobles took Honey's side in the drama, and the Princes honored their old alliance and sided with them. But even the combined support of both factions and the Buccaneer Trail employees were no match against the power of social media, the Loves' law firm, and Mrs. Pittman's gossip network. Charlie's story held sway with most of the Paradise residents, except for a small group of tourists and newcomers who had no idea what was going on.

A few days after Peter and Ben retrieved Honey's furniture, the guys returned to Charlie's house to try to talk some sense into him. Charlie gave them a reluctant audience from his gaming-chair throne, where he had been playing a new sandbox game with an unusual degree of obsession. He couldn't understand why Peter, who had seen exactly what Charlie had seen, had suddenly turned against him. Peter's argument that the couple they had seen was not Honey, but someone else pretending to be Honey, seemed like denial at best and delusional at worst. Ben hadn't been at the bachelor party — he had gone to bed early, pleading jet lag. So at least his confusion made sense. But it was still weird that Ben would side with the girls instead of him.

The thing that occupied most of Charlie's thoughts was — who was the man that Honey had cheated on him with? He had been so shocked by the sight of Honey that he remembered almost nothing of the other man, except that he'd had unusually long blond hair, because her hands had been in it. Whenever he went out, he searched the face of every guy he saw, even the ones who didn't fit that description, wondering, *Is it him?* But he could be long gone, just some stoner she'd picked up off the beach...

Peter and Ben's visit was followed by a visit from a small contingent of the Buccaneer Trail Productions staff, who missed Honey bitterly. Whenever she had come to visit Charlie, she would bring baked goods, enthusiasm, and encouragement to the crew. The company's only female programmer, Mina, relied on Honey's moral support against the overwhelming tide of testosterone. Honey had introduced Steve from accounting to his girlfriend and organized a meal train for Stan the janitor's elderly grandmother. Their pleas that no one as kind and caring as Honey could have hurt Charlie on purpose fell on deaf ears. This was mostly because Stan the janitor, due to an unfortunate coincidence, had unusually long blond hair. The only outcome of their conversation was that Charlie cross-questioned the hapless Stan and fired him.

Charlie was next visited by Pastor August, who felt partially responsible for the disaster. In addition to being one of his son's closest friends, Charlie's family had gone to his church for years, through its various permutations from Baptist to nondenominational. August had mistakenly assumed that he understood Charlie. He gently suggested that some grace towards Honey on Charlie's part would go a long way. Charlie retaliated with a long rant of a kind that the pastor had heard many times before. He decided that he'd had worse pastoral calls and planned to try again next week.

As soon as he was gone, Charlie went down to the Angry Lizard for a drink. It was the sort of place frequented by depressed old men, complete with a broken jukebox and a giant plastic lizard residing on a moldy pool table.

Johnny found him there. He bought Charlie another drink and listened with apparent sympathy to his account of his day.

"Man, it really sucks that Peter and Benny betrayed you like that," said Johnny.

Charlie shifted uncomfortably on his stool. "I don't know if I'd say they betrayed me. They just…can't believe the truth."

"I wouldn't be so sure of that," said Johnny, taking a long, slow sip of beer. "I'd say your best interests aren't exactly at the top of their priority list anymore."

"What do you mean?" said Charlie, leaning forward.

"Let's just say that Peter's got some good reasons for taking Honey's side instead of yours," said Johnny.

It was a risky move, but it had the desired effect. Charlie's face was blank with confusion for a moment, and then slowly darkened. "Well, he can have her."

Johnny bought them another round. "You know," he said, "If you really want to get back at her, you should make it very clear that you've moved on."

CHAPTER TEN

The Language of Flowers

Flowers for the Rest of Us

By Johnny Donahue
Friday, February 9, 2018

Everyone knows that red roses mean love. But that's just the beginning of a whole entire language devoted to flowers. Floriography—encoding symbolic messages in flowers, had its heyday in the Victorian era, but the practice has existed for thousands of years. There are several ancient Greek myths that claim flowers originate from the bodies of dead lovers. And since Valentines' Day is never quite as fun as greeting card companies say it is, sometimes your floral sentiments are a little more...complicated. So, if you've ever wondered how to say, "I hate you," or "why don't you like me?" or "let's be mortal enemies" with a bouquet, enjoy the following tips from our local florist, Juliet Gardner, owner of A Rose by Any Other Name:

I hate you: basil (hatred); thistle (defiance); peony (anger)

You're cheating on me: yellow rose (unfaithfulness, jealousy); lavender (distrust); peony (anger); nettle (cruelty); columbine (folly),

Let's be mortal enemies: Amaryllis (pride); basil (hatred); fern (sincerity)

Why don't you like me?: hydrangea (coldness)

Rejecting someone: yellow carnation (rejection); hydrangea (frigidity and heartlessness), snapdragon (presumption)

I'm breaking up with you: marigold (pain); lantana (sharpness); white rose (I would be single)

For those of you who pretend to enjoy being single:

I'm single and I love it: white rose (see above); narcissus/daffodil (self-love)

And finally, for you basic greeting-card people:

Declaration of love: tulip

affection: honeysuckle

roses: love and beauty (do I really need to tell you this?)

pine: daring

— from *The Paradise Post*

There were two things Johnny hadn't counted on when he'd begun planning his sabotage of Bea's job at the *Post*. The first was Elaine's stubborn refusal to retire. The second was that she made him cover Bea's beat — all the fluffy stuff, like Valentine's Day. Rookie mistakes, really. At least everything else was going according to plan.

• • •

Bea wasn't able to devote as much time as she would like — or really, any time at all — to figuring out Johnny's plot. She was too busy trying to make a living. Thankfully, as word got around that she was now "fully self-employed," (as she put it), more and more clients sprang up, wanting senior pictures, engagements, maternity shoots, weddings, or ads. Meg was also, apparently, busy trying to make a living, because she never returned any of Bea's texts or calls. When Bea finally did get in touch with her, Meg was decidedly evasive. She had gotten a short-term job as a makeup artist for a touring show, which had required a lot of traveling, and now had an interview for some big, long-term work—although she wouldn't say what it was. "Tell you what—I'll make you an appointment at the salon, and we can catch up then. I've got availability about a month from now, and I'll give you an extra discount for the wait." Bea calculated it out in her head—she had enough photography gigs scheduled between now and then to justify the expense—and agreed.

For Bea, Valentines' Day was a working holiday that passed in a blur of sappy engagement photo shoots. It felt especially surreal this year. She hoped none of the couples would come to a disastrous end like Honey and Charlie, but she wasn't optimistic. Most of them were difficult and self-centered.

She did come home to flowers. Ben had canceled his subscription to *The Paradise Post*, so he didn't know about Johnny's somewhat dubious floral advice and wouldn't have followed it if he did. What Ben did know was that Bea loved hibiscus flowers. She had several different varieties on her back balcony, because they flourished in Florida's blistering climate and attracted hummingbirds (who were also small and feisty). So, he had left a small hibiscus tree on her doorstep with a note that said, *For your collection. I know better than to bother you when you're in work mode, but meet me at Pirates' Cove tomorrow night (after editing). Love, Bandersnatch Crinklefries.*

• • •

Honey also received flowers. She had burst out of her apartment, running late for work, and almost collided with Peter, who was carrying a large bouquet.

"Oh, it's you!" he said. He held out the flowers, clearly flustered. "These are for you. From, uh, the Buccaneer Trail crew."

"Oh," she said. It took a minute for all this to register, and then she took the flowers from him. "That was, uh, sweet of them."

It was a rather unusual bouquet, tulips and honey-suckle and pine branches for greenery.

He rubbed the back of his neck and avoided her eyes. "They, uh, miss you a lot. And they figured that today — I mean, you'd be surprised what an impact you've had on them."

"Thank you," she said. To her embarrassment, she felt her eyes fill with tears. She buried her face in the bouquet and inhaled deeply, trying to get a grip. It smelled like Easter and summer all at once. "Tell them thank you for me."

He wrung his hands anxiously, and for a moment she caught a glimpse of the scar down the middle of his palm. He heard the catch in her voice and wanted nothing more than to hold and comfort her. Instead, he nodded, said "I'll tell them," and was gone.

She stood there for several minutes, looking at the flowers.

• • •

"So," said Ben, sitting down beside Bea in the sand at Pirate's Cove, and looking very pleased with himself. "For which of my bad qualities did you fall in love with me?"

He had built up a big bonfire on the beach and brought down hotdogs and marshmallows to roast. The beach faced out onto the river that flowed between Paradise Island and the mainland, so they could see the sun setting over the marsh.

She looked him over, pretending to consider. "They're all so terrible, how could I possibly pick a favorite? When you put them all together, you've reached the Platonic ideal of a terrible human being."

"Mm. So I'm perfectly imperfect, then?" he asked, sliding closer to her.

"Platonically," she said, grinning.

"That is a bit of a setback," he replied, putting his arm around her, and kissing her forehead. "Fortunately, I never read Plato."

To cover up her sudden shyness, she said, "So, for which of my good qualities did you first fall in love with me?"

"Oh, your gravity, definitely." he replied.

It took her a minute, and then she groaned. "You did not seriously just make a falling pun."

He shrugged. "Look, even I can't be brilliant *all* the time."

For a moment, they sat in silence, watching the leftover ribbons of color from the sunken sun, and listening to the waves lap against the shore (and to the dull grinding roar of the paper mill in the background), breathing in the scent of the campfire.

"Are we allowed to have fires out here?" asked Bea as she put a hotdog on a roasting stick and held it out over the campfire.

"Probably not," said Ben. "I expect we've got about, oh,

half an hour before the park rangers find us."

Just then, a small motorboat appeared in the distance, its lights bobbing on the water, and started heading towards them.

"It kinda looks like Fish and Wildlife might find us first," said Bea, setting down her roasting stick.

"Frick!" said Ben, scrambling to his feet. "Save yourself!" He sprinted down to the water to fill up a bucket to douse the fire.

"I'm not leaving without you, you idiot," she said, grabbing a second bucket and running after him.

They scrambled to douse the fire and gather up their things. But, of course, in the midst of dousing the fire, Bea accidentally got splashed by Ben's bucket. So, of course, she had to retaliate. By the time the Fish and Wildlife boat got within shouting distance, they came upon an extinguished fire and two soaked lovebirds who were helpless with laughter.

The Fish and Wildlife officer gave them a long look of extreme disapproval. He said, "I see y'all are old enough to know better but not old enough to do better."

Ben gave him a jaunty salute. "Yes sir."

Fish and Wildlife cast his eyes to the heavens, and then turned the boat around and continued on his way.

• • •

Honey and Bea's families responded to all major life events, tragedy or triumph, in the same way: food. Honey hadn't yet exhausted her supply of casseroles, but she'd eaten all the comfort food she could stand. So, she'd gone on a quest for fruit and salad and hummus at the grocery store. But now Johnny was standing in front of her favorite hummus, Mango-Habanero Burning Bliss, apparently engrossed in trying to make a selection. Like every normal socially anxious person, Honey pretended to contemplate the gourmet cheeses on the opposite side of the refrigerated case while she waited for him to go away. But apparently, he couldn't make up his mind, so she mustered up the nerve to say, "Excuse me," to him.

When Bea had told Honey her suspicions that Johnny had orchestrated a plot to ruin her wedding, Honey had been so distraught that it barely registered. She had, by this point, become accustomed to people either reacting to her with pity or with thinly veiled judgement. Johnny's reaction to her was neither of these.

"Oh, hello," he said, turning and looking down at her with what, for him, was a gentle smile. "I was just trying to make up my mind between the Sweet and Smoky Sriracha" — he held it up with a flourish — "and the Mango Habanero Burning Bliss," he finished, gesturing with the latter.

"The second one's my favorite," said Honey.

"Oh! Well, then, I'll defer to your expertise," he said, with a small smile as he put it in his cart. He reached up and handed one to her, his enormous hands brushing hers briefly. "There you are, Burning Bliss."

"Uh, thanks," said Honey.

"That's a nice dress, by the way," he said. "Did you just come from work?"

Honey looked down to see which dress she was wearing. It was the appallingly cheerful yellow one with the pineapples on it. "Yes. Thank you." She glanced at him, trying to decide if there was anything she could compliment him on in response.

He looked, as always, like he had just come from a polo tournament or a yachting expedition. Today his shorts had tiny crabs on them. It appeared that he had gotten a haircut recently. Deciding a compliment might be too risky, she said, "I've been teaching the kids about Captain Cook."

Johnny squinted. "He was the one who was afraid of alligators, right?"

"No," said Honey, with a small smile that might have had a hint of derision in it. "He actually existed."

"Did he? You'll have to educate me further." He leaned back against the shelf and slicked back his hair. "You know, there's a new restaurant down by the water that's supposed to have really good hummus. If you wanted to join me."

For a moment, she half-considered accepting. She was so tired of spending evenings alone in her room, crying more often than not. But the truth was, she had no more emotions left to spend on anyone, least of all Peter's weirdo brother. And suddenly she was thinking of Peter, big and awkward, standing there with flowers, with a scar on his hand.

She retreated back to her cart. "I appreciate the offer, but I think I'm all set."

At that moment, Mrs. Pittman walked by, saw them, and exchanged a significant look with one of her acquaintances across the way.

"Come on," purred Johnny. "What's the good of having a fake bad reputation if you can't have some fun along with it?"

She started to walk away, then paused. "You believe me?"

"Of course I believe you," he said, moving towards her. "Anyone who didn't would be crazy."

That was when she saw the façade slip, saw the hungry, wolfish gleam in his eye. She gripped the handles of her cart, said, "Have a good night," and made her exit.

• • •

The next time Honey went to the store, she asked Bea to come with her, because she was tired and didn't want to deal with Johnny. Pretending to be warm and cheerful for her students at the elementary school every day was exhausting. For some tragedies, she could have asked for time off. But not this kind. *In Victorian novels,* she thought, *when your heart gets broken, you can waste away on a divan, the life's roses draining from your cheek until you pass into tragic repose, or go mad, or die heroically defending your former lover, to your glory and their eternal shame. But in the real world, there are bills to pay. And someone has to teach these kids how to read.*

It was a strange grief. She felt she had spent a large part of her life in a happy dream, and suddenly woken up to find herself in an alternate reality that was harsh and colorless. But slowly, she began to explore this new world. As she went on, she began to find pockets of warmth, of color. Like the flowers from the crew.

She leaned back against the passenger seat of the Wagon, thinking of all these things, and glad that Bea was with her.

Bea was thinking that this was the first time she and Honey had done anything together since the wedding disaster. She said, "I'm glad to have you back in the land of the living."

Honey smiled. "It's good to be back." Seeing a gardenia bush outside the window, she asked, "Didn't you do a paper on the language of flowers in college? I wonder what the crew's bouquet means."

Honey had canceled her subscription to the *Post.* Bea had never needed one, since she copyedited most of it, and certainly didn't intend to start now, so she was also unaware of Johnny's flower article.

Even without the article or her research paper, Bea had a pretty good idea of what these flowers meant. *Bother Peter.* She wondered if he was counting on Honey's knowledge or her ignorance. She decided to play it safe: "Remember, these are from the computer geeks. They've probably never heard of the language of flowers. It's probably something random like 'presumption' and 'quadrille.'"

"True," said Honey. "So, catch me up. I want to hear about everything not Charlie-related."

"Everything?" said Bea hesitantly.

"Start with Ben," said Honey. "Mom said she saw you guys making out in the parking lot?"

"Well, about that," said Bea, turning pink. She carefully narrated the events of the past week, making sure not to say anything that might make her friend feel like she was responsible for Bea getting fired. She tried not to gush too much about absurdly fun dating Ben was turning out to be, but it wasn't easy. By the time she had finished, they had accomplished about half of their grocery shopping, and Honey seemed in much better spirits. Bea paused in front of the pasta sauce, considering the dizzying array of options, and asked, "How are you feeling, really?"

Honey shrugged and pressed her mouth into a tight line. "It sucks. It sucks a lot. Sometimes I think I'm getting better, and then sometimes it's worse."

It was late afternoon, and the store was bustling with people—sunburned tourists, gossipy old ladies, moms with kids, middle-aged men buying beer. Bea and Honey kept adding things to their cart — ground beef for tacos, ice cream, mangoes, cilantro, tomatoes.

As they made their way through the produce section, Bea said, "I don't know how far you want to venture into the land of the living, but Peter said he's more than willing to start up a fresh campaign without Count Charles the Execrable. He's got a new Renaissance set."

Honey smiled. "Maybe." She perked up slightly, like a plant that's just been watered. "I want to do a new character. An explorer, or an illegal actress. Or a Scottish witch who's made it her mission in life to terrorize James I."

"Ooh, that would be fun," said Bea as she gently squeezed the avocados, trying to find a ripe one. "You could have a cat whose power is to be as inconvenient as possible."

"Yes! And make a cameo in *Macbeth*, before sailing away with Sir Francis Drake to escape my imminent execution." Honey added a spiky-looking fruit that looked like a deformed relative of a dragon fruit to the cart.

Bea was about to tell her that Francis Drake was long dead at that point, when she saw two older ladies who were friends with the Loves look furtively in their direction and begin whispering. It was clear from the way they fluttered and gasped that they were gossiping about Honey. She tried to steer Honey around a corner so she wouldn't see them — but it was too late. Bea saw the joy drain from her friend's face. She took Honey's arm gently. "I think we've got enough for the day."

Then Bea gave the old ladies a withering look. "Looks like this place is already infested with witches," she said, making sure her voice carried all the way across the produce to the gossiping women. Honey allowed Bea to steer her towards the checkout line.

But escape would not be so easy. Even the fifteen-year-old girl at the cash register looked askance at Honey, and both women saw the questioning glance she gave the cashier across the way — *that's her, isn't it?* — and the cashier's smug nod.

"I got this," whispered Bea. "Give me your card, and you can go on to the car."

Honey squared her shoulders. "No, I'll stay. They'll just have to put up with me."

She went through the line with her head held high, and Bea felt a rush of pride for her friend. "You're braver than any of us," she said when they were safely back in the car.

"Thanks," she said. "But I'm seriously considering curbside grocery shopping."

Bea nodded. "The future is now."

• • •

Meanwhile, Ben and Peter had assured Stan, the distraught janitor, that Charlie did not have the authority to fire him, and that they very much wanted him to stay. Peter and Ben were unable to devote much time to proving Honey's innocence because they were having to do all of her ex-fiancé's work. Charlie's absences had increased with an alarming frequency. Ominous rumors floated around the Buccaneer Trail Productions galley — supposedly he was spending lots of time with Johnny (Ben was pretty sure he spent most of it playing the new hybrid video game), and more than one rival gaming company had hinted that they had made Charlie generous offers — and he was considering them. After the last unsuccessful visit, Ben had decided to leave Charlie alone for a while. He still sent him texts and emails reminding him that he was, in fact, still an employee, and that he was supposed to be planning their booth at the Kissimmee First Annual Renaissance Faire and Fandom Convention.

In mid-March, Charlie stopped showing up entirely. Ben decided to pay him another visit. He was shocked by what he saw.

The pretty little house that Honey had lovingly painted and decorated was completely trashed. A controller was sticking out of one wall from where it had been thrown. One window was broken. There were empty candy wrappers, takeout containers, and beer bottles everywhere, and it stank. Charlie hadn't bothered to replace the furniture, so most of the room was just bare.

"Charlie, it's me," Ben called into the darkened room, but Charlie did not respond. As Ben waded through the trash, he was reminded of the weekends he'd spent on the Gulf Coast a few months ago, cleaning up from Irma. At least Charlie was alive. He was sitting where Ben had last seen him, sunk in the giant gaming chair, which was now stained with soda and food. His hair was long, and he'd grown a scraggly beard. Ben decided that the rumors going around about the new sandbox game being unusually addictive were probably true.

Enough is enough. Ben switched on the bright overhead light and switched off the screen. "Playtime's over, Charlie."

Charlie started, then stared at him blearily. "Says who?"

"I do," said Ben, walking towards him. It looked like Charlie was just drunk, not on drugs or anything. He could deal with drunk Charlie. "Give me your controller."

Charlie pulled away, like a small child. "No."

Ben put on his best Pastor Dad voice and held out his hand. "Charlie."

Charlie sullenly handed him the controller. It was sticky. Ben set it gingerly on the coffee table and wiped his hand on his jeans. Then he took his friend by the hand and pulled him out of the chair. In the end, there was nothing for it but to make Charlie go to bed, check his room for any extra stashes, and guard the living room to make sure that he didn't resume his gaming. Ben texted Peter and Bea a short explanation, and then began cleaning up the living room. He wasn't going to sleep in this mess.

The next morning dawned upon a deep-cleaned living room and Ben dozing in a less-used recliner against the wall. He woke up hungry and decided to make breakfast. It looked like Charlie had kept getting groceries, at least, so that was a good sign. Several hours later, a somewhat more lucid and showered Charlie emerged.

"Morning," said Ben, who was on his second cup of coffee. "There's coffee and a plate for you by the microwave."

"Why are you here?" said Charlie groggily.

"You haven't showed up for work in weeks," said Ben.

He waited on any further conversation until after Charlie had some coffee, water, and most of his food. Then he said, "Charlie, you're an adult. You have responsibilities. You've made promises to your friends and the people who work for you. You need to either start showing up for work or give notice. Don't think that I won't fire you just because you're my friend."

Charlie's expression was stony. "Fine. I quit. I'll work my notice, and I'm outta here. I've got companies rolling out the red carpet for me."

"Not if you keep living like this, you won't."

Charlie nodded in begrudging agreement.

Ben got up to leave, and his shoulders sagged in defeat. "You can take today off, but so help me, Charlie, if you're not there tomorrow I will drag your sorry ass in myself."

He rose to leave, feeling hollow. When he reached the door, he turned back to look at Charlie. He was sitting at the bar, drinking coffee, apparently unconcerned.

• • •

When Ben walked into the office, and Peter saw the look on his face, he knew immediately what had happened.

"I'm sorry, Pete," said Ben, sinking down into his desk.

"It's not your fault," said Peter.

They sat there in silence. They would survive without Charlie in about the same way that you survive after losing a leg.

Peter ran his hands through his hair and stared at Charlie's vacant desk. "You still want to ask Bea to join the team?"

"I do," said Ben. "She could use the work, and we need another hand."

"She doesn't know anything about video games."

"But she knows us," he said with a small smile.

Peter raised an eyebrow. "You're sure you're not doing this just so you can hang out with your girlfriend more often?"

"Of course I'm doing it so I can hang out with my girl-friend more often," he replied. "But she also happens to be trustworthy and hardworking and insanely smart. And… she's also best friends with your crush."

Peter covered his face with his hands and groaned.

···

Bea was more than a little surprised when Ben offered her the job over a breakfast date at Tropical Bob's, Paradise's retro diner. On the mint-green walls, velvet paintings of 50's pop icons vied with pink flamingos and decorative surfboards. There were fake palm trees in every open space, and surf guitar music jangled over the sound system. Bea and Ben were the youngest people in the diner by a good 40 years. Bea loved it there.

Ben said, "I know it's not your line exactly, but it definitely pays better than the *Post*. And it'll help with networking."

"Won't I be a distraction?" she asked.

"Oh, you're very much a distraction," he said with a wicked smile. "But I think I can live with it." He looked down at his steaming pink mug. "Besides, we could actually really use the help." He lowered his voice, even though almost everyone else in the diner was wearing hearing aids. "Charlie's leaving the company."

"Oh," said Bea, trying to keep her voice neutral. "Is that good or bad?"

"It's pretty bad." he said, making a face. "We can get along without him—we've got a few people who do story stuff, although the more brains we have in that department, the better—but it's always been me and Peter and Charlie. And now..." He shrugged.

"I'm sorry," Bea said. "I didn't know." The three guys' friendship had survived the transition from high school to college and after. As bad as the situation with Charlie and Honey was, she never thought it would change that. "He'll probably change his mind once he realizes what he's missing."

"I don't know," said Ben. "I mean, it's normal for people to grow apart—it's just not usually quite this ugly." He looked so desperate that Bea would have said yes even if she didn't need the extra work.

"You do realize I know almost nothing about video games, right?" she said.

He smiled. "We can fix that."

• • •

The inner sanctum of Buccaneer Trail Productions was a place that few had ever seen, mostly because it had only become fully safe to work in a few weeks ago. Due to the company's emphasis on collaboration, Peter, Ben, and Charlie shared one large office, if you could call it that. It looked like no office that Bea had ever seen. For one thing, there was a massive TV equipped with every gaming console known to man. The room resembled nothing so much as a futuristic world in an 80's movie. The walls were dark, but there was color everywhere—neon signs, LEDS along the floor, movie and video game posters along the walls, a big kitchen table for meetings, a vintage record player in the kitchen. There were toys and memorabilia from various science fiction movies, a hammock in one corner, and a gigantic, transparent smartboard with a fainting couch under it (so that Ben could throw himself on it dramatically whenever there was the slightest inconvenience).

Then there were the desks. The wall above Peter's desk was plastered with old theater posters, some of them signed, and he had rigged up an old spotlight to use as a floor lamp.

Charlie's desk was flanked on either side by surfboards, decorated with an enormous photograph of a pipeline wave, and cluttered with stacks of surfboard wax. Neither Peter nor Ben had the heart to clean it out yet (although Peter had confiscated one of the boxes of wax). There were no photos on his desk, only a gapingly empty spot in one corner.

Ben's desk looked like it belonged to a steampunk pirate, partly due to the large aquarium in the place where the window should have been. His desk was lined with books, along with a few carefully curated action figures and starships, a large pirate flag in one corner, and a steampunk lamp. A plush red velvet armchair on a makeshift swivel platform sat in front of it.

There were also two empty desks near Ben's. "We usually use these when we've brought in other people to work on stuff," said Ben. "When Charlie's—when you come in in person, you can pick his or one of these. Also, it can get kind of loud in here sometimes, so we've got quiet rooms for individual work down the hall."

"Okay," said Bea. She sat down tentatively at the empty desk nearest to Ben's, which had a window overlooking the front entrance. The freshly planted garden outside looked a bit spare and awkward, like a group of college freshmen, but she could tell it would be lovely once the plants got settled in.

There was a glistening work computer, so it didn't look like she would need her laptop. "So, did it take you a long time to get your desk looking like that, or did it just kind of spring out of your briefcase unbidden?" she teased Ben.

"Well, it sprang out of my old office in Orlando," said Ben, leaning against her desk. "We encourage people to do it to help boost creativity. Nate in Accounting is using the remains of a ruined grand piano, complete with a creepy candelabra and a masquerade mask, although the cleaning crew's been threatening to call an exorcist about it."

"I'm surprised you don't have a working organ in there somewhere," she said.

"I won't say I haven't thought about it," he replied with a grin. "But I have been told that it might be pushing it, just a little." He walked around her chosen desk, sizing it up. "I'd say there's enough room here for your life-size Christopher Marlowe cutout."

Bea went pink. "I don't think I have it anymore."

"I mean, I don't blame you. No one can compete with Marlowe," he said.

"You certainly talk a lot more," she said, rolling her eyes.

"I also have the benefit of being three-dimensional," he said, leaning towards her.

Peter cleared his throat. "It might be helpful if you explain to her a little more about her job," he said.

"Right," he said, standing rigidly at attention. "So first we'd like you to do some research on the original game, with an eye towards brainstorming some ideas for a more multi-audience game..."

"What do you mean?"

"Well, you've mentioned once or a hundred times that *Swashbuckleriad* is rather lacking from a feminist perspective," he said.

"Now you're just making fun of me," said Bea.

"No, we really want your help."

Peter went back to his desk and kept an eye on them from his vantage point under the window. He wasn't entirely sure about having Bea on board. He was also somewhat startled that his ploy to bring the two together had actually worked. He was certain that at any moment the two would start fighting. Or flirting (again). Or Generally Not Getting Things Done. And there was a lot to do to get ready for the thing in Kissimmee.

To his surprise, the two settled down quietly to work, and he went back to working out the bugs in the rendering of a fight scene between his video game alter-ego, Captain Gallant, and some zombie pirates. When he looked up again, the two were having lunch at the kitchen/meeting table, debating the merits of the latest movie they'd seen. Bea steadfastly maintained that the book was better. They exchanged insults with cheerful abandon, but they were laughing with each other instead of at each other. Peter felt a stab of jealousy mixed with pride. He wasn't sure how long he should reasonably wait before confessing his feelings to Honey, but he was pretty sure that a month and a half wasn't it. He had just made up his mind to take a working lunch when Bea said "Peter, how do you think y'all's movie is going to go?" and waved him over to the table.

Bea's long friendship with the guys kept her from being utterly at sea in the video game world, but she found she needed a lot of training to be anything like a functional employee. She kept applying to other places, because the job still felt a little bit like charity and a lot like nepotism. But it was interesting, particularly after a few years of churning out articles. And it was fun. Ben insisted that, as a company devoted to games, they incorporate the spirit of play whenever possible, which meant office-wide nerf wars, game nights, elaborate versions of Capture the Flag, and ongoing variations of Assassin. But she still kept her photography business going on the side. She also started a new blog, in hopes that it would boost her marketability — and because there was part of her that missed the biweekly announcement of news to her small world.

• • •

The time went by quickly, and the day came for her fateful hair appointment with Meg. It was more than a little exasperating, she thought, to no longer have the excuse of being a journalist when you wanted to poke your nose into other people's business. Of course, she had the excuse of being Meg's friend (frenemy? God, it was like high school all over again), but somehow, she didn't think that would get her very far.

She was right. Meg was nowhere to be found.

The receptionist did her best to be helpful. "Meg? Oh, yeah, she left about a month ago. She got a job working for the renaissance fair. Or the nerd convention. Didn't say which one. I can set you up with somebody else, though."

Bea quickly said, "No, that's all right. I'll just uh, come back another time." With that, she retreated.

Outside, she saw Mrs. Ophelia sitting in a camping chair in front of Beau's Bridal, drinking a margarita and soaking up the late-afternoon sun. When she saw Bea, she waved. "Just got through dressin' another of Pearl's granddaughters," she said, gesturing with her glass.

"She came back?" said Bea in surprise as she walked over to join her.

"'Course she came back," said Mrs. Ophelia, taking a sip. "She's too cheap to go anywhere else. But this was a different granddaughter."

"I'm not sure if I should apologize or not," said Bea. "To you, I mean."

The older woman grinned. "There's always some excitement when it comes to weddin' dresses. That's why I went into the business. You want me to fix you one of these?"

Bea was about to refuse, but something in the older woman's expression made her say, "Yes, thank you."

She hoped Mrs. Ophelia's margaritas were better than her coffee. The older woman got out of her chair with some difficulty and led Bea inside. She went behind the front desk, pushed aside a rack of wedding dresses and ushered Bea into the breakroom. If possible, the breakroom was even more crowded than the store itself. A large sewing table and a gigantic antique sewing machine took up most of it. There were piles of fabric, scattered spools of thread, scraps of trimming and pearls and lace. The other half of the room was occupied by a mini bar, a boxy old TV set, and two squashy armchairs, one of which was covered with dirty laundry.

"My husband, Beau, used to watch football over there," she said, brushing the laundry out of the chair and kicking it into a dark corner. "Before he passed away. Now I watch all the wedding reality shows."

Bea stifled an uncomfortable laugh. "You do?"

"It's important research," she said, her eyes crinkling as she threw the margarita ingredients in the blender. "Lets me know where all these girls' notions are comin' from. Watteau trains and glitter fabric and corset things that no one in my generation would have walked around in outside. Always makes me feel like a rebel." She smiled gleefully. "And some, they've got their own style. Those are the ones I like best. Like Honey."

Bea sat down in one of the chairs and hoped it wasn't

the dead husband's.

"Poor thing," said Mrs. Ophelia. "She looked so lovely in that dress. One of my best."

"It was," Bea agreed.

"Meg helped me with the alterations. I taught her how to sew, you know. When she started doin' her cosplay stuff. I'm gonna miss her help."

"Do you know where she's working now?" asked Bea.

Her forehead creased in concentration. "I heard it was one of those theme parks. Doin' makeup for one of their shows." She poured up Bea's margarita and brought it over, then sat down in the chair opposite her.

Through the wall, there came the muffled sounds of a hair dryer. "Beauty parlor's next door," said Mrs. Ophelia, patting the wall. "You hear all kinds of stuff, comin' through there. I try not to listen in too much—that's why I have the TV, but sometimes…" She took a sip of her margarita.

Bea sat up straighter, realizing this was why she'd been invited into the inner sanctum. "Oh?"

Mrs. Ophelia lowered her voice. "The trouble with bein' old is that you can remember what happened when you were seventeen, but not what you ate for dinner, or what happened a week ago. A while back—maybe November? December? I don't know exactly, but Johnny came in for a haircut. I could tell by the sound that Meg was the only one workin'. It was a slow day. Anyway, they got to talkin' about a weddin', and of course I listened then out of professional interest."

She looked so prim that under any other circumstance Bea would have started to laugh.

Mrs. Ophelia went on: "What made me think of it, you see, was that Leonata is good friends with my daughter,

Emily, who's best friends with Emma Prince on account of their names bein' so similar. And Leonata told Emily that she had seen Johnny Prince, who's staying at the mo-tel, at the grocery store, and he was buyin' champagne. So, Emily asked if it was on sale, because you know her birthday is comin' up and she always throws a big party down at that fancy high rise because Bob is the manager there — you should have seen her dress when she got married. Sewed it all myself, right down to the last seed pearl — anyway, the champagne wasn't on sale because you know it never is, but anyway Leonata asked Johnny what the champagne was for, and he said his girlfriend had got a new job and they were celebratin'. And that's what made me think of it."

Bea had gotten lost somewhere around trying to remember who Bob was. "Think of what?"

"Well, when Johnny came to get his haircut, he said — I don't know if this is exactly right, but he said to Meg, 'I think I know of a way where we can both get what we want. But it requires your particular expertise.'" Mrs. Ophelia looked down at her hands, which were calloused from so many years of sewing. "I didn't think much of it at the time, because that's just Johnny's way with girls — But then, when I heard about the champagne, I began to wonder."

It took Bea a while to untangle the meaning from all this. Meg's particular expertise, of course, was costuming. Disguise. And she was a master at it. She was about the right height and build to pass herself off as Honey. But... Meg was their friend. She lived down the hall, and watered their plants while they were gone, and they helped her set up her pop-up shop, and had watched her dog when she was on vacation and went to see all the shows that she'd done costumes for, even the really awful ones. Could she really do something like this? Maybe Johnny had just manipulated her...Or maybe Johnny was just moving on to Meg, and that was all there was to it. But, given Honey's account of his behavior in the hummus section, he hadn't moved on for long. Or he was just a player...*If only I had majored in investigative journalism, I might actually be good at this*, she thought ruefully.

Then she realized that she was completely ignoring Mrs. Ophelia. "Thank you for telling me," said Bea.

The older lady shrugged. "Figured you oughta know."

But of course, Bea wasn't getting out of there that easily. Only after several hours of hearing about everyone else's gossip, including a lot of other wild things Mrs. Ophelia had heard while eavesdropping on the hair salon, a side-track into her decades-long passive-aggressive feud with Mrs. Pittman, her opinions on college football, and the various doings of Mrs. Ophelia's children and grandchildren did Bea escape, more determined than ever to find Meg.

• • •

As part of her training, Peter told Bea to play through the entirety of the first *Swashbuckleriad* game to get a feel for the original storytelling and to note room for improvement—and to note her reactions to the game as a relative outsider. Sometimes, after school, Honey would bring her grading over while Bea played. At first, Honey had been worried about the memories that the game would dredge up, but it was strangely therapeutic to have Bea's sarcastic criticism of Charlie's creative choices in the background as she worked. It took a while to play through it all, since the game had multiple storylines that depended on in-game choices. It was, Bea thought, like a choose-your-own-adventure novel. One afternoon, she found something in the game that set the pieces in motion for Honey's vindication.

The storyline she was currently playing followed the adventures of Scarlett Blood. *Swashbuckleriad* did have a few okay female characters — the Anne Bonny-like Captain Kate (Ben's contribution) and the indomitable Empress Song, modeled after Ching Shih. Scarlett Blood was not one of those characters. Everything about her made Bea's skin crawl — from her clothes to the way her walking was animated. Scarlett's adventures were catalyzed primarily by her relationships with a long and circular string of unsavory men, both pirates and members of the Royal Navy. Bea had written a strong critique of almost every scene. She doubted whether they would actually listen to it, though.

She had just finished a level that concerned Scarlett's achievement of the dubious title of mistress to the Admiral of the English Royal Navy. Her rise in position was abruptly derailed when she was captured by the crew of Captain Coldheart (whose heart was, apparently, less cold than his moniker). Fuming, Bea pressed X to swoon into the arms of the nearest pirate and proceed to the next level.

The obliging pirate, Steve the Stymied, revealed to the once-again conscious Scarlett that Captain Coldheart was the true ruler of these waters, and that the true second-in-command was not the first mate, Paul the Pernicious, but the captain's mistress, Pretty Polly (who was, in fact, a person and not a parrot). This led to two choices — press A to convince Steve the Stymied to cause a mutiny; or press Y to seduce Captain Coldheart.

"Mutiny or seduction, Honey?" asked Bea.

"Well, mutiny almost always gets you killed, unless you've got really good charisma stats," said Honey. "Besides, seduction's, like, a guaranteed win for Scarlet."

Bea muttered some choice words under her breath, and pressed Y.

To oust Polly, Scarlett talked Steve (who, incidentally, had unusually long blond hair) into becoming her accomplice. She then stole some of Polly's clothes and made herself up to look like Polly.

"What the…" muttered Bea. What a weird way to go about it. But it sounded eerily familiar, somehow.

Scarlett got Polly drunk and concealed her in a place that would be convenient for later, dressed herself in some of Polly's clothes, and, with Steve's help, staged a scene in which it looked like Polly had…found herself a new captain, as it were, in Steve.

"This is disgusting," said Bea.

"It gets better later on," said Honey without looking up.

There was a brief cutscene showing Captain Coldheart watching the woman he thought was his mistress betray him, the lovers silhouetted against an open window in his cabin. He gripped the mast and swayed drunkenly. "No," he said. "It can't be."

When they made the original game, Buccaneer Trail Productions didn't have money for voice actors, so the guys had recorded the lines themselves. Captain Coldheart was voiced by Charlie.

Bea gave a small, sharp gasp as the story connected. "Honey, look at this." With some difficulty, she went into the settings and found the "replay cutscene" button.

Honey's brow furrowed with concern as she left her

grading and joined Bea on the couch. "I forgot about this level. It's awful, isn't it?"

Bea sat back on the couch, thinking furiously. It was here, in the game, the game Charlie had helped create years ago. This was the piece that she needed. She wasn't sure how it had got there, or why, or what it meant. How did it end? *Press Y to continue.*

Outraged and heartbroken, Captain Coldheart denounced Polly to the crew — here Scarlett very narrowly avoided discovery by substituting Polly for herself and fleeing to her bunk. The captain forced Polly and Steve to walk the plank.

"You know they didn't really make people do that," Bea couldn't help saying.

"Keep playing," said Honey, a strange urgency in her voice.

Scarlett "awakened" and came up onto the deck to see the spectacle. She draped herself against a mast and watched with heaving bosom.

"He would go for *that* angle, wouldn't he," Bea muttered.

When the commotion had died down somewhat, Scarlett was there to lend a sympathetic ear — and whatever else might be required — to the Captain, and the level ended. At this point, you could either stay as Scarlett, or switch and play as Polly. Instead of drowning, Polly was taken in by the sea sirens and had the option of became a siren herself, luring pirates and admirals alike to their deaths.

Bea paused the game and turned to look at Honey.

All color had drained from Honey's face. "My God. She's *me*. Polly." She sat there for a few moments, stunned, then turned to Bea and demanded, "Why is she me?

"I don't know," said Bea. "Let me think." She got up and began pacing around the living room and kitchen. "Has Johnny ever played *Swashbuckleriad*?"

"He had to," said Honey. "Peter makes everyone do it when they join the company. And I think Johnny might have borrowed this copy of the game from me a few months ago. Said he'd lost his, but I think he was just trying to get my attention."

Well, this rules out Peter, Bea thought with relief. No one would set up an elaborate illusion like Fake Honey and then continue pointing everyone towards its origin. "There has to be something to this. Maybe the guys will know more." She got up from the sofa. "Let's go find out. I think they're upstairs setting up the campaign." In an effort to shake things up, they had switched the weekly game night to Thursday.

Honey followed Bea out the door, her thoughts racing. Honey had never really talked about the Scarlett Blood arc with Charlie, or really even given it that much thought. The guys all had pirate alter-egos in the game. Ben was, of course, Captain Constant, and Peter was Captain Gallant. But Charlie wasn't Captain Coldheart. He was Admiral Love, who rescued a pink-haired mermaid from the East India Company and was branded as a pirate in response. But of course, there was no reason why he couldn't be both...

She was so preoccupied with this creepy new piece in the nightmare of her life that she almost didn't see Charlie making out with Diana Pittman in the doorway of his apartment.

CHAPTER ELEVEN

Fare You Well, Boy

This time, it was no publicity stunt. Time seemed to slow down. It hurt, hurt so badly that it was difficult to breathe. She was dimly aware of Bea's arm around her shoulders, steadying her. This was worse than the things he'd called her, worse than when he'd struck her, worse than the way the wedding played over and over in nightmares, haunting her dreams. Then, as if he realized he was being watched, Charlie pulled away from Diana, and looked up, looked at Honey. When their eyes met, she knew he had been waiting for this, waiting for her to see him. He looked as if he had aged five years in a matter of months. There were dark shadows under his eyes, and new, hard lines on his face, around his slavering mouth. Whatever remained of the wide-eyed, enchanted lifeguard who'd saved her was gone.

Along with the pain came a strange sense of liberation. The feelings that had bound her to him, even when he had cast her off, dissolved, and the weight on her lungs lifted.

She might wish things were different, but she didn't love him anymore.

When she had bought her wedding dress, a lifetime ago, Mrs. Ophelia had taught her how to walk in it, how to walk when all eyes are on you. *Most of the time, we walk through the world like it's someone else's house, and we're just visitin'. But now you want to walk like the world belongs to you. You don't have to smile. Just hold yourself strong in the center. Shoulders back, head up high.*

It was a lot easier when she was wearing the most beautiful dress she'd ever worn in her whole life, instead of a t-shirt and leggings and sneakers. But Honey managed. She strode past him and Diana, down a concrete walkway that felt miles long, until she reached Peter's apartment, and knocked on the door. Peter opened it, and then she went in. Bea followed after her.

Peter had seen the change from onstage face to offstage face too many times not to know something was wrong. "What is it?"

Bea answered for her, her voice seething with barely contained rage. "It's Charlie."

Peter's jaw clenched. He went out the door, and Bea followed him, leaving Honey alone with a very confused Ben, who was in the middle of setting up the game when Honey had entered. He rose, uncertain as to whether he should help Honey, somehow, or follow Peter and Bea.

Honey sat down on the sofa. "You'd better go after them and make sure they don't do something stupid," she said. "Don't worry if I'm not here when you get back. I need a couple minutes to myself."

"Okay."

Ben arrived just in time to hear Peter say, "What the hell, Charlie?"

Diana braced herself against the doorway and assessed

the situation rapidly. Her innate love of drama battled with her impeccable sense of dramatic timing. Dramatic timing won out, and she made a quick exit.

Charlie turned to face Peter. "You got a problem, Pete?"

Ben sighed. "Several, actually. Would you like me to list them in chronological or alphabetical order?"

"Don't answer for him," growled Charlie.

"You've done enough," said Peter. "Leave her alone."

"Bastard!" Charlie spat, lunging towards Peter. Ben moved in front of Bea—both to protect her from Charlie and to protect Charlie from her.

Charlie said to Peter, "You just want her for yourself! It's all your fault!" He raised his fist, and was about to attack Peter, when Bea cried out— "No!"

Ben held her back as she went on: "It's all because of that stupid game! Johnny found out about Scarlett Blood and has been playing you just like Scarlett played Captain Coldheart."

Charlie, Ben, and Peter turned to stare at her.

The memory of the Scarlett Blood level returned to all three with ruthless precision. Peter felt a little sick. *Of course.* That was why the whole scene at the bachelor party had seemed so surreal and strange. He had seen it before, had debated the storyboarding with Charlie, had painstakingly worked it over to make sure everything was running smoothly, had fixed the jerky glitching of the lantern lights (at least, it was mostly fixed). Then some sicko, probably his own brother, had decided to bring it to life.

Charlie was unfazed. "The only reason that scene is there," he said, "is because I knew, deep down, the truth about what women are really like. That's what that game is—the truth!"

"No! Don't you see? He's gotten in your head!" said Bea.

"Prove it," demanded Charlie.

"Proof isn't going to be worth anything if you don't see it now," said Bea, throwing up her hands in exasperation. "Can't you see how you've been manipulated?"

Charlie said, "Oh, I can see how I've been manipulated all right, by you three! Only Johnny had the decency to tell me the truth."

He turned to leave, and then stopped to look at Ben. "You know, I never thought that you were the sort of guy to abandon his friends just because some girl told him to."

Ben looked at him and shook his head slightly. "I never abandoned you," he said. "You're abandoning us."

Charlie turned on his heel and left. The three friends watched him go with a mixture of sadness and relief. Mostly relief.

• • •

They met as a council of war around the gaming table. Bea wanted to check on Honey, but it seemed pretty clear that she wanted to be alone. So instead, she gave the guys a detailed explanation of what she'd just seen in the game and told them Mrs. Ophelia's story. She and Ben were sitting on the window seat, which Peter had mentally renamed the Lovebird Bench. At the moment, though, they seemed pretty focused on the situation at hand. Bea had borrowed Peter's laptop and was scouring the internet for traces of Meg. Ben was mapping out various plans of attack on the campaign board, using a tiny plastic palm tree for the Paradise Motel and a small ceramic castle for Meg's unknown new employer. Peter passed around the snacks and worried about Honey. Now, more than ever, he felt responsible for what had happened.

"I just can't believe I was so stupid," he said aloud, burying his face in his hands. "Of course. It's all there, in the game."

"Just because it makes sense doesn't mean it actually proves anything," said Ben.

Bea said, "I've thought of a way we could prove it… but we need Meg. I've searched all over, trying to figure out where she lives or where she's working, but I can't find anything."

"Sounds like Johnny's been cleaning up after her," said Peter grimly.

The beginnings of an idea flashed into Ben's mind. "Maybe we're thinking about this the wrong way," he said, leaning forward. "Maybe instead of us trying to find her, we need to get her to come to us." He moved the castle towards the palm tree.

"And how are we going to do that, exactly?" asked Peter, who was absently munching on cheese puffs.

"Well, what it all comes down to is, what does Meg get out of this?" said Ben. "And it seems to me that— aside from whatever weirdness is going on with her and Johnny—what she really gets out of this is a better job. So why don't we offer her an even better job as a makeup artist for the *Swashbuckleriad* movie? It would at least get her to talk to us."

"It's not going to go into production for another year," said Peter. "At least."

Ben rolled his eyes. "I think we should rename your character Captain Buzzkill."

As they bickered, Bea continued searching. Suddenly

her eyes lit up. "I found her! Look." She turned the laptop around so they could see the screen. Sure enough, there was Meg, standing onstage with a look of ghoulish glee as she appeared to slice into someone's arm. "She's with some kind of special effects show, and it says she's going to be at the Kissimmee First Annual Ren Faire and Comic Con."

"Excellent," said Ben. "That's this weekend. We're going to have a booth there. And they've offered us guided special access to the whole thing."

"You know, for an entitled millionaire, you're pretty tolerable," said Bea, kissing his cheek.

He turned towards her. "You're not too bad yourself, for a psychopath ex-journalist."

Peter tried to keep them on topic: "So we're going to Kissimmee then?"

Bea replied, "Yep. If Honey's okay with it, that is. I'll go check on her and tell her what we've come up with." She disentangled herself from Ben, and then stopped. "Actually…wait, no. I've got an idea."

CHAPTER TWELVE

Hurt/Comfort

From *Faint Hearts and Fair Ladies: a* Swashbuckleriad *fanfic*

By: theladyhero205

After a devastating betrayal, The Lady Hero no longer knows whom to trust. Can she put her faith in the mysterious Captain Gallant?

Tags: hurt/comfort/romance - Captain Gallant x OC - Chapters: 9 - Words: 30,000 - Updated March 9, 2018.

"Haven't you ever imagined what life is like beyond the walls of Paradise?" asked Captain Gallant.

"Of course I have," said the Lady Hero, throwing up her hands. "But I can't just leave. Especially not with you. I've got responsibilities."

"Why not with me?" he asked, gazing at her intently. "Because I'm a pirate?"

"No," she said, turning to look out over the walls at the outskirts of the settlement and the sea beyond. "I mean, yes, but—"

"Because of the admiral?"

"No," she said scornfully. "That was all over long ago." She sighed. "You don't know what it's like," she said. "If I go—I can never come back."

"I came back," he said.

"But you're leaving again," she said.

"That's true," he said. Something of the old aristocratic reticence seemed to come over him. "But I…would prefer not to leave without you."

She twisted one of the rings on her elaborately bejeweled hands. "I've spent my whole life thinking I knew exactly how it would turn out," she said. "And now…I don't."

He took a step forward, the afternoon sun burnishing his golden hair and tanned face. "Then why not embrace it? It's only a great leap into the unknown."

The Lady Hero could see it vividly in her mind's eye—running before the mast, every day a new horizon, doing and learning and being things she'd only imagined in her wildest daydreams. With the strange, gentle captain at her side. Could she trust him? Could she trust herself to survive? Could she trust herself not to fail?"

"Think about it," he said. "We sail on the next tide." He took her hand and kissed it, and then leapt over the wall.

[To be continued…]

–from a popular fanfiction site

It was the end of another very long day of teaching. Honey was tired of feeling so dead inside. Her heavy bag was cutting into her shoulder as she made her way to the end of the grim institutional sidewalk. Hopefully, her car would be out of the shop soon. Right now, her mom was picking her up after school. It was close to destroying whatever shreds of dignity she had left. Just then, a shiny SUV that most definitely did not belong to her mom pulled up in front of her. The window rolled down to reveal Bea in the driver's seat, her eyes sparkling with mischief. "Get in," she said. "We're going on an adventure."

Honey found herself smiling back as she opened the passenger door. "Whose car did you steal?" she asked as she climbed in.

"Mine," piped Peter from the backseat. Honey started and craned her neck around to see Peter and Ben sitting in the back. They waved awkwardly. Honey fastened her seatbelt. "Where are we going?"

"Kissimmee," said Bea as she pulled out of the parking lot.

"City of magic," intoned Ben from the back seat.

"And bad traffic," added Peter as he handed Honey a bag of takeout from Tropical Bob's.

"Why?" asked Honey as she took it. "For how long?" She opened the bag and began pulling out her dinner.

Bea grinned. "For the weekend—your mom packed your clothes. We're going to clear your name once and for all."

"Where? How?"

"At the First Annual Renaissance Faire and Fandom Convention," said Peter.

Then, of course, Bea had to explain everything as they drove off into the setting sun.

The truth was, that up until yesterday, Honey had been ambivalent about whether people believed that she was innocent or not. She appreciated her friends' determination, but she didn't think anything would change Charlie's mind. And even if it did, things would never go back to the way they were. But his sheer nastiness yesterday had roused her fighting spirit. It would be something to make everyone see the truth.

"Look in the glove compartment," said Bea. "There's a surprise in there."

"I'm not sure how many more surprises I can take," said Honey, but she opened the compartment and found a bunch of CDs.

Bea said, "Your mom found these with the Christmas decorations."

"Oh *no!*" she giggled. "My road trip CDs!" These were Honey's favorite songs in high school, which she had carefully compiled and painstakingly burned onto discs. Soon, all four of them were belting cheesy early 2000s pop songs at the top of their lungs.

It was only a two-hour drive to Kissimmee (on the outskirts of Orlando), but Bea stopped to let Peter drive before they reached I-4. After Bea's stunt driving on their trip to the airport, Peter was taking no chances. The I-4 corridor was one of the most dangerous and crowded roads in the southeast, packed with tourists streaming to the theme parks and hapless locals trying to get to work. It was always under construction and there was almost always a wreck somewhere.

Honey found herself in the front with Peter. She glanced in the rearview mirror and saw Ben offer Bea one of his earbuds. The two were soon snuggled up together listening to music and watching the streetlamps zoom past. Honey whispered, "Can you believe it?"

"No," he said. "Never in a million years did I really expect it to work."

"It's so weird," she said, shaking her head in amazement and sneaking another look at them. "What even."

"Don't worry, they'll start bickering in about twenty minutes," he said.

She looked out the window, thankful for her friends and their harebrained schemes. They passed the I-4 Eyesore, a gigantic unfinished building that looked like a cross between a skyscraper and a rocket ship, with none of the good qualities of either. It had been under construction as long as anyone could remember, and much like I-4 itself, it didn't look like it would be finished anytime soon. It felt so *good* to be on the road, going away from stupid Paradise and all its tiny petty people. For a few days, she would be blissfully surrounded by crowds of strangers. No one would whisper, and no one would stare.

Peter asked, "Do you want some more music?"

She shrugged. "I don't know, I feel like I've subjected you to enough of my angsty teenager music—although you do know all the words."

"I mean, I was also an angsty teenager," he said. "Thank God that's over."

"Yes," she said, leaning back against the seat. "But the angst keeps going."

"True that," said Peter with a sigh. "I was mostly in my theater phase then."

"Phase?" repeated Ben from the backseat, who forgot that he was supposed to be ignoring them. "*Phase?* You made me listen to the entirety of *Pirates of Penzance* last week. Twice."

"I didn't say it had ended," said Peter, grinning.

"You were good," said Honey. "I'm pretty sure you carried the theater program through high school. Bea and I had the best time going to see those plays." She looked over at him. "Why did you stop?"

"There were too many plates to balance," he said. "Trying to do college and get the business off the ground. And, after you do enough love scenes, you get tired of… pretending to fall in love."

"Oh," she said, surprised. "I can see that."

Before her, the lights of downtown Orlando glimmered on the horizon, a deceptive front of ordinary-looking sky-scrapers with the usual paraphernalia of highway over-passes, backlit by the last rays of the setting sun.

"What's your favorite song?" she asked.

"From *Pirates of Penzance?* Or of all musical theater?"

"Out of all of them."

He groaned. "I can't pick just *one!*"

She grinned. "You can do it. I believe in you."

Then, it was out of his mouth, almost before he had time to think: "Well, it's not really a musical theater song. We did it in our version of *Persuasion.*"

"Oh, I remember!" said Honey. "Loch Lomond."

"You remember?" he said.

"Of course I remember," she said. "It's my favorite Austen novel."

"I didn't know that," he said.

She looked thoughtful. "I suppose it's because it's about second chances. There's just something about the stories where it seems like everything is lost—and then it isn't." She looked out the window, momentarily lost in thought. Then she said, "Will you sing it for me?"

Peter went bright red. "Oh. Um. Sure. But only if you'll sing along."

"All right, then," she said, reaching for his phone. His lock screen lit up, revealing a photo of Peter buried in the sand, surrounded by his gleeful nieces and nephews. Peter gave her the code to unlock it, and she pulled up the song.

Peter had heard the song enough times that he knew exactly where to come in. His warm, golden voice floated over the delicate strumming of the folk band.

By yon bonnie banks and by yon bonnie braes
Where the sun shines down on Loch Lomond

Honey closed her eyes to listen. She had forgotten how much she loved this song. It was amazing, really, how much emotion he could pour into the words without practicing.

He had to keep his eyes on the road; he couldn't look at her. It was almost better that way.

She joined in on the chorus, quiet and timid at first, but steadily growing stronger.

You take the high road (and I'll take the low road)
And I'll be in Scotland afore ye
But me and my true love will never meet again
On the bonnie, bonnie banks of Loch Lomond

Peter was so surprised that he missed a measure but recovered himself in time to join on the last line.

The wee birdies sing and the wildflowers spring
And in sunshine the waters are sleeping
But the broken heart it kens, nae second spring again
Though the woeful may cease from their grieving.

They finished out the final chorus. The sound hovered in the air, blended with the ancient cluster of folk musicians, and dissolved into silence.

"You were a great Captain Wentworth," Honey said quietly, surprising both of them. Remembering back on it, she wasn't sure that was strictly true. He never quite had the same level of spite and bitterness as Wentworth. But he'd had the yearning part down.

Peter wondered, for the hundredth time, if he really

did have a chance with Honey. Bea had told him to wait until after they found Meg. Honey needed that closure. But after—he wouldn't ask anything of her, but he needed her to know.

From the backseat, there came the distant sounds of Bea and Ben squabbling. This recalled Peter to the road. The really dangerous stretch of I-4 was drawing close.

"Kids, behave yourselves, we're about in the thick of it," he called to the backseat. They ignored him. He gritted his teeth. As the road grew more congested, the cars around him fell into the familiar rhythm of "speed up and then violently slam on the brakes."

Honey found herself stealing glances at Peter, wondering why the song had felt different. She had always thought he was nice-looking, in a comfortable sort of way. It had never really made an impact before. But there was something about his voice, something about the song that…got to her, somehow. She wanted him to keep singing, and yet was afraid of it at the same time. Afraid of what? Of Peter? Never.

And yet as she found herself looking at him again, her heart seemed to turn over. This was insane. Ridiculous. Her heart was broken, wasn't it? And yet a small, strange voice, a voice that belonged to herself but that she hadn't really noticed until after everything had happened, said, *but why not?*

For now, there was no more singing. They had to navigate the rest of the Orlando traffic and the more uncharted wilds of Kissimmee. The south side of Orlando was where things got exciting. Honey did her best to look out the window at the increasingly carnivalesque scenery and not think about Peter's face, which, now that she was not thinking about it, really was handsome. They passed the skyscraper where Buccaneer Trail Productions used to be located. There were the crazy off-brand amusement parks with illuminated rides that seemed to fling their occupants into the void; water parks; putt-putt places; the massive creepy gift shops.

She knew the road very well, partly because of visiting Charlie, but mostly because of her grandparents, who loved theme parks. "At home, we're surrounded by old farts," Grandpa Noble had said to her on one of their many trips. "So, we like to go where there's a lot of young people and we can pretend we're not old farts ourselves." Honey was the nearest available grandchild, and the one whose parent could least afford it, so she became their usual companion. When they got too old to walk several dozen miles a day, they became the sort of people who would chase down unwitting tourists on their scooters. Her mom sometimes grumbled that the money might be better spent on a college fund for Honey, but there was something to be said for years of good memories. It was like building a house out of cinderblocks, she decided. When the storms came, at least the walls remained.

The hotel they were staying at was to the Paradise Motel as a gourmet supper club was to Tropical Bob's Diner. The building towered. The grounds were vast and immaculately manicured. The lobby was almost blinding in its understated opulence. But growing up as she had, there was a delicious sense of hominess to Honey in all hotels.

"So, do we actually have a plan, or are we just supposed to wing it?" asked Peter. He was somehow carrying all four of the group's overnight bags and the cooler. He refused to let the others carry any of it as they made their way down one of the endless hallways of the hotel. The bellhop looked on in disapproval.

"It's simple," said Ben. "So, the event is divided in two parts—there's the renaissance fair part, which is outside, and the convention part, which is inside. I've arranged for us to get a tour of the inside part tomorrow, and tonight we'll scour the fair for signs of Meg. And then after that...I guess it depends on how it goes, and whether or not we get kicked out."

They stopped in front of the girls' hotel room. "But how are we going to get her to tell us what happened?" asked Honey as she unlocked the door.

"I don't know," said Ben, taking his luggage from Peter. "I've got a few ideas...but mostly I'm hoping the element of surprise will carry us."

None of them were really thrilled by this plan, but since they didn't have any better ideas, they didn't say anything.

"Isn't it going to be dark?" said Bea.

"What better than an adventure by torchlight?" said Ben cheerfully as he disappeared into the guys' hotel room to get ready.

They had, of course, planned costumes for both nights. As Peter and Ben were suiting up for the ren fair portion of their expedition, however, Peter realized that he had a serious problem. He had put most of his efforts into his futuristic space-pirate costume for the second day, since they were at least in theory representing the company, and had ordered a ren faire costume online at the last minute. It left, however, much to be desired. "Oh frick." He rummaged around in the packaging in growing alarm. "Where's the rest of it?"

A few minutes later, he emerged out of the bathroom with a look of deep dismay. "Ben, what am I going to do?"

Ben burst out laughing.

"It was supposed to be a woodland warrior!" wailed Peter.

Instead, his costume consisted of a short kilt made of cheap fabric leaves, some skintight leggings that ended just below the knee, and a leafy sash. That was it.

Ben wiped tears of laughter from his eyes. "I told you not to order online," he said.

Peter cursed. "What am I going to do? I can't go out like this."

"It's the ren fair. People are going to be wearing a lot less than that," said Ben, still laughing. He did his best to be serious. "Don't think I've got anything that'll help you. I'll ask Bea."

"All right," said Peter, sitting down in the swivel chair in defeat. "Just don't let Honey see me like this."

A minute later, the room door clicked open. As soon as she came in, Bea also burst out laughing. "Well, this is a new look for you," she said. She was dressed as a forest witch, with many layers of jewel-toned fabrics, thrifted scarves and assorted crystals and talismans, which were all gathered with a leather utility belt that was stocked with tiny glass jars of potions.

"Please help me," said Peter.

Bea surveyed him critically, hands on her hips. "Least you've got the body for it. Let me see what I can find." With that, she went back to her room. When she returned, she handed him a bottle of body glitter and a flower crown. "Put these on. You're lucky. Honey had an extra one." She turned to Ben. "Give me your hat."

Ben's pirate outfit had undergone a significant upgrade since October. It was, somehow, even more piratey than before. His boots were taller. His shirt was puffier. The neckline was deeper. The hat in question was a massive, richly embroidered pirate hat with a huge feather.

Ben handed her the hat. Instead of giving it to Peter, as he had half-expected, she put it on her own head, adjusted it, and surveyed herself in the closet mirror. "I like this hat. I'm keeping it. You can wear my hat."

Ben made an inarticulate sound that Bea ignored. She turned back to Peter, who was awkwardly applying body glitter to his arms like sunscreen. "Do you know how to do eyeliner?" she asked.

"Sort of," he said. "It's been a hot minute."

Bea did not look convinced. "Better get Honey to do it," she said. "She's better at it than I am."

Peter spluttered in protest and alarm, but Bea the pirate-witch was already gone. He turned to Ben for help, but Ben was staring after Bea openmouthed, his eyes shining, clearly unfazed by the loss of his hat. "She's amazing," he said.

And so it was that, several minutes later, Peter was summoned to the girls' room to get his eyeliner done.

Bea had, between bouts of laughter, explained Peter's costuming difficulties to Honey. Even so, Honey still wasn't quite prepared for the sight of him in all his glory. She clapped a hand over her mouth, but a giggle escaped anyway. It wasn't like she'd never seen him shirtless before. Maybe it was the body glitter. Or the fact that he was tall. But wow. What a look.

"Uh, thanks for helping me out," he said, sitting down awkwardly in the swivel chair by the desk. "And lending me your crown."

"Oh, it's no trouble," said Honey. "I always bring an extra one." She was dressed as a flower fairy—she had made the costume for the Paradise masquerade a few years back. She smoothed down the giant petals of her skirt, took a deep breath, and dipped her brush into the makeup.

Behind them, Ben had put on Bea's witch hat and was admiring himself in the closet-door mirror.

Bea was, more or less, sitting on the bed, eating popcorn, and watching the drama go down.

"It's been a while since I've done other people," said Honey, getting to work in a matter-of-fact way. There was nothing for it but to stand close to him, occasionally resting the edge of her hand on his cheek to steady the brush. "Meg's much better at it. I wish I knew why she…" Honey trailed off, evaluating the effect of green shimmer. Peter was used to getting makeup done and held himself very still. "You've got really nice lashes," she said, adding careful, dramatic eyeliner wings stretching almost to his ears, with parallel lines above them for an otherworldly effect, wishing that her eyelashes were as thick and fluffy as his.

"Thanks," said Peter, who felt that he was having trouble breathing.

His eyes were nice too, she thought as she added in more shading. A warm golden brown. Not really wicked enough for Oberon or Puck. But then his eyes looked into hers and something in them made her catch her breath. For a moment, she stood in front of him as if rooted to the spot, and then turned away. "I think that should do it."

Dazed, he turned to face a weird, unearthly figure in the mirror. "Wow," he said. "It's really good."

"You like it?" she said, her voice rising.

"It's like magic," he said, with a small, nervous smile.

A few hours later, the four adventurers found themselves inside the gates of the First Annual Kissimmee Ren Faire and Fandom Convention, which was situated in a forested area that backed up to one of the ubiquitous shallow artificial lakes of central Florida. It was dark by now, but the buildings were hung with twinkle lights and lanterns spread across the street. Torches flickered at the corners. There were people everywhere, of all different shapes, sizes, and varieties. Wizards, monsters, pirates, Vikings, thieves, mushrooms, dragons, and more. The air was thick with the scent of pine needles, incense, beer and mead, roast meat and fried fair foods, and it rang with the sound of folk music and vendors hawking their wares. The sensory overload was a little dizzying.

They made their way through the crowded streets with no clear plan in mind—just exploring any stalls that seemed likely to be Meg's place of employment. As they did so, they acquired an assortment of extraordinary merchandise—leather gauntlets, elaborately carved candles, a fearsome masquerade mask, and a sword. Honey spent a good portion of the money left over from the wedding gifts on an enormous pair of elaborate light-up fairy wings to replace her frayed paper ones. The fair's layout was rather circular and maze-like. After having traversed what seemed like all of it without any sign of Meg, they stopped for apple cider doughnuts.

"Hey guys, we should totally go up in the balloon," said Peter, pointing to the round balloon moored on the edge of the lake.

"Ooh, yes, I've always wanted to do that," said Honey.

Bea and Ben exchanged glances. "Eh, I think I'd rather

be on the ground," said Ben. "Maybe check out the whirli-gig. You guys go ahead."

"Bea?" asked Honey.

Bea shrugged. "Someone has to keep him out of trouble."

Peter and Honey exchanged glances. "Suit yourselves," they said. They gathered up their share of the doughnuts and wandered off towards the balloon.

After Peter and Honey were out of earshot, Bea whispered, "I ship it."

Ben grinned. "Oh, definitely."

They turned to face the teeming street. "C'mon, let's go back to the blacksmith shop," said Bea. She grabbed his hand, and they darted off into the night.

• • •

Peter and Honey didn't have to wait long for the next balloon ride. In a few minutes, they were standing next to each other in the basket, which felt increasingly flimsy as the balloon slowly climbed higher and higher. Honey gripped the railing with the resigned dread she usually reserved for roller coasters.

"You okay?" Peter asked.

Honey gave a short, nervous laugh. "It's not the bal-loon, it's just — I'm afraid."

"Yeah?"

She was silent for a moment, and then said, "I don't know if I want to know the answers. I already have a pretty good idea of what happened and — it makes it more real, somehow."

The balloon had risen just over the roof of the adjacent tavern. They could see Bea and Ben disappearing into a shop below. Fiddle music wafted up to them from one of the clusters of street musicians down below, in the cool, delicious dark. They were playing "Loch Lomond."

"Don't get me wrong," said Honey. "I appreciate all you guys have done. You've worked miracles, really. I just want it to be over."

"I can understand that," he said.

She had relaxed a little bit, her arms resting on the rails now instead of gripping it tightly. She had wound flowers and vines around her arms like gloves. He was always surprised by how at home she looked in costume.

Now they could see the full length of the lake, shimmering in the warm flickering lights of the fair on one side and the bright neon lights of the convention on the other.

"Two houses, both alike in dignity," murmured Honey thoughtfully. Her glowing fairy wings fluttered in the breeze.

"Which is to say, no dignity at all," said Peter, laughing.

"I wonder why they decided to separate them," she said. "I mean, the Venn diagram between people who go to renaissance fairs and people who go to cons is practically a circle."

"I don't know," he said. "Maybe…"

A sudden gust of wind caught the balloon, and the basket lurched. Honey lost her balance, and, without thinking, reached for Peter's hand to steady herself. In the process, she nearly hit him in the face with her wings, but he had the presence of mind to duck. They were perfectly safe, of course. At least, as safe as anyone dangling from a giant balloon can be. She didn't think about it or look over at him, until the balloon leveled out and she felt the unfamiliar, steady warmth of his huge hands. When she did look over at him, his eyes were wide. "Sorry," she said, letting go.

Peter decided that the best course of action would be to pretend like everything was perfectly normal. "Don't be," he said with a small shrug. "It's, uh, it's definitely a lot shakier than I thought up here."

Honey was left to interpret this how she might. She looked over at the weird eldritch creature who was also Peter. The costume had come together really well, in spite of itself. He looked fantastic. Although some of the credit was definitely due to his physique.

The balloon pilot announced that they had reached their peak altitude; they would descend in a few minutes.

The vast, shimmering landscape of Greater Orlando spread out before them; the world refracted by a dizzy disco ball. Rivers, docks, stacks of hotel windows twinkling in the night, blue glowing swimming pools, tiny golden fountains, a small sea serpent, ferries making white foaming trails through the water. And then, in the distance, fireworks. Bursts of red and gold and purple and green, shooting stars in every shade.

"This was a good idea," said Honey, unconsciously moving a bit closer to Peter.

The quiet joy in her voice was like music.

• • •

The next day dawned crisp and clear, one of the few remaining days of nice weather before summer set in again with all its oppressive glory. The four friends stood on the fringes of the elaborate airport-like awning of the convention center, examining the map. Even more people milled around them than they had seen last night—superheroes, aliens, and anime characters joined the ranks of pirates, knights, princesses, fairies, etc. from the day before.

"Look," said Honey. "There's a special effects makeup class. I bet that's where she is." She was immensely pleased with her new wings and had decided to combine them with her 60s-inspired space girl outfit, with striking effect.

"Looks like the makeup show's not far from here," said Bea. Today, she had joined the ranks as a space-pirate riff on Captain Kate. She had not given Ben back his hat.

"Can we stop for coffee?" asked Ben, tugging at the map.

"Not now!" said Bea, swatting his hand away. "We've got more important things to do."

Peter looked up from checking his phone to see if there were any messages from the tour guides. "Did Bea really just say there were more important things than coffee?"

Ben grinned. "Write it down."

"Oh, shut up," said Bea, laughing in spite of herself.

Peter shaded his hand with his eyes and searched the bustling entranceway for the tour guides. "A Mr. Berry and a Mr. Stephens are supposed to meet us here shortly…"

"Mr. Prince?" A man in in an official-looking golf shirt came bounding across the entryway. He had a pointed, gingery beard and horn-rimmed glasses that gave him a look of perpetual surprise or benevolent superiority, depending on his mood.

"Yes, that's me," said Peter. "And you must be —"

"Doug Berry," the man said, shaking Peter's hand enthusiastically. "And this is my assistant, Virgil Stephens."

"My friends call me Verge," said his companion, also shaking his hand. He was a very earnest-looking, clean-cut kid. "I'm a big *Swashbuckleriad* fan, sir."

"We're your tour guides for today," interrupted Doug, who sounded like he'd definitely stopped for coffee this morning. "And this must be your girlfriend," he added, shaking Honey's hand with equal enthusiasm.

"No, ah—you must have got me and Ben confused," said Peter, turning red. "These are my colleagues, Ben Constant and Beatrice Bright. They're dating. Honey's a mutual friend of ours."

"So sorry—definitely got that mixed up," said Doug. "Er, well, no time like the present to begin. I'm head of security, so I know everything there is to know about the convention."

"Security? I had no idea we were so important," said Ben, trying not to sound alarmed. Evading tour guides was one thing, but evading security guards (with weapons?) was another matter entirely. He exchanged a worried glance with Bea.

"Last-minute change," said Doug cheerfully as they dodged around a quartet of terrifying clowns. "The flu's been going around pretty badly, so all the usual guides are out sick. But don't worry, we'll do our best to make sure you have the best experience. I know everything there is to know about the inner workings here, if I do say so myself. You'll have a fantastic look at what goes on behind the scenes. We'll start off with a bang at the panel on videogaming in space."

"Uh, if you don't mind," said Peter, "We'd like to go the special effects panel." He gestured in the opposite direction, towards the artists' section. From where they were standing, they could just see the sign for it.

"I'm afraid we were given a very strict itinerary," said Doug, steering him down the aisle in the opposite direction.

"Because of course there's *your* panel after that."

"Oh right," said Ben. "The panel." Had he brought his notes with him?

"If you're interested in the special effects makeup panel, I can try to get you in at 3:45" said Verge helpfully. "Although it'll mean missing lunch."

"Please do," said Bea firmly.

"Right," said Doug cheerfully, leading them up a large glass escalator jam-packed with an entire army of fictional soldiers. "And of course you're scheduled to do a signing after the panel."

"Hey, there's our table," said Peter. He waved apologetically to their long-suffering staff as he and the others were carried slowly out of sight.

Doug, meanwhile, was giving a cheerful account of the origins of the convention. "You see, it really happened due to a scheduling error," he said. "The fair and the convention were both scheduled for the same day, and the organizers got wind of it and decided 'why not do them together?' It promotes a spirit of fellowship among the diverse fan communities. They both got a discount for not making a fuss about the error. The fan convention has actually been going on here for several years, although it's often overshadowed by larger events in Orlando…"

Doug did not stop talking for the remainder of the tour, except for a brief interval when he and Verge had to stop to break up a fistfight between a superhero and an individual in full astronaut gear who turned out to be, in fact, a real astronaut. Doug was seconded in his narrative by enthusiastic agreements from Verge, who also asked for Ben's autograph. Resigned, the captive tour followed along, gawking at the ever-changing array of extraordinary sights. At one point, dozens of drones designed to look like spaceships raced above their heads.

The pugilistic astronaut turned out to be the keynote speaker at the first panel they were attending. He had apparently been the game's consultant on living in zero-gravity. He gave a lively account of his time on the space station in the 80s. They never did find out what the fight was about.

Their panel was next. Honey settled into the audience, beaming with excitement as Peter, Ben and Bea took the stage.

Bea had been conflicted about whether to be on the panel — really, it was more of a roundtable. "I'm just filling in," she'd said to Honey.

"Well," said Honey. "You've done more filling in for a few months than Charlie did in a whole year."

Bea had folded her arms and said, "From what I've heard, you've done more behind the scenes there than Charlie ever did. Everybody there loves you, you know."

Still, Honey was content to sit in the audience and cheer on her brilliant friends. It was wonderful to see the way they lit up when talking about their work. Ben had the natural animation of someone who has succeeded far beyond his wildest dreams. Bea had the cheerful spark of satisfaction with her work, and Peter had a quiet joy about him as he detailed their plans for the next game. She recognized the others on the panel from various work events she'd attended with Charlie.

After that came the signing. Peter and Ben gravely answered questions from the flock of middle and high schoolers that wanted to know about making their own video games and took pictures while Honey and Bea snuck off to scope out the nearer merch tables.

Then, finally, it was time for the panel they'd pinned all their hopes on. Even then, Doug made his best effort to make scheduled stops at sponsored merch booths, but this time they insisted. Once they had gotten Doug onto the desired course, however, he was amiable enough. "The special effects makeup workshop is a new event for the convention this year. They've brought in talent from all over the country, from the greatest artists of Hollywood to up-and-coming locals, along with some fantastic props and historic prosthetics."

The room where the workshop was being held looked more like a film set than a conference room. It was dimly lit. An assortment of monstrous prosthetic heads was arrayed along the back wall like the trophies of an intergalactic big-game hunter. Alien and human limbs were scattered around, along with large buckets cheerfully labelled "BLOOD" and "SLIME" and "GUTS."

Honey shifted uncomfortably in her seat, a sense of dread creeping over her. There was something about this setup that had "audience participation" written all over it. And they were in the front row.

At that moment, the lights went out completely. Eerie music played, and an eldritch creature emerged from the darkness. It looked to be at least eight feet tall, with massive, alien antlers and glowing eyes and extra arms.

"Hello everyone," it said in a cheerful voice that Honey recognized only too well. "Welcome to the special effects makeup workshop, where we turn men into monsters, and vice versa." An assortment of other equally terrifying creatures emerged onto the stage around her. "We're a team of makeup artists from around the nation, and we're here to give you an introduction to some of the tricks of the trade."

Honey didn't really listen to the rest of the spiel, because her mind was racing. The creature was Meg! She was sure of it. But how were they going to catch her?

And then, from another one of the eldritch creatures, she heard the dreaded words: "I'm going to need a volunteer from the audience."

Meg's co-worker, who looked like a cross between an alligator and a Pteranodon, decided that the nervous girl in the front row with bright pink hair would be a perfect volunteer. Despite Honey's protests and Meg's frantic attempts to catch his eye and signal against her, he brought Honey up onstage to be their victim.

Her friends tried to interfere, but the alligator man was oblivious. Honey tried to give him the benefit of the doubt. Maybe his hearing was impaired by his prosthetics.

Honey hated being onstage, even in the best of circumstances. Being teased and frightened by displays of fake severed limbs (all in good-natured fun, of course) made it infinitely worse. Several of the creatures began peeling off their prosthetics with a macabre glee, gradually revealing the human underneath. She looked around for the exit; but she couldn't see it in the glare of the stage lights. She couldn't see the faces of her friends, but she was terribly aware of the audience of strangers, staring at her, laughing at her, whispering. Like people had been for the past few months. *That's her, isn't it? The girl who cheated on Charlie Love? Wasn't it on her wedding night?* She couldn't hold her head up in this hellscape like she owned it. She closed her eyes for a moment, trying to think of something happy that would get her through this. Nothing came to mind, except the sheer determination that she was not going to let Meg see her cry. And then she thought of Bea in the grocery store. *You're braver than any of us.* Given that her hands were shaking so that she could hardly move, she was kind of skeptical, but Bea usually didn't say things like that if she didn't believe that they were true. Honey took hold of Bea's words and used them to steady herself...

Meg had to duck backstage for a quick change, swearing under her breath as she did so. They had found her, damn them. A quick succession of images flashed through her mind — Honey at the wedding, unconscious, her face streaked with tears. A patch of makeup had been removed by Charlie's blow, and a bruise was beginning to form on her cheek. And then, further back, high-school Meg recoiling back from Charlie's slap, holding her hand up against the bruise. A few weeks ago, Johnny pinning Meg against the window of Honey's apartment, kissing her with a kind of ruthless passion. She wasn't sure if he was actually good at it or if it was just the sheer ecstasy of knowing that Charlie's perfect world was about to go up in flames, but it had been worth it. She bounded back onstage in a clean t-shirt with her company's logo on it. The show must go on.

Her co-worker, meanwhile, was chatting with Honey while prepping for the stunt, which would make it appear like Honey had been stabbed. It was an old trick, really, old as the theatre. Simple but effective. This was usually his favorite part because he was allowed a certain amount of improv. He went through the usual questions — What's your name? Where are you from? "Paradise," she stammered, forgetting to add the crucial "Florida."

"Paradise?" he said. "So, did it hurt when you fell from heaven?"

This elicited loud groans and a few giggles from the

audience.

"It did," said Honey, staring straight at Meg. Honey briefly touched her hand to her own cheek, where Charlie had hit her.

The alligator man forged ahead: "So what did you come here for?"

"I came for this, actually," Honey said, still keeping eye contact with Meg. "I wanted to learn about what's going on behind the scenes."

Meg gripped the plastic knife a little harder. She wasn't going to make it easy on her.

The co-worker asked Honey to practice screaming. That, she could do. She felt a little better after that. He took her aside for a moment, gave her a thick poncho-type garment to protect her costume from the blood, and provided some whispered instructions on what would happen next. As he did so, Honey noticed a bowl of small fake blood capsules beside a pile of tentacles. Then she was brought back front and center for the stunt. Without further ado, Meg stabbed Honey.

Even though he knew how it was done, knew she was more or less all right, Peter was half out of his chair when Ben put a hand on his arm to pull him back.

It was a weird sight, Honey thought, seeing the fear and guilt in the eyes of someone who is apparently succeeding in murdering you. The sword collapsed in upon itself, but as it did so it struck a small packet of fake blood, which spurted dramatically onto the stage. The sight made Honey a little sick. Cheers and laughter from the crowd.

Finally, finally, after the trick was explained, Honey was free to go. She fled the stage amid raucous applause and anchored herself in her seat. Then she reached for

Peter's hand.

To his surprise, Peter felt her slip him something small and pill-shaped. Just as the show was coming to a close, he realized what it was.

When the show was over, they were hustled out of the auditorium by the combined forces of the crowd, the staff, and Doug and Verge pulling them towards the next attraction.

Bea thought fast and talked faster: "Doug, do you think you could show us what it's like backstage here? You see, I write for a travel blog, and I know the readers would love to hear more of your expertise."

"Well, I don't know," said Doug, who had been looking forward to sharing his vast trove of knowledge about the various vendors.

Verge suddenly connected the dots. "What's the name of it?" he asked. "Is it Beatrice's Guide to Paradise?"

She blinked in surprise. "Yeah."

Verge explained to Doug: "One of my coworkers recommended it when I got the job here — it's hilarious. I just always assumed it was written by a really salty soccer mom" — here Ben snickered, and Bea glared at him — "anyway, Sir, it's got a really good following."

Doug puffed out his chest. "Well, I suppose it wouldn't hurt to take a look around. For the fans. No pictures, though." He strutted off and led them through a side door concealed behind a large potted plant, and into the bare, utilitarian hallways backstage.

The only problem with Bea's plan was that she now had Doug and Verge's full attention. It would be nearly impossible for her to slip off to find Meg. She'd either have to find her with Doug and Verge in tow or leave it to the others. That was when Doug opened the door into the makeup show's breakroom, where Meg was frantically gathering up her things in one corner to make her escape.

As they went in, Peter caught Honey's eye, and winked. Then he bit down on the blood capsule she'd given him, gave a little groan, and collapsed against the wall, blood pouring out of his mouth.

Honey cried out in unfeigned alarm. Even as she realized what was doing, her heart was in her throat at the sight of him apparently dying. *God, he's good.*

Doug uttered a highly unprofessional exclamation. He and Verge rushed towards Peter. "We'd better get him outside. Everybody stay put until we get back."

It took the two of them and Ben to carry him out.

Stunned, Bea and Honey stared after him.

"I suppose I deserved that," said Meg. They turned towards her. She crossed her arms and smiled. "We used to play that prank on the new kids all the time."

She still had on bits and pieces of the eldritch creature costume, but it was clearly her face underneath.

"Look," said Honey, recovering herself. "I don't want to hurt you or get you in trouble. I just want to know what happened the night before my wedding."

"Well, I didn't think you'd come to say hello," said Meg, sitting down in a conference chair. "You know, it isn't going to take them long to figure out that's fake blood."

"Talk fast, then," said Bea, her arms folded.

Meg sighed. She picked up her fake knife and began pulling the extended blade in and out as she spoke: "I'll tell you what I will do, since you're so persistent. I'll come back to Paradise in a few days and give a demonstration on how we did it."

"What makes you think we'll trust you to keep your word?" asked Bea.

"Let's just say I've got my own reasons for seeing Johnny's dreams crushed," Meg replied, with a nasty look at Honey. "Besides, I want to see the look on Charlie's face."

"Why did you do it?" said Honey.

Meg put down the knife and looked her in the eye. "Because I wanted to hurt him like he hurt me. He hurts people. You know that."

"No!" cried Honey. "He never hurt me at all, until you decided to—interfere."

"You never made him jealous before," countered Meg. "I did." She reached up to touch her own cheek gently. "Let's face it, sweetie, you're better off without him. Johnny told me about how Charlie's treated you since I left."

Honey clenched her fists and lunged towards Meg. "How *dare* you," she said, her voice choked with rage. "How dare you assume that you know what's best for me?"

It has been a while since Bea had seen Honey get truly angry. She knew better than to get in her way.

"Well, to be honest, I was more thinking about what's best for me," said Meg, backing away.

They heard the muffled sounds of Doug and Verge running down the hallway.

"Y'all are gonna have to work this out later," said Bea. "Meg, can you be at the office on Tuesday, at about 10 am?"

"I'll be there."

At that moment, Doug and Verge burst through the door, with Ben and Peter (still trailing blood) hot on their heels.

Doug drew himself up to his full height, panting from the run. "Ladies, I'm going to have to ask you to leave."

CHAPTER THIRTEEN

The Final Performance

From *Faint Hearts and Fair Ladies: A* Swashbuckleriad *fanfic*

By: theladyhero205
Updated: April 9, 2018

[Sorry it's taken me so long to update, guys, things have been absolutely insane]

The Lady Hero made her way swiftly through the darkened streets. As she approached the harbor, a gray dawn was just beginning to show itself on the horizon. There it was — the ship *Effervescent*. She quickened her pace as she heard the men on board getting ready to shove off. But just as she reached the gangplank, she hesitated. So much had happened last night. Was she the same person? Was he?

No, she realized. And that's why she had to go. "It's only a great leap into the unknown," she murmured.

"Oi!" said the pirate at the head of the gangplank. "Are you coming or not?"

"Yes," she said, catching up her skirts and scrambling up it. Just when she had nearly reached the top, she stumbled, and a strong hand caught her. And she looked up into the eyes of the gallant pirate. "Welcome aboard," he said.

-from theladyhero205's fanfiction blog

Bea, Ben, Peter, and Honey probably should have gotten in more trouble than they did. As it was, Doug demanded a full explanation as he and Verge escorted them out. He issued them a trespass warning, effectively banning them from the event for the next four years.

Verge was torn between official disapproval and awe—his internet heroes were just as brash and reckless in real life as they were online. Besides, he now had a fantastic story to share around the breakroom.

The four friends returned to their hotel, exhausted, sunburned, and glad to have the First Annual Renaissance Faire and Fandom Convention in their rearview mirror. After changing back into civilian clothes, Bea and Honey went over to the guys' room to debrief. The hotel was ritzy enough for the room to have a distant view of one of the theme parks and a small sitting area, but since the furniture was the standard uncomfortable mid-century modern stuff, the girls took possession of the bed near the window and the guys took the other. It gave their conversation a strange sleepover feel.

"Don't you ever scare me like that again, Peter Prince," said Bea. Most of her hair had already fallen out of her braid, so she began taking the rest of it out.

Peter raised his eyebrows and pointed to himself with exaggerated innocence. "Me?"

"I'm with Bea on this one," said Ben, looking up from where he was ordering pizza on his laptop. "For a minute, I thought you were really dead."

Peter grinned. "Yeah, we used to get in a lot of trouble doing that. I'm sorry, I didn't know what else to do. Honey slipped me the capsule and—"

"Honey?" said Bea and Ben at once. All eyes turned

towards her.

Honey shrugged. "I don't know, I was kinda desperate, saw there were a bunch of them, and thought it might be helpful in creating a distraction. I didn't know exactly what he would do with it."

Ben whistled. "You've got guts."

"I could have told you that," said Bea, beaming at her with pride.

Honey curled up so that she could rest her chin on her knees and slightly mask her embarrassment, then looked up at Peter. His brown eyes were shining with warmth and admiration.

She held his gaze for a moment, then turned away, towards the window. As she gazed out at the glittering enchanted city that they'd seen from the balloon the night before, she still felt his eyes on her. Without bothering to consult her brain, her heart began to beat faster. It was like something between a warm hug and downing an espresso.

Ben tossed Peter a bottle of aloe vera. "Hey Pete, I think you got some sun." Peter caught it, but otherwise ignored him.

Ben closed his laptop. "Do you really think Meg will actually show up?"

Bea shrugged. "I don't know. She might have said that just to get rid of us. Offering to pay her for her time might do the trick."

"I think she will," said Honey, turning back towards the group. "Something happened, between the beginning of the show and finding her backstage. She...changed, somehow."

They talked long into the night, making plans and speculating. The next morning, they slept late, and then piled in Peter's car and drove back to Paradise to recuperate and make plans for Meg's visit.

• • •

Bea was tasked with talking Elaine into making sure that Johnny would be in attendance. And so it was that Bea found herself in Elaine's office bright and early on Monday morning. It was strange to be standing there as an outsider, wearing the same green kimono that she used to wear to work. The *Post's* smell—fresh coffee and newsprint and the mustiness of the old building—filled Bea with longing.

"And what makes you think I'm going to go along with this?" said Elaine, who was grimacing as she sorted through Johnny's blurry and badly framed photographs. Her eyesight was getting worse, and it was easier to look at the physical prints than the digital versions. "Buccaneer Trail Productions is old news. We've got much more important things to cover."

Bea glanced at the galleys on Elaine's desk. "Like the shuffleboard tournament?"

Elaine wrinkled her nose. "You'd be surprised at how much impact it has on certain social circles."

Bea glanced out the window of the office door to make sure Johnny wasn't nearby, and then turned back to her former boss. She put her hands on the front of Elaine's desk and lowered her voice: "Look, this isn't about me, it's about Honey."

"Honey's a sweet girl, but I don't owe her any favors just because she used to bring us doughnuts," said Elaine as she unceremoniously deposited all of Johnny's photos in the trash. A reminder dinged on her phone. She squinted at it, and then grimaced. "Tell you what. Mrs. Pittman's coming in about ten minutes to complain about the article we printed on the restoration of the Main Street Saloon. If you can get through that without losing your cool, Johnny and I will both come to whatever it is you're planning."

Bea started to thank her, but Elaine raised her hand for silence. "If you can't keep your head, I'll send Johnny on an all-day assignment to Jacksonville tomorrow."

Bea pursed her lips. "Okay." *We're doomed.*

"Good. Just sit over there." Without looking up from the galleys, Elaine gestured to a chair in the corner which was used for particularly unwanted guests. "Make yourself look useful. Take notes or something."

Bea obeyed. Once settled in, she pulled out a notebook and began drafting her next blog post on some of the spots that had inspired the visuals for the *Treasure Island* game.

Mrs. Pittman appeared to be running late. Elaine continued reviewing the galleys. An awkward silence fell over the room.

Elaine cleared her throat. "I, uh, don't suppose you went to see that new superhero movie that came out." She still did not look up from her work.

Bea looked up from her notebook in surprise. "I did."

"What did you, uh, think of it?" said Elaine.

"Oh, I cried," said Bea.

Elaine looked up, unable to hide her surprise. "You?"

Bea met her eyes. "Yes. I...always get a little too emotionally invested."

Elaine went back to reviewing the galleys. "Johnny says that since everyone has access to the bigger review websites, local film reviews are redundant."

Bea went back to drafting. "I suppose they are."

Another awkward silence.

Elaine said, "I got an email, from Ophelia, last week, saying that she missed your reviews. She said you never steered her wrong, except once, about that wedding movie."

Bea smiled in spite of herself. "Tell her thank you from me."

Elaine sighed. "I don't suppose you would ever consider—"

Suddenly, Mrs. Pittman burst through the office door. "Elaine, you better have a good explanation for why the saloon restoration wasn't on the front page last week!"

"The history section's on page 3B," said Elaine, turning back to her computer.

"That saloon was the site of some of the most significant events this town has ever known," said Mrs. Pittman, flouncing into the chair in front of Elaine's desk.

"That's odd," said Elaine. "Because I believe you said that in your previous articles about the gas station and the Old Post Office. And the liquor store."

A laugh escaped Bea. Mrs. Pittman craned her neck around, searching for the source of the sound. With an enormous, feathered sun hat perched atop her permed gray hair, she looked a little like an irritated cockatiel. "I thought you didn't work here anymore," she said.

"She's doing a little freelance work for me," Elaine replied.

"Hmph," said Mrs. Pittman. "Couldn't find work elsewhere, so you had to come crawling back, I see."

Bea put down her notepad and met Mrs. Pittman's gaze. "Actually, I work for Buccaneer Trail Productions now."

"Oh yes, I heard that you had taken up with that sleazy

game developer. Can't say I'm surprised after the way you fawned over him in all your articles."

Bea nearly choked trying to suppress her laughter and was forced to cough instead.

Mrs. Pittman adjusted her hat. "Now, I'm not one to repeat gossip, but *some* people are beginning to think you're quite the gold digger."

Elaine leaned back in her office chair and watched them with narrowed eyes.

For a moment, Bea felt anger tightening in her chest. She'd been worried about what people would think, when she took the job—not Mrs. Pittman, but people. But it was just too ridiculous. *Yes, I seduced him by displaying my violent hatred of him every time our paths crossed.* She took a deep breath and replied, "That's unfortunate. Do you have anything you'd like us to put in for next week's edition?"

"I don't think so," said Mrs. Pittman. Then, with a triumphant, sharklike grin, she added, "But perhaps Elaine would like to run up a little story about you getting banned for life from that thing in Orlando after you and your friends attacked a security guard."

"Is this true?" Elaine demanded, leaning forward in her chair.

Bea winced, then pulled herself together, sitting up straight like a queen. Like Honey. "I'm afraid your sources were not quite correct, Mrs. P. We received a trespass warning after trying to talk to an old friend in a backstage area. Our actions were not particularly wise,"—here she smiled—"But I assure you, no one was hurt."

The feathers on Mrs. Pittman's hat fluttered. "Are you calling me a liar?"

"Just misinformed," said Bea, smoothing out a wrinkled

page in her notebook. "It happens to the best of us."

Mrs. Pittman sniffed. "Maybe people would be less likely to be misinformed if you didn't spend so much time with that little tramp, Honey Noble. They say that she slept with a different man every night the week up to her wedding, and that now she's taken up with *both* of the Prince boys. Charlie's lucky he got rid of her when he did. He doesn't deserve her."

Bea ran her fingers over the binding over her notebook, thinking about how she would like to throw it at Mrs. Pittman's head. The nastiness of this woman knew no bounds. Honey, who'd had to endure so much in the past few days alone, to say nothing of the months beforehand, even though she'd done nothing wrong. The image of her friend, quiet and self-possessed, walking with her head held high past the grocery clerks, past Charlie and Diana, somehow keeping her grace and her nerve in front of the raucous makeup show. If sweet, timid Honey could brave so many hostile audiences, Bea could find enough restraint not to tell Mrs. Pittman to go to hell. But she couldn't resist having a little fun in the process.

"You're right, Mrs. Pittman," Bea said, in a voice that was eerily cool and polite. "Charlie doesn't deserve her."

Mrs. Pittman raised her eyebrows, but she said nothing. She turned to Elaine. "You know, Elaine, I don't know why you bother hiring her, even for freelance. She clearly can't see the truth of anything even if it's staring her right in the face."

Elaine glared at Mrs. Pittman over the top of her bedazzled reading glasses. "And what would you know about it?" she bristled. "I've had enough of you telling me how to do my job. Get out."

"I beg your pardon?" said Mrs. Pittman.

Elaine got up, walked around the desk, and opened the door with a flourish. "Remove thyself. Skedaddle. Vamoose. Depart."

Mrs. Pittman left, squawking, "I'll have your job for this!" as she went.

"Don't let the door hit you on your way out," said Elaine. She slammed the door, gave a brisk nod, as if agreeing with herself, and then turned to a surprised and grateful Bea. "Johnny will be there tomorrow. And so will I."

Bea wanted to run over and hug her, but she didn't think Elaine would let her. "Thank you," she said instead.

"Don't make me regret it," Elaine replied, but her eyes were twinkling.

• • •

The next morning, an all-staff meeting was called at the office. Most of the staff, except for Charlie, arrived before Peter or his friends, and clustered in the back, murmuring anxiously amongst themselves. The email that had summoned them had been rather vague, which was usually not a good sign. The main office was set up as if for a presentation on the big TV, with chairs in rows with one main aisle down the middle. The usual meeting table had been moved front and center beneath the screen. Bea's life-size cutout of Christopher Marlowe had taken up residence in the corner and had acquired an eye patch and a pirate hat. Peter and Ben came in through a side door, and Peter sat down on the big wooden table to address the staff.

His voice carried easily through the room. "Good morning. I know you're all wondering why you're here today. I assure you there's nothing wrong with the company, or anything like that. I've invited you here to ask for your help."

This created more murmurs of alarm. Peter raised his hand for silence. "Most of you know Honey Noble. And you all know what an amazing person she is."

The staff murmured enthusiastic assent. "We miss her!" said Mina from the back row.

Peter nodded. "And I'm sure you've all heard the rumors that have been going around. A few months ago, she had her reputation smeared in a very public way, and things have been really difficult for her since then. It was partly my fault, and so I'm trying to do everything I can to make amends. She decided that it would probably be best to have the truth explained in a way that was equally public. If you have other things to do, or you'd rather not get involved in this, feel free to go. This isn't a business meeting. It's personal, and it's messy." He paused, and then held out his hands. "But, as your friend, as Honey's friend, I ask you to be our witnesses."

The room broke into a buzz of chatter. A few people who had other places to be that day left. The rest got coffee and settled in to watch whatever drama was about to unfold. Peter thanked them, and then went to sit by Ben in the front row, stage left. The staff knew things were getting serious when not one, but two reporters came in—Peter's brother, Johnny, and a grumpy-looking older woman. The experienced staff members whispered to the newer ones about Johnny's sudden departure from the company.

Charlie arrived a few moments later. He hadn't particularly felt like going to the meeting, but he knew that if he didn't, Ben would come and get him. He had enough self-respect to be ashamed of the way Ben had found him last time; he didn't really relish the thought of another visit. As soon as he saw Johnny and Elaine, he had a feeling he'd been summoned for some kind of reckoning. He took one of the few remaining seats on the front row and waited apprehensively.

As per instructions, Elaine had told Johnny that they were going to the meeting because the company was about to announce bankruptcy. Johnny settled into his seat, relishing the uneasy tension sweeping through the room, thinking that he had a front-row seat to the end of his brother's company.

Then Peter got up to speak again. "Thank you again for coming," he said. "Now, without further ado, I'd like to introduce the very talented Meg Smith. She's a makeup artist, and she's going to give us a little demonstration inspired by an episode in the original *Swashbuckleriad*."

It was then that Johnny realized that he was in deep trouble. It was probably not the most trouble he had ever been in, but it was definitely enough trouble for him to start looking for available exits.

Meg strode up the aisle carrying a large makeup box. Johnny caught her eye, but she just gave him an icy smile. If he left now, it would only confirm their suspicions. Johnny braced himself. *Play it cool. No reason to lose your head yet.*

Meg was a consummate performer, and she reveled in the knowledge that all eyes were on her. She turned and smiled to the crowd, and then set her box on the table.

Bea and Honey slipped in quietly and sat down in the back row.

"Thank you all for having me," said Meg. "Today, I'm going to do a little demonstration on disguise." She opened up her box and began arranging the many drawers and compartments. Then she washed her hands and put in some colored contact lenses. "A few months ago, someone approached me with a very intriguing creative challenge. I was asked to disguise myself as someone that most of you know well, and then act out a little scene."

She pulled out a bottle of primer and began applying it to her face with a makeup sponge. "I had a key to her apartment from when she asked me to water her plants while she was traveling. The night before her wedding, I put on my disguise."

Picking up another sponge, she began applying a foundation that was much darker than the one she normally used. "I broke into her apartment with the man who'd asked me to disguise myself. I disguised him as well, but I don't think he'd be willing to sit down quietly and let me demonstrate. Which is too bad, really, because it was some of my best work."

Johnny realized what she was doing. If he interrupted her now, everyone would know it was him. There was a small chance that maybe she wouldn't tell them. He had grossly underestimated her. All he could do was sit there and sweat as Meg brushed on a faint, rosy blush that would match the bubblegum-pink wig.

"It's all in the contouring, really. Rearranging light and shadow," said Meg, demonstrating as she went with the help of a mirror in the box, sharpening the lines of her face, subtly shifting its apparent structure. "The main difficulty was not waking her or her neighbor up. I put sleeping pills in some chocolates and left them in her mom's apartment. That part was far from foolproof, but neither of us could think of anything better." Then came highlighter. "We got into Honey's apartment, turned on some appropriate mood lighting, and staged our little scene."

Meg fell silent for a minute — even she couldn't talk and do liquid eyeliner at the same time. "Of course, it wasn't actually as bad as it looked. We just made out pretty…thoroughly." She made eye contact with Johnny as she ran the perfectly pink lipstick slowly over her lips, then pressed them together to make sure the coating was even.

It had the desired effect. For a moment, he forgot entirely about how much danger he was in.

Then she began brushing on a few layers of eyeshadow — most of it was very light, but the shading had to go in just the right places to give the illusion that her eyes were larger and belonged in Honey's face. "We bribed one of Charlie's cousins to get his attention because we knew he wasn't coming back in town. The rest, as they say, is history." She finished the eyeshadow and mascara. Then she slipped on the wig cap and the pink wig. It had taken her weeks to get it dyed and styled to match just right. Once she was sure it was in place, she nodded to Bea, who dimmed the lights. Meg fluffed out her wig, and said, "And there you have it, folks. The one and only Honey Noble."

The effect was uncanny.

Meg-as-Honey sauntered over to Charlie. "Hello sweetie," she said. "Miss me?"

The look of shock and horror on his face was well worth it, she thought.

Meg said, "Can I get a volunteer from the audience? Honey, darling, why don't you come up and let everyone see how well I did?"

Honey rose and walked down the aisle towards this uncanny shadow of herself. This time, the strength in the way she carried herself came from a deep and seething rage. When Honey reached Charlie, Meg stepped back and watched Charlie writhe, watched the remorse work painfully through his pretty face as he looked from her to the real Honey and back again.

"Oh, God," said Charlie, covering his face with his hands.

Honey's voice was thick with grief and anger as she turned to Meg. "Why? Why did you do this?"

Meg turned to her with tears in her eyes. The cool professionalism vanished from her voice. "Because I hated you," said Meg. "Sweet, perfect, little Honey Noble. Everyone loved you. Any man I ever wanted ended up wanting you instead." Her gaze lighted briefly on Charlie, on Peter, on Johnny. "All my life I've heard people sing your praises, and I've heard what they whisper about me when they think I'm not listening. *She goes through men like nobody's business. Can't keep them, though.* I wanted you to know what it felt like to be me. And, like I said," — she looked back at Charlie, and her hands curled into fists — "I wanted to hurt him."

She took a deep breath, to keep the tears at bay. "But then…I got exactly what I wanted. I got to watch you break. Watch your dreams shatter into a million pieces. And it was hell."

Her eyes were pleading now, haunted. "So, I ran away. But then you found me. And I saw what you had been through, what I had done to you. And somehow, in spite of it all, you were still — And I knew that if I didn't tell you the truth, that it would haunt me." She looked away. "I'm not asking you to forgive me. I just wanted you to know."

Honey closed her eyes for a moment, trying to make sense of it all. She had a sudden, overwhelming desire to be as far away from people as she could possibly be. But when she opened them, she was, of course, still onstage. Again.

She was still trying to find words to say to Meg, when Charlie cut in: "Meg, who asked you to do this?"

Some of the vindictive, theatrical spark returned to Meg's eyes. A sardonic smile played over her lips. "Of course it was Johnny."

Johnny was out of his seat before he could stop himself. "Don't be ridiculous, Meg," he said, walking towards her. "You're just bitter because I broke up with you, that's all."

Meg raised her eyebrows. "I think you must be mistaken," she said, sauntering over to meet him. "As I recall, *I* broke up with *you* after I saw you flirting with Honey in broad daylight in the middle of the grocery store."

Johnny smiled triumphantly. "You have no proof that I was involved in this — charade."

Suddenly, Meg wrapped her arms around Johnny and kissed him hard. She was gratified that Johnny kissed her back, in spite of himself. He knew what she had done, and he might as well get a few last moments of pleasure out of it. From this angle, in her disguise, Charlie and the others could see beyond a shadow of a doubt that they were the couple he had seen the night before the wedding.

Then Johnny pushed Meg away from him and made a break for the exit. But Peter and Ben were waiting for him. "Hate to see you leave so soon," Ben said, reaching out to grab him.

Johnny turned and darted back down the aisle. Peter and Ben raced after him, but they stopped short when Johnny threw himself at Honey's feet. He grabbed her hands, and his eyes were wild as he looked up into her face. "Please! I couldn't help myself. It was all for you. I love you. I knew if I could get Charlie out of the way, make you see what a terrible person he was, I knew that you would love me."

In that moment, whatever compassion Honey had felt for him at first evaporated. She pulled away from him, her face a mask of anger and disgust. "Don't touch me." She pulled away, but his grip tightened. "Let go of me!" She cast a panicked look towards her friends, and her eyes met Peter's.

Johnny sprang to his feet and caught her in his arms. "Please, try to understand—"

Peter was there. He grabbed Johnny by the shoulder and wrenched him away. As Johnny staggered back, Peter stepped in front of Honey, and said, in a low, even voice, "Leave her alone."

"You just want her for yourself!" cried Johnny.

Peter didn't rise to the bait. "That's enough, Johnny."

"I'll show you enough!" cried Johnny, lunging forward.

He'd been living inside his head, plotting and scheming and fantasizing for too long. He'd been so close to the object of his desires, and Peter had gotten in his way. To hell with hurting people emotionally. He wanted to draw blood and break bones.

Peter threw up his arms, staggering under the force of Johnny's impact. Johnny had played football. Peter had not. All Peter could think as he struggled to keep Johnny's hands away from his throat was that stage combat had really not prepared him for this. In stage combat, everything was planned and prepared and precise. This was sloppy. Arms flailing, knuckles stinging, the sickening crack as one of Johnny's punches landed. Peter's lip split. His jaw was somehow both numb and aching. Johnny's hands were around his throat. He couldn't breathe.

Then, somehow, he had wrenched himself free. He was breathing. Like oxygen to a fire, with his breath came his anger. His fist slammed into the side of Johnny's face. Pain shot up Peter's arm. Johnny staggered back, but not for long.

Honey was rooted to the spot, staring at Peter and Johnny with a mixture of shock and fear. She felt Bea shielding her, pulling her off to the side so she wouldn't get hurt. Honey grabbed hold of Bea's hand — more to keep Bea from going off to join the fight than for reassurance.

From her vantage point at the edge of the room, Honey saw Ben and Charlie dash into the fray. Ben seemed to be trying to break it up. Charlie was not. He went straight for Johnny, his face twisted with hatred as he did his best to throttle him. His best was not very good, she thought. At least it kept Johnny from hurting Peter and Ben.

And then, as suddenly as it began, it was over. Peter struck Johnny, and he crumpled to the floor. He was still conscious, but he did not get up, just lay there with his hands over his nose. The mess of arms and legs that had been the fight untangled itself. Peter looked up at Honey. There was blood trickling from the corner of his mouth. Split lip. Real blood, this time. Strange.

He dropped his eyes and wiped it away with his sleeve, his face flushed with the heat of the fight or with embarrassment.

She took a deep breath. This was her part. She walked towards Johnny, who was now sitting up, still holding his hands to his nose. Broken, probably.

Honey was no longer afraid. She was angry.

"Did you get all that, Elaine?" she asked.

"You bet," said Elaine, gesturing with her phone.

"Great video. I think we might go viral."

"Okay," said Honey, turning back to Johnny, putting her hands on her hips. "Here's how this is going to work. You're going to leave, Johnny. Get out of Paradise and never come back."

"Or what?" he said in a muffled voice.

Bea spoke up. "We'll go public with this. 'Florida Man Attacks Game Developers.'"

"I like that," said Elaine, emerging from the crowd. She walked over to look down at Johnny. "You're fired, by the way."

"You can't...fire me," wheezed Johnny.

Ben matter-of-factly thrust a handful of paper towels at him. "Don't get blood on the carpet."

"Oh, I most certainly can," said Elaine. "In addition to the spectacle you've made of yourself today, you fabricated a news story and published it under a pseudonym with a rival news source *after* signing a noncompete agreement. And lied to me about your embezzlement scheme. And conspired to get my best journalist fired. I will happily share this information with all the business owners in town."

"And you're being evicted from the motel," said Honey, handing him the notice. "Unauthorized entry into another resident's apartment is a direct violation of the leasing contract. Mom's usually pretty prompt about confiscating people's stuff, so I suggest you get moving."

Johnny swore. He searched the hostile faces of the crowd for a weak link. But he found no one. Not even Peter. Especially not Peter. He could always create a little chaos by telling Honey about Peter's feelings for her, but there were too many ways that particular grenade could blow up in his face. As things currently stood, he could probably count on Peter throwing some money at him to make sure he stayed away. Leonata sure wouldn't have pity on him. She was probably in the process of cleaning out his stuff as he spoke...

He cursed again as he got to his feet. Then he said, "Fine." It wasn't much of a note to end on. He turned to go.

Bea took charge. She called a few of the sturdier-looking staff members over and directed them to take Johnny to the doctor to get patched up. They couldn't keep him away forever, not really. But it was a start.

Charlie watched them go with glassy eyes. Then he turned to Honey. He looked smaller than she remembered. A bruise was forming on his cheek in about the same place where he had hit her on the day of the wedding.

For a few moments, all that could be heard was the sound of the air conditioning and the distant hum of the traffic on the road outside.

Finally, Charlie spoke. "I'm a monster."

Honey wrapped her arms around herself, as if she was trying to keep from falling to pieces. She did not answer. She didn't need to.

Charlie crossed towards her slowly, his hands open, pleading. "Is there any way you can ever forgive me?"

Honey swallowed, and blinked back tears.

"Please," he said. "I'll do anything that I can to make it right."

Honey held herself tighter and shook her head. "I forgive you. But there's nothing you can do to make it right." She put a hand to her face. "It's over, Charlie. We're done."

He opened his mouth to protest, but no words came. There was nothing he could say.

To his surprise, he felt the gentle pressure of Ben's hand

on his shoulder. Charlie bowed his head and felt hot tears of remorse trickling down his cheeks. He turned and left the room. Ben followed him out.

Honey watched him go. For a few minutes, the old hollow grief returned in all its force. And then she felt nothing but relief. It was over.

• • •

Late in the afternoon, Honey decided to go for a walk on the beach. It looked like it was about to rain, which suited her mood exactly. As she climbed the weathered boardwalk stairs, she spotted Peter coming back from the beach. She gave him an awkward wave and started towards him.

"You ok?" he asked, stopping in the middle of the boardwalk.

"Better than I was," she said. She looked at him. "Are you?"

He shrugged. "I will be."

"That good, huh?" she said, with a half-smile.

"I'm sorry," he said. "I didn't handle things with Johnny well at all. I didn't mean to make things worse for you."

She looked out at the sand dunes. "I probably shouldn't say this, but I'm kind of glad you broke his nose."

He made a strangled sound that might have been a laugh. "I think that's the most bloodthirsty thing I've ever heard you say. Outside of a campaign, of course."

"Good," said Honey. She leaned against the weathered railing. "Listen, Peter. About what Johnny said—"

"Oh," he said, reddening. "You heard that." He stared down at the boardwalk. "God knows what you must think of me."

She twisted her hands, and then held them out as if she

was trying to grasp words in the air. "I'm not…upset with you. I just—I need some time. It's all so much, right now." She sighed. "I think I'm going to go away, for a little while. But I…" She trailed off, unsure how to proceed.

"Look," he said, still very red. "If you decide it's… what you want, all you've got to do is say the word." His eyes met hers. For a brief moment she saw all the love and longing in them as if illuminated by a flash of lightning. He went on, "But… if not, you don't have to bring it up. I won't bother you about it, ever. I promise you. The last thing you need is another guy who won't leave you alone."

And she knew he meant it.

"Okay," she said, her shoulders slumping in relief. "Thank you."

They stood there for a moment as if they had become attached to the boardwalk like barnacles.

"So…uh…where are you thinking of going?" he asked, making a desperate attempt at sounding casual. "If you don't mind telling me, that is."

She looked back towards the motel. "I've always wanted to go to the Pacific Northwest," she said. "You know, whales and big rocks, and forests and vampires. And coffee. I've got a cousin with a coffee shop in Seattle. She's always asking me to come visit."

"Sounds nice," he said.

The wind billowed through the dunes, whistling in the sea oats. A gopher tortoise eyed them judgmentally from the entrance to his hole.

"I should go," he said.

"Me too," she said, brushing a strand of hair behind her ear. She turned to go, all too conscious of his footsteps going away from her, echoing hollowly on the boardwalk.

CHAPTER FOURTEEN

The Geography of Treasure Island

Your Burning Questions Answered: Is there anything for kids to do here?

By Beatrice Bright
Friday, May 4, 2018

Several of you have asked me what there is to do in Paradise for kids. To be honest…there's not a whole lot. If you want excitement, you should probably go elsewhere. But I can tell you what I did as a kid. At the risk of sounding like a salty soccer mom, we had to create our own excitement. Some of us took this more literally than others. Of course, things have changed since we were kids. There's a putt-putt course now, and there's going to be an arcade. But mostly we were outside.

Pirates' Cove

Supposedly, this is the spot where the fabled Captain Constant eloped with Minerva Hedges. It's a beautiful, secluded bay on the river, just south of the Governor's House. It's great for picnics and launching kayaks. And sword fighting. It's on the very edge of John Hedges State Park, so no campfires.

The Treehouse Village

According to my self-created lore, this was the hideout of Jim

Hawkins, Robin Hood, or Camelot, depending on the day. It was originally just a ramshackle playground that looked a little haunted, but a few years ago they replaced it with an awesome new one that makes me wish I were six again. As you might guess from the title, it's got lots of shade from these lovely ancient, enormous oak trees. There are also some really big vines for channeling your inner adventurer (don't try this at home, kids).

Mermaid Springs

This is on private property, so I can't tell you a whole lot about it, except that the owner says that if her kids sell it to the state parks, she will come back specifically to haunt them. Anyway, there's a freshwater spring there, and we used to have the best time swimming in it.

—from *Beatrice's Guide to Paradise,* later reprinted in *The Paradise Post.*

Elaine was a little disappointed that Johnny kept to the terms of the agreement and left Paradise the next morning without further incident. The confrontation she had filmed would have made a fantastic article and brought some much-needed traffic to the *Post's* ancient website. Of course, there was always the chance he'd slink back later. Then she'd really have some fun.

But Johnny did not come back. His talent for manufacturing fake information and selling it with a smile quickly landed him a job at one of the broadcast news networks in Orlando, and he seemed content to create chaos on a more institutional level. Since Bea owed her a favor for agreeing to participate in their exposure of Johnny, Elaine asked Bea to turn one of her blog posts into an article. She discovered that her readers liked Bea's chatty, somewhat irreverent blog voice. Meg returned to her traveling show and her eldritch critters. She always felt apprehensive whenever her partner went out to fetch a volunteer from the audience—and half-hoped for those familiar faces, all the same.

• • •

The morning after the confrontation at the office, Ben found Charlie loading up his car in front of his house. The almost-summer sun shone down on the immaculate wet lawn, blanketing the neighborhood in air so humid that everything was clouded with steam.

"You here to gloat?" said Charlie, slamming a pile of boxes into his trunk and wiping the sweat off his brow.

"I thought you might need some help," said Ben. He walked over and put the last box in the trunk.

Charlie scowled. "Just can't wait to get rid of me, can you?"

"You know that's not true," said Ben.

Charlie slammed the door of the trunk shut, and leaned against it, his shoulders sagging in defeat. "Movers got most of it yesterday. Not that there was much to begin with. Just a couple of suitcases left."

"I'm on it," said Ben, heading towards the house.

Charlie followed after him. "It's in the living room."

Ben knew that Charlie had been planning to move for a while, but, somehow, he had always thought that he would change his mind, at least about leaving the company. Inside, the house was startlingly clean, empty of almost all traces of its former inhabitant. The walls had been repainted in Real Estate Beige and Millennial Gray. The granite countertops sparkled in the morning sun, ready for a retired couple or a family of four. It was really happening. All that remained were a large suitcase and two smaller bags.

Ben picked up Charlie's suitcase. "So. California. You'll have to tell me what it's like, out there in the big time."

"Yeah?" said Charlie. He grabbed the two smaller bags.

Ben smiled. "Got to keep up with the competition, after all." They went out, back through the empty house, over the threshold, down the driveway. After Ben wrestled the suitcase into the backseat of Charlie's car, he said, "But seriously, Charlie, if you need anything, you can call me."

Charlie walked over to the opposite side of the car, put in his bags, and then stared at Ben over the roof of the car. "Look, man, why are you doing this?" he asked. "After everything I've done—Why do you keep coming after me?"

Ben just looked at him, shrugged, and said, "We've been friends too long to stop now." He walked around the car to Charlie. "You sure that's everything?"

"Yeah," said Charlie, opening the door to the driver's side. He was about to get in, then stopped and turned back to Ben. "Thank you," he said. "For...everything."

To Charlie's surprise, Ben hugged him. "Take care of yourself, man."

Something like a sob escaped Charlie. Then he let go and got in the car before Ben could see him cry.

Ben stood in the driveway, watching, as his friend drove down the hazy street, out of the neighborhood, out of Paradise.

• • •

A few days later, Bea came into the office. When she arrived, she found Ben sitting at her desk. The office was strangely quiet, especially compared to the last time she'd been here.

Ben spun around in the swivel chair. "I've been expecting you," he said in his best cartoon villain voice.

"Well, I should hope so," she said, setting her bag down beside the desk. "You told me I could come in today."

He sprang up and offered her the chair with a flourish. "Yeah, I need someone to tell me I'm an idiot periodically. It keeps me from getting too cocky." He sat down at his desk in his ridiculous-but-awesome swivel armchair. Then he pushed off with his feet, sending himself careening across the room, pushed off against the far wall, and screeched to a halt in front of Bea's desk.

"I've been telling you that for years and it hasn't made a bit of difference," said Bea, trying not to laugh. "Where is everyone, by the way?"

"Peter went out to Orlando to help Johnny move into his new apartment—and to keep an eye on him in case he's thinking of causing any more trouble. Charlie's somewhere in California, and I think the rest of the staff are in the galley because Steve brought bagels."

"Well, what are we still doing here, when there's bagels?" asked Bea, jumping up and starting for the door.

"Hold on," said Ben, taking her hand to stop her. "I've got a surprise for you."

Bea raised her eyebrows. "A surprise?" She allowed herself to be led back to the chairs as Ben went on: "Yes, and it should be coming through the door in about, oh"— he looked at his watch—"five minutes."

"What is it?"

"You'll find out," said Ben, with his most maddening smile.

She crossed her arms and sat back in her chair, trying to guess what it could be. There was, honestly, no telling with Ben. Then, as she looked out over the empty office, her face fell.

"What is it?" asked Ben.

Bea sighed. "I feel like I've messed everything up here."

"Well, you certainly keep things exciting," he said, spinning around in the armchair, and then coming to an abrupt halt beside her. "But I don't think you can really take any credit for messing things up. We did that all on our own. I miss Charlie, but...I didn't realize how on edge we all were, until we—weren't, anymore. Things have been unbelievably better here in the last few days. Mostly thanks to you and your everlasting stubbornness—with a little assistance from yours truly. And, you know, everyone else."

"We do make a pretty good team," she said. She reached out and took his hand and laced her fingers through his.

Ben had just leaned in to steal a kiss when the door opened and Elaine came in. It was hard to say which was more surprising—Elaine herself, or her outfit. She had forgone her usual professional wear in favor of a Hawaiian shirt and pink pastel shorts, and a massive sun hat.

"Excuse me," said Elaine, pushing her sunglasses on top of her head and giving them a judgmental squint. "I thought this was supposed to be a business meeting."

Ben just squinted judgmentally back at her. "Well, you know what they say. Two's company, three's a business meeting."

"Don't make me regret my decision, young man," she said, shaking her finger at him.

"What's this all about?" said Bea.

"Elaine is trying to take you away from us," said Ben. He got up to grab a chair for Elaine.

"Well, I'm kind of running out of staff," grumbled Elaine, waving the chair away impatiently. "I mean, the other folks aren't bad, but most of them already have one foot in retirement. And I want to go to the Bahamas and spend time with my grandkids."

Bea gripped the arms of her chair. "You mean —"

"I want you to run the *Post*," said Elaine.

Bea was about to spring up and hug her, but then hesitated. "I want to, definitely, but…I don't want to create any more chaos here than I already have."

"I think we can work something out," said Ben, smiling. "There's a long line of people wanting to work for us. Still…" He winked at her. "I fully intend on coming to bother you whenever we get really stuck."

Bea rolled her eyes at Ben, then jumped up and clasped Elaine's wrinkled hands. "Count me in."

"Thank goodness," said Elaine, pulling away and checking her watch. "Now, if you'll excuse me, I've got a plane to catch." She started towards the door.

"Wait, now?" said Bea, following her. "Don't you want to like, train me or something?"

"What do you think I've been doing for the past year and a half?" said Elaine, who was already halfway out the door. "You'll figure it out. Just don't forget to get everything in by Wednesday night."

They watched her go in astonishment.

"Did that — did that really just happen?" asked Bea, still staring at the door.

"I think so," said Ben.

Bea made an alarmed pterodactyl sound. "I gotta go!" She darted back to the desk, grabbed her bag, and started for the door. Then she stopped and darted back to kiss Ben on the cheek. "Thank you," she said. Then she was off like a shot.

He couldn't keep from grinning as he watched her leave.

• • •

And so began Bea's career as Editor-in-Chief of *The Paradise Post*. The first few weeks were more than a little chaotic. The cranky part-time retirees that comprised the rest of the staff put up with her. This was mostly because she was willing to listen to them, whether they had advice, complaints about the paper; or just wanted to ramble on about their grandchildren, the vintage car show, or the wild days of their youth. She had a knack for discovering a feature story amid their ramblings, and started a weekly column devoted to the reminiscences of the older islanders. Eventually, late in May, Bea began to feel less like she was drowning and more like she was working a normal job.

One afternoon, when things were slower than normal, except that someone had taken out a classified ad stating that they wanted to rent their apartment to aliens (they refused to clarify whether they meant illegal or extraterrestrial), Honey stopped in for a chat. She found Bea in Elaine's old office, editing photos from the shark fishing tournament. The office looked more or less the same, except that Bea had added a large bulletin board plastered with her photos of her friends and family, Ben, and the island's beautiful scenery. A postcard from Elaine was wedged in one corner — one of the terrible cheesy ones involving a trio of shirtless men.

"I'm on my way to Mermaid Springs," said Honey,

who was wearing her painting clothes. "But I thought I'd stop in and say hi first."

"It's a day for visitors," said Bea, happily closing her laptop. "Peter was in here a few minutes ago with a press release."

"He was?" said Honey, glancing around the office as if he might still be here. "I'm sorry I missed him."

"Are you now?" said Bea with a teasing smile.

"Yes," she said, with a faraway look in her eye. "It's always nice when he's—" Then she realized what Bea was getting at, and backpedaled. "I mean, I just would have like to uh, ask him about whether or not I could take the kids on a fieldtrip to the offices."

"Mm." said Bea. "Maybe you should just take yourself on a fieldtrip there and see what you can find out."

Honey's cheeks turned as pink as her hair. "I—I can't. It hasn't been that long since—and I don't want people to think—"

"The good people of Paradise have minds that are dirtier than motel gutters after a hurricane," said Bea, holding up this week's stack of Letters to the Editor for emphasis. "Don't let that stop you."

Honey got up and walked over to the window, which looked out on Main Street. "I just…don't trust my judgment anymore."

"I mean, that's fair," said Bea. "But you were right about Johnny being the worst, so you've got 50% accuracy as far as judging guys goes."

Honey laughed and turned back to her friend. "I'm pretty sure that's not how statistics work."

"All I'm saying is that you could do a lot worse than Peter," said Bea.

The faraway look returned to Honey's eyes. "Yeah."

• • •

Ever since Charlie had jilted her, Honey had taken to spending more and more of her time at Mermaid Springs. That wasn't its real name, of course. It was just "the spring" in Mrs. Ophelia's property on the mainland. It was one of the few freshwater springs that hadn't been taken over by the state parks. Before he died, Ophelia's husband, Beau, had bought the property with the intention of building a house there so that they wouldn't be in quite as much danger from the hurricanes. His wife had never been particularly excited about this plan since it would mean a longer commute to her shop. They compromised and added a small mobile home (plus a generator) so that they could use it as a retreat for weekends and hurricanes. Now Mrs. Ophelia kept the property as a guesthouse for her grandkids when they came to visit.

When Honey and her friends were younger, Mrs. Ophelia recruited them to keep the property up for her. In exchange, she let them come and go from it as they liked, swimming in the spring, making campfires, playing make-believe, and generally having a good time. Thanks to Paradise's wealthy and enthusiastic cycling community, there was a decent bike trail from the motel to the mainland via the old fishing bridge, so Honey and her friends could bike there. After she started dating Charlie, they didn't come quite as often. By then, they and their friends had their driver's licenses. There were too many other places to explore and things to do. Even so, the friends would still drop by every week or two to mow the lawn, clean the trailer, or clear tree limbs from the driveway.

Here, underneath the shade of the towering cypress trees and the strong, green-gray arms of the twisting live oaks, with their rich draperies of Spanish moss and resurrection ferns, Honey's swirling world seemed to fall into place. Instead of gossipy neighbors, there was the earthy music of the cicadas. Instead of small, adorable (but needy) students, there were yellow-bellied slider turtles perched on logs in the sun with their feet splayed out like little fans. But mostly, there was the spring itself, clear, fresh water bubbling up from the limestone caverns and rivers deep, deep below, icy cold, even in the summer. The fissure through which the water bubbled up was deep blue, and the shallow, sandy edges seemed almost to glow aquamarine in the afternoon light, mottled by patches of turtle grass. The air smelled clean, washed by water and perfumed by cypress, with a hint of the musty earth-damp of the plants that crowded up to the water's edge.

Usually, Honey brought her sketchbook, or, if she was feeling really ambitious, her traveling easel and paint set. Today she was feeling ambitious. She was trying to paint the lagoon not so much as it was, but as it existed in her mind — the enchanted place it had been in her childhood, where mermaids swam, and pirates buried treasure. As she painted, she thought about how strangely disparate the challenges of painting landscapes and painting human (or human-ish) figures were. Landscapes were more forgiving of error — a few strokes could smooth or blur away a stray brushstroke. But a wrong stroke on people could leave them looking scarred or seriously deformed. Which was all very well with pirates, but less so with mermaids. But perhaps, she thought, as she scraped off some of the paint with her palette knife, mermaids would be a bit like manatees in that way — scarred from the tumultuous business of underwater living and interactions with often-hostile humans. But even these artistic challenges could not keep her mind wholly occupied. Her thoughts drifted, as they often did these days, in the general direction of Peter.

The trip to Seattle had been very much needed. It had been such a relief to get away from Paradise and all its gossip and claustrophobia. Everything was different there — the land, the buildings, the sky. She had begun to feel more like a person again. She wandered through markets and in and out of coffeeshops, went on long hikes and angsty walks along the rocky coast. Despite her determination to put the scene between her and Peter on the beach out of her mind for a while, she couldn't help coming back to it again. And again. Half of her kept wishing that she had told him how she felt there and then. The other half had been unsure. She had been so wrong before.

But the more she thought about it, the more she found that she very much wanted Peter in her life. She was drawn to his gentle presence, his kind, handsome face, the strong music of his voice — and to his quiet capacity for mischief. There had been a reckless, intoxicating quality to their adventures together in Orlando. There had been moments, then, and later, when all she wanted to do was run into his arms and let him hold her. She had been half tempted to rush to him as soon as she'd gotten back home, but she hadn't quite had the nerve. Besides, she had found out that he was traveling, too — gone to visit his other set of grandparents in Naples. People would talk, of course. It would probably be wiser to wait until she was sure of — something.

There, these highlights on the tail flukes would actually work, the accidental scars turning into the shimmer of sunlight on the water.

She glanced up at the water for reference—and nearly dropped her brush. As if her thoughts had summoned him, or her paintbrush had brought him into existence, Peter himself appeared on the opposite side of the spring. He stopped when he saw her, and put a hand on a nearby cypress tree, as if to steady himself. The sunlight that came through the edge of the clearing burnished his golden hair.

Honey shyly raised a hand to wave, and he smiled and started towards her, walking on the overgrown trail around the edge of the spring. He looked like he had come to do yard work, in athletic shorts and a dry-fit shirt that was almost the same color as the spring.

She wasn't sure, at first, whether she should go to meet him, or wait for him to come to her. After a moment, she decided to go to him. She felt, suddenly, that she was tired of shrinking, tired of letting her fears govern her life. Each step felt strangely momentous, as if she had found a way to walk through the canvas and into the world of the paint-ing—or had really been in the painting her whole life and had finally found her way out.

Then he was standing before her, astonishingly real. And all she could think of to say was "Hey."

"Hey," he said, rubbing the back of his neck, like he did when he was flustered. "I uh, didn't know you were out here—just came to do the lawn."

She tucked a loose strand of hair behind her ear. "Yeah, I've been coming out here when I need a break from people."

His face fell. "Oh. Well, I can come back and do the grass another time—" He turned to go.

But then she put a hand on his shoulder to stop him,

and said, "You don't count as people."

He turned back to her, his brown eyes searching hers as he realized there was something more behind the statement. "I don't?"

Her hand remained on his shoulder. For the first time, she allowed herself to feel the full weight of the hope and longing in his face, and it filled her with a courage that she did not know she possessed. "No," she said.

She took a deep breath. "You said...all I had to do was say the word."

He nodded.

"I couldn't say it then," she said. "But I'm saying it now." She was vaguely aware that she wasn't making much sense, but it was all she could manage.

Her hand traveled the short distance from his shoulder to his cheek, prompting a very quiet "*Oh.*"

Up this close, she could see the little sunlines around his eyes, the surprising redness of his lips. His eyes were big, and a little scared. She ran her thumb gently along his cheekbone—and then realized she still had paint on her hands, leaving a blue streak like a river on his skin. His hand reached up and covered hers, his face filled with a fierce and lovely joy.

She heard his sharp exhale, felt the softness of his breath on her cheek.

"I wanted so much to tell you," he said.

"Tell me," she said, as he leaned in closer.

And then he found that he didn't need words after all.

• • •

When the Pirate Festival rolled around again in early September, Bea found herself once again sitting on her favorite wall, documenting the action. Despite Mrs. Pittman's comments the year before, Bea was once again dressed in her "practical Floridian" outfit—purple *Paradise Post* t-shirt and mint green shorts. This time, however, she had company. Her small niece, Emma Beatrice, was visiting for the weekend. Bea had let Emma Beatrice put her hair into a messy braid while they waited for the parade to start. Now her niece was listening with unusual focus as Bea instructed her in some of the basics of photography. The streets were once again bustling, since the parade was just about to begin, and the air smelled of ice cream and funnel cake.

Bea leaned over and showed her niece the huge camera, pointing out the parts as she went. "Now this button here, this is called the shutter. That's what takes the pictures. And this big telescope-looking thing on the end is called the lens—don't put your fingers there. And this is the viewfinder—that's how you look through the lens to see what the picture's going to be. Do you want to look through it?"

"Yes!" said Emma Beatrice.

This was a bit more complicated than Bea had originally planned. She ended up having her niece sit on her lap, while Bea put her arms around her so that she could look through the camera without holding it, since the camera was almost bigger than Emma Beatrice.

"All right," said Bea. "Now put your finger on the shutter, like I showed you. Good. Now, look through the tiny window, and tell me what you see."

"A puppy!" said Emma Beatrice.

Bea looked up. The "puppy" in question was an enormous black Great Dane with floppy ears, which had escaped its leash and was bounding towards them with unbridled enthusiasm. Emma Beatrice got a great action shot just before the dog's owner grabbed its leash, bringing it to a screeching halt.

"I'm so sorry," said its owner, who Bea recognized as Crystal Prince, Mrs. Pittman's other granddaughter, reeling in the dog. "Stay, Cannonball!"

Emma Beatrice's eyes were big, but, like her aunt, she wasn't afraid of much. "Can I pet him?"

"Sure!" said Crystal, patting the big dog until he sat down. Emma Beatrice disentangled herself from her aunt and the camera, and then jumped down off the wall. Bea set her camera aside, ready to leap into action if she needed to, but Cannonball happily accepted Emma Beatrice's petting, his huge tail thumping the ground.

"I'm sorry if I scared you," said Crystal. "We just got him, and we're still working on getting him trained. But I'm glad I ran into you! I've been wanting to talk to you about the Paradise Motel."

"The motel?" asked Bea, surprised.

"Yeah. I don't know if you heard, but I'm the new chair of the Historical Society."

Oh, no, not again, thought Bea. Aloud, she said, "Really? Is — your grandma okay?"

Crystal laughed. "She's fine — she's on a cruise in the Bahamas, actually." She kept talking faster and faster as she grew more excited. "After the rest of the society found out that Elaine had kicked her out of *The Post,* they decided that it was time for some new leadership. I was really surprised when they asked me, because I'm only on there because you have to be if you're an architect and you want to get anything done in this town. Anyway, they told me about you and Leonata wanting to restore the motel. I'm kind of obsessed with 50's architecture—it's what I did my final project on. We talked it over, and we'd love to help you raise the money to restore it, if you're still interested."

It took a moment for Bea to process all this. "Wow, that's—amazing. Leonata's the one you want to get in touch with, though—text me, and I'll give you her number."

"Great," said Crystal. "Here, hold Cannonball for a sec." She took out her phone and began typing while Bea gripped the very thick leash firmly and prayed that Cannonball didn't get distracted and try to run off again. She breathed a sigh of relief when Crystal put her phone away and reclaimed the leash.

"Thanks," said Crystal. "I'll be in touch! Come on, Cannonball." She tugged at the leash, and Cannonball bounded after her.

The parade had just started when Emma Beatrice gave a cry of "Ice cream!" and darted off towards Ben. He was dressed as a pirate, as usual, and was trying to carry three waffle cones at once. He handed the strawberry cone to Emma Beatrice, and they made their way back to Bea. She put away her camera when she saw them coming.

"Never understood what you see in green ice cream," said Ben. He handed a mint chip cone to Bea, then picked up her niece and put her on the wall so she could see over the crowd.

"Says the man whose favorite flavor is 'trash can,'" replied Bea as he sat beside her.

Ben shrugged. "It's got everything in it. What more do you ask of an ice cream cone?"

"Sophistication," said Bea.

For a while, the three of them were absorbed in trying

to eat their ice cream before it melted.

"Mmm," said Ben, who now had ice cream all over his face. "This is way better than last year."

Bea passed him a handful of napkins; and was about to reply when they heard the booming of the cannon. "Look! Here they come!"

This year's float had somehow managed to be both more tasteful and more ostentatious than last year's. Now that Bea was captaining *The Paradise Post*, Peter and Ben had asked Honey to take Charlie's place in the company. Despite her initial hesitation, she was a natural fit in the company — the crew loved her, and she found she loved the work as well. She still volunteered at the school, but it was a relief not to have to get her livelihood from it. She and Peter had pulled out all the stops on the company's float. Peter had put his theatrical skills to work, using 2x4s and plywood to turn the hull of an old ship into the *Hispaniola* from the new *Treasure Island* game. It looked surprisingly like a historic sailing vessel, except that a shimmering golden topcoat had been applied to the whole thing, making it almost blinding in the afternoon light. This time, it was crewed by adorable pirate children. Some were the children of the Buccaneer Trail crew, but most were from an after-school program that helped the kids of Paradise Elementary learn about technology. Peter and Honey stood at the helm of the ship, holding hands, and looking completely radiant. When they saw Bea and Ben, they waved enthusiastically. Bea waved back, and Ben gave them his best Captain Constant salute. When they had passed by, Bea and Ben fist-bumped in silent celebration. Two could play at that game.

EPILOGUE

The Grand Chain

Bright-Constant

Timothy and Christine Bright announce the engagement of
their daughter, Beatrice Minerva Bright, of Paradise, FL, to
Benedict Dante Constant, also of Paradise. He is the son of
Pastor August Constant and Julia Constant. Bea is the Editor-
in-Chief of *The Paradise Post*. Ben is the spokesman and creative design manager for Buccaneer Trail Productions. They
plan to be married in March of 2022.

— from *The Paradise Post*

It was March of 2022. Assorted disasters of a local and
global nature had come and gone, but the Paradise Motel
was still standing, and so were its inhabitants. In fact,
the Paradise Motel looked better than ever, thanks to the
efforts of Crystal Prince and the Hysterical Society (who
had decided to make the name change official).

No one was more relieved than Pastor August
Constant, who officiated the ceremony, when Bea and Ben
Constant were married without any dramatic objections or
revelations. Peter was the best man, Honey was the maid
of honor, and Emma Beatrice was the flower girl. Honey

caught the bouquet.

After the wedding was over, and they had processed elegantly out of the church sanctuary, Ben whispered, "Quick, in here before someone sees us." Giggling, the bride and groom ducked into a side closet that was used to store folding chairs. Ben breathed a sigh of relief. "I just— need a minute, to let it sink in before we go face every-body," he whispered. "We did it!"

"We did!" she whispered back. She cradled his face in her hands, contemplating the joyous gravity of it all. "You're stuck with me now."

"I can live with that," he said, grinning.

Shortly thereafter, the bride and groom, Honey and Peter, and Bea's small niece Emma Beatrice gathered around what may or may not have been Peter's campaign table covered with a white tablecloth in the courtyard of the newly renovated Paradise Motel. Everything was trim and freshly painted. Emma Beatrice was thrilled that she got to sit at the grown-up table.

"Don't get used to it," Ben warned her. "At Thanksgiving, we got stuck at the kid's table so long that it became another grown-up table."

"What did you think, Emma Beatrice?" asked Bea, noticing that she was looking a little overwhelmed by all the excitement. "Did you like being a flower girl again?"

Emma Beatrice considered this as she licked icing off her fingers. "It was nice. But it took a long time. And Pastor August is kind of scary."

"You have no idea," said Bea, trying her best not to laugh.

"The cake is good though," she said. "Can I have another piece?"

"Of course," said Bea.

"Okay," said Emma Beatrice. She slid down from the table and bounded off in her very poufy dress.

Peter raised his glass for a toast, his eyes sparkling with mischief. "So, how does it feel to be Ben Constant, the married man? Out of all of us, I never guessed you'd be the first to go."

"Mmm," said Ben. "You know, I'm going to level with you. Remember that day when we realized that we were famous?"

"Yeah," said Peter.

"Well, it's way better than that," he replied, with an incandescent smile. Bea took his hand and twined her fingers into his. Then Ben said, "And oh, while we're on the subject, we totally figured out that you guys set us up."

Peter choked on his drink. "You what now?"

"Almost instantly," agreed Bea. "Once we started comparing notes, anyway." She took another bite of cake and savored their stunned expressions.

"But then how are you still..." Peter asked, looking completely baffled.

"Well, we both realized that we had believed it so easily because we both wanted it to be true," said Bea. "And it kind of—helped us to see what had been there all along. Underneath, you know, fifteen layers of arrogance and sass."

"I believe there were at least seventeen on your side," said Ben.

"I mean, obviously it was against my better judgement," she replied.

"And mine," replied Ben.

"Really, that's your best comeback?" she said.

"No," he replied. "This is." He kissed her.

Peter and Honey exchanged flabbergasted looks. "Well," said Peter. "As long as it works, I guess."

Suddenly, there came a sound like the last wail of a dying elephant.

"What was that?" asked Peter, startled.

"I think that's Grandpa Noble," said Bea, laughing. "He's been threatening to break out the bagpipes."

Bea listened for a moment as the squawks sorted themselves into music. "Isn't that 'Mairi's Wedding?'"

"It is!" said Honey, laughing. "It's his favorite. There's a dance that goes with it, but it's complicated."

Peter glanced around. "Yeah, I don't think this crowd is sober enough for that."

Ben counted the time signature off on his fingers. "I think we can do the Carolina Promenade to this."

"I think you're right," said Bea.

Ben rose and offered his hand to Bea with the same exaggerated flourish he'd used at the Halloween party a few years ago. "Let's have a dance, then, shall we?"

They had turned the parking lot into the dance floor for the evening (much to the chagrin of the neighbors). Peter convinced Grandpa Noble to pause for just a moment. Ben led Bea into the center, and then they called their friends and family to the floor and explained the steps. As country dances go, the steps were fairly simple. This was a good thing, because no sooner did they finish explaining then Grandpa Noble was off again, and there was nothing for it but to dance. They all took hands, weaving in and out of each other in a great circle that seemed to spread out into the very stars, breathless under the wavering fluorescent lights of the Paradise Motel.

CREDITS

Information for "Flowers for the Rest of Us" taken from

Dumont, Henrietta. *The Language of Flowers. The Floral Offering: A Token of Affection and Esteem; Comprising the Language and Poetry of Flowers*. (Philadelphia: H. C. Peck & T. Bliss, 1851). *Hathitrust.*

Tyas, Robert. *The Language of Flowers: Or, Floral Emblems of Thoughts, Feelings, and Sentiments* (London: George Routledge and sons, 1875). *Hathitrust.*

ACKNOWLEDGMENTS

This book is a dream come true, and I am deeply grateful to all the people who helped make it possible.

Many thanks to Apprentice House Press, especially to my editors, Rory Durso and Molly Clement, marketing manager Kate Tourison, graphic designer Maxx Lao, and Dr. Kevin Atticks for their invaluable support through this process.

I am deeply grateful to the incredibly talented Karen Samuelson for her beautiful cover art.

Welcome to the Paradise Motel began as a creative thesis project at Baylor University. Special thanks to my advisor, Dr. Greg Garrett, who has continued to encourage me in the publication process, as well as to the members of my defense committee, Dr. Jacob Shores-Argüello and Dr. Deanna Toten Beard.

I would also like to thank my first readers: Dr. Alli Reising, who showered me with enthusiasm, patience, and fantastic reader-response feedback; and Fr. Jonathan Kanary from the Graduate Writing Center, who helped me make sense of the first draft. Thank you also to the students in Dr. Shores-Argüello's Crossing Borders and Genre class: Samantha Kiser, Daniel Smith, and Maddie Wayland, who provided me with invaluable feedback.

I would also like to thank the people who helped me as I began sending my book out to publishers, including Dr. Maura Jortner. Additional thanks to Laura Semrau and the Baylor University Libraries for allowing me to do a preview reading as part of their Shakespeare 400 festivities, and to the students from Dr. Sean Benson's class, whose enthusiastic response to the reading helped me believe that people would actually want to read this book. I also want to thank Becky Presnall and Laurel Samuelson for their help during the revision process, as well as the many other English graduate students who cheered me on throughout this process.

I am also deeply grateful to my parents, Mark and Teresa Taylor, and my brother, Matthew, for their love and support in this project and in all my endeavors.

This book is dedicated in memory of my dear friend Kayla Harris, who passed away suddenly in 2021. She was a kind and loving person who taught me so much about friendship. Bea and Honey's best qualities are indebted to her fierce and caring spirit. She helped me talk through the story as I wrote and helped me develop the characters visually. The quote in the dedication was one of her favorites, because she interpreted it as being about God's grace.

"Sixth and lastly," I end with thanks to God for his many gifts—"thy grace being gained cures all disgrace in me."

ABOUT THE AUTHOR

Olivia Taylor grew up in Fernandina Beach, Florida, which has a healthy population of pirates and community theatres. In college, she lived in a motel-turned-dorm that inspired the Paradise Motel. She now lives in Waco, Texas, where she is a graduate student at Baylor University and one of the editors of the *Mark Twain Journal*. She enjoys painting, cozy videogames, and exploring local coffee shops. Her poetry has appeared in *The Avalon Literary Review*, *The Lamp*, and *Living Waters Review*.

Apprentice
House Press
Loyola University Maryland

Apprentice House is the country's only campus-based, student-staffed book publishing company. Directed by professors and industry professionals, it is a nonprofit activity of the Communication & Media Department at Loyola University Maryland.

Using state-of-the-art technology and an experiential learning model of education, Apprentice House publishes books in untraditional ways. This dual responsibility as publishers and educators creates an unprecedented collaborative environment among faculty and students, while teaching tomorrow's editors, designers, and marketers.

Eclectic and provocative, Apprentice House titles intend to entertain as well as spark dialogue on a variety of topics. Financial contributions to sustain the press's work are welcomed. Contributions are tax deductible to the fullest extent allowed by the IRS.

To learn more about Apprentice House books or to obtain submission guidelines, please visit www.apprenticehouse.com.

Apprentice House Press
Communication & Media Department
Loyola University Maryland
4501 N. Charles Street
Baltimore, MD 21210
Ph: 410-617-5265
info@apprenticehouse.com • www.apprenticehouse.com

www.ingramcontent.com/pod-product-compliance
Lightning Source LLC
Chambersburg PA
CBHW051335020726
47501CB00007B/2099